GLOOM'S LIGHT

THE
EVERS SAGA
BOOK 1

GLOOM'S LIGHT

BL PARKER

Book Cover by Vivian Reis

Edited by Maryssa Gordon

1st edition 2024

Print ISBN 978-0-6459760-0-7

To Sam, Tanner and Heath,
Thank you for letting me
decide on many different careers.
Hopefully this one sticks!

I started to relax a little. I lifted my head to feel the sun on my face and felt the tension slowly start to melt away. I walked past the small wooden houses that comprised the town and looked at the bright wildflowers that had found a way to grow and bloom in this horrible place. Woodmere was in a clearing near the Jagged Thorn Forest and would be a beautiful place to live if you removed the people.

I pushed open the door to the temple and stepped inside the cold, dark space. It was a large square room with pews lined up nice and neat. At the front of the room, there were a few instruments and a large wooden throne-like chair that had padded pillows on the seat. That was where Matthew sat and delivered his sermons. Today, I ignored all that and walked to the back of the cleaning closet and set about making sure the temple was clean and ready for this afternoon's message.

I got to scrubbing the floor with the stiff wooden brush, and it wasn't long before my hand and shoulder were aching, but I didn't stop. I knew if it wasn't done right, Matthew would relish in punishing me. He never let an opportunity pass to tell me I couldn't do anything right and that I wasn't enough. It didn't help that he was right. Everything I touched seemed to fall apart.

The morning went slowly, but I managed to get the whole room clean. I looked outside and realised it was later than I thought, and I had missed lunch. I sighed as I packed away my things and headed out to my next chore for the day. I walked to the produce shed and saw all the food laid out to give to Awe the Sun Ever. Ripe fruit, loaves of bread and pastries were all laid out on a tray, and my mouth started to water. It had been so long since I had had a pastry, and my fingers reached out to take one. I snatched my hand back and looked around, making sure no one had seen.

I was out there alone, and a treacherous thought slipped in. No one would know if I took one. There were so many there, and did anyone really think the Evers cared about our sacrifice? I was sure that someone just went out at night to collect this and make it look like the Evers had taken our offerings.

One more glance around confirmed I was alone. I reached out and took one of the apple tarts and smelled it. It glistened in the sun, and I knew exactly how it would taste. I hesitated a moment, then before I could think, I took a bite. Flavour exploded on my tongue, and I almost cried. It was delicious, and I couldn't remember the last time I had tasted something with so much flavour. I rammed the whole thing in my mouth and moaned out loud, lost in the taste of it.

"Amelia! What is this?" a voice said from behind me.

I whirled around, almost choking on the pastry, and my stomach dropped. Diana was standing there, her grey eyes squinting with hands on her hips.

"Are you *eating* one of the gifts for Awe? I can't believe you could be so stupid. Don't you ever learn?"

I tried to swallow, but the once lovely pastry was clogged in my throat. How could I have been so foolish? Fear flooded me as I realised Matthew would hear of this. He had just warned me about not causing trouble, and now I knew my punishment would be bad.

Finally, I got the pastry down, and I begged Diana, "Please. Don't tell anyone. I won't ever do it again. I missed lunch, and I was so hungry. I promise I'll do a double shift of chores; just don't tell him."

I saw in her eyes she didn't care. She was going to tell Matthew, and I would be locked in the hot box or beaten. Coldness started to tingle in my fingers, and I closed my eyes, willing my body to listen to me, for once. Diana was still reprimanding me, but I shut her out, trying to stop myself from losing control. A sob escaped from my mouth as I felt the tether slip. I looked behind me as the tray of food started to rot and mould. The beautiful ripe fruits grew holey and black until there was nothing left but black and grey mush on the tray.

Diana started screaming, and I retreated into myself. I knew what was to come, and I buried my mind deep inside me and ignored the hands pulling me towards my room and locking me in. I lay on my bed waiting to hear from Matthew so I could endure my punishment. Hours went by, and no one came, but I didn't care. I lay there and stared at the ceiling deep within myself. I could hear people trying to replace the food I had destroyed with my power and get it ready for Awe tomorrow. People walked past my hut and whispered terrible things to me, but I ignored it all as I prepared my body for what was to come.

I stayed like that until morning, when there was a knock on the door. My heart hammered despite my calm, and I walked on shaking legs to the door. I opened it, expecting someone to grab me, but it was Jeremy standing there with a tray of food.

"Here," he said as he pushed the tray at me and then left.

I stood holding it for a moment, looking out into the sunshine. Not a person was out. Everything was quiet, and something tip towed down my spine. This wasn't right. By now, people should be out harvesting and washing clothes. The children should be exercising and doing chores. Where was everyone?

I stepped inside and closed the door. I sat at the table and looked at the food in front of me. Porridge and water. My stomach felt sick from all the anxiety I had been holding all night, but I knew I should eat something if only to keep my strength up. I knew from past experiences that it was important. I took a mouthful of the bland food and swallowed it. It settled like cement in my belly, but I took another one and eventually finished the bowl. I leaned back in my chair, feeling weak. I should have gotten some sleep last night.

Now, I was tired and drained. I went to have a drink but realised my hand would not move. I tried again, but nothing. Panic speared through me as I tried to move my other arm, and it stayed still. What was happening? I tried to stand, but all I managed was falling out of my chair and landing on the cold wooden floor. Had they drugged me?

Then everything went black.

TWO

Amelia

The pole they tied me to was hard.

It dug into my back like knuckles digging into my skin. My eyes were covered and the blackness made my anxiety soar. The rope chewed into my wrists and ankles. I knew I wouldn't be going anywhere soon. Still, it didn't stop me from straining and trying to loosen the rope enough to get out. My wrists were raw and burning from trying to escape. Whoever tied me up did their job well. It took a moment to calm enough to notice that I could see a little sliver of light around the edge of the mask, but I was still blind.

My brain was finding it hard to process the people I had lived with for the last eighteen years would be okay with sacrificing me to the Sun Ever. I struggled against my bindings again as my brain began to defog and clear. They must have drugged me, probably at breakfast this morning. Was this the same day? I swallowed and could taste something bitter coating the back of my throat. I swallowed again, trying to get rid of the taste, but my mouth was so dry the taste lingered.

Matthew had been the centre of my problems since I was a child. He had ruled over Woodmere since his father died thirty years ago. From what I had heard, his father was kind and gentle, but Matthew was your typical cult leader. He wanted control over everyone that lived in that community, and he had it. He did not like things not going his way.

I knew he had been trying to get rid of me, but this was a little extreme. He had never made it a secret that he didn't like me. I had always been his favourite example of what a woman should not be, even though I tried so hard to be obedient and run a household, but something inside of me had always rebelled and said, 'that's not for you.'

My mind cleared enough to realise the situation I was in. I was tied to the sacrifice pole, which meant it was only a matter of time before Awe would be here to claim his sacrifice. I bet he would be surprised to see me instead of the usual cow and produce. I thought about yelling out to see if someone would save me, but I knew I was too far from the village for anyone to hear. Would they help me anyway? It scared me that I didn't know. If I believed any of the Gods cared about us humans, I would have prayed to them, but I wasn't sure they were listening.

My heart started to beat as panic speared through me. Coldness spread through my body, my hand tingling. *No, not now*, I thought, but it didn't work. I heard the familiar crackling sounds around me, and I knew I had lost control again. I closed my eyes, tried to focus on calming myself, and ignore the predicament I was in. My mind raced, thinking about what was going to happen to me out here. Maybe this was a punishment for yesterday, and someone would come and collect me when they deemed I had suffered enough? I knew better than to disobey Matthew and his orders.

After a few deep breaths, I pushed past my panic and calmed myself slightly. I knew getting worked up did me no favours, but it was hard to rein it back in. Being there made me so vulnerable. Especially where I was. I knew I was on the edge of The Jagged Thorn Forest, a place famous for ripping our clothes on the thorns of the bougainvillaea plant that wrapped around everything in there and where the people of my village tended to be careful of. I could smell the pine needles and earth. Scents that usually would comfort me, but not today.

Over my rough breathing, I could hear things rummaging on the forest floor. Creatures moving about, and it frightened me that I couldn't see them. Everyone knew there were all sorts of beings in the forest, and not all of them were nice. Stories of pixies, boggles, and redcaps had been repeated over and over at night-time to scare the children from going into the forest. Most of the time, the stories worked. The forest had a long history of looking after itself and dealing with the people who entered and harmed it.

It was well known that the Forest Ever, Gloom, was unforgiving and uncompromising and did not take people who harmed the forest lightly. I could name a handful of people that had ventured in and not returned. Some were never to be seen again, and some were found in...bits. Injuries made by something with teeth and claws. I had grown up near the forest and had always been respectful of it, as strange as that might sound. I had never had any trouble in there, but I would be lying to myself if I said it wasn't still frightening to be tied up on the edge of it blindfolded, not able to see anything that could be watching me.

My calm slipped, and my panic started increasing again. What was going to happen to me? I was so used to being told what to do all the time I was tempted to accept my fate and wait for Awe to arrive. I had always been told to be obedient, and for the most part, I was, but there was something buried deep and battered inside of me that wanted to fight and get free. The cold threatened to rise again, but I gritted my teeth and held it back. My whole life, my grandmother had told me to leave no evidence of my curse. Push it deep. Don't hurt anyone. Don't be different.

Something whispered inside of me. It whispered this was a blessing in disguise. This was my opportunity to escape and to get out of the oppressive cult leader, Matthew. To live the life I wanted to live and the life my grandmother had wanted me to have. Thinking about her brought a smile to my lips and a tear to my eye. If she was here right now, she would tell me to "toughen up and make the best of it." I missed her so much.

This could be my chance to go out into the real world. I could live in an apartment, drive a car, and own a mobile phone! All the things that were banned in Woodmere. Matthew wanted us to be one with nature and obey the laws of the old Gods. I must admit I liked that part. I liked being in tune with the natural world, but I knew the village could have benefited from those modern conveniences. Getting off this post could be how I got what I secretly wanted. Free. I had longed to be free of Woodmere and the small-minded people forever. All I had to do was get off this stupid post before Awe, or a creature from the forest, got here to claim me.

The people in my village would believe he had taken me, and I could get out of there without consequences. I could vanish into a city and never be found again. I would worry about the how of it later. I struggled against the bonds that held me with determination that had replaced the fear. I tried again to loosen them enough to slip a hand out. Even though it was the start of autumn, the sun was beating down on me, and I could feel my shirt sticking to my skin. After what seemed like hours, the rope was no looser, and I knew my wrists were raw and skinless.

"Shit," I muttered.

Instantly, I clamped my mouth shut and inwardly berated myself for cursing. I flinched involuntarily, waiting for the slap that was the usual punishment for cursing in Wood-mere. It took me a moment to realise none was coming. For the first time in a long time, I wasn't being watched, and I was by myself. Even though I couldn't see, I glanced around.

"Shit, shit, shit," I whispered with a smile on my face. I enjoyed the moment of mischief but then got serious.

I tried to get free again, spurred on by the little taste of what I could do if I was out of there. Why wouldn't this rope give up its hold on me? The stress rose, and the coldness returned. This time, I couldn't hold it back, and it was released. I felt it flow out of me and into the ground. My heart picked up speed, and I squeezed my eyes shut and clenched my jaw with the effort of trying to control it, but I couldn't. I had broken my most important rules: Don't lose control. Don't be different.

THREE
Gloom

My mind wandered as we trudged our way through the darkening forest. We had been walking through the trees for hours now, and I was getting to the end of my patience. Flying insects and creatures buzzed around my head, and I swatted them away from my face. There were much better things I could be doing. Bilvog, my most senior advisor, was next to me, prattling away about the other Evers and how we should handle this feud with Ashes and the mage.

I couldn't care less. I thought it was Ashes' problem, not mine. I had enough things to worry about. If he wasn't so arrogant, he would have fewer problems dealing with people. I didn't say this to Bilvog, but eventually, he must have seen the look on my face because he fell into a disgruntled silence. I could sense the disapproval radiating off his small gnome body. That seemed to be the only emotion he felt lately. Time to put an end to that.

"Bilvog. It is getting late, and we haven't found any symbols. I think it's time to go."

Bilvog screwed up the fat squat nose on his face and frowned with his bushy eyebrows. They were so low I was surprised he could see past them.

"Yes, well, if you want to get back, it's your choice, Master," he said, crossing his arms over his small gnome body. "We will have to find another night when you are unoccupied and have the time to come into the mortal realm and investigate. I know we have had plenty of reports of them being out here, but it is probably nothing. Just some ominous symbols withered into plants and bushes featuring the head of a legendary creature that wreaked havoc on the land. I'm sure it can wait until you have another break in your busy schedule," he said in his croaky voice.

I closed my eyes for a second and held in the sigh that threatened to escape. I looked at him and made sure he knew I wasn't happy. I saw some uncertainty enter his eyes when he saw I was not impressed.

"Fifteen minutes. We will look for fifteen minutes, then we are going, symbols or not."

"Yes, Master, very good idea," he said with a slightly smug look on his face. "I'll search over here and report back in fifteen minutes."

I watched as his squat little legs managed to get him through the challenging forest with relative ease. I let out the sigh I had been holding and rolled my eyes. The things I let him get away with sometimes even surprised me. As I turned to continue through the trees, my jacket got snagged on one of the millions of thorns that wrapped themselves around every tree and bush in this place. I cursed as a small tear appeared in my jacket. I unhooked myself and headed off to look for those symbols.

The forest was getting darker, even though it was mid-afternoon, and the usual mist that never seemed to evaporate was rolling in thicker. Throughout the green, it was punctuated with the purple flowers of the bougainvillaea. As I freed myself from yet another tangle of thorns, the never ending list of tasks I had waiting for me back at Toleran pressed down on me. Some days, I wished someone else could take on some of the burden of ruling Toleran, but I knew it eventually would come down to me, so I might as well do it myself. These symbols were troubling, but I needed to get to the bottom of them and find out why they had been left and what they meant.

I dragged myself from my head to focus on the job at hand. Having already found a few of these symbols in Toleran, I knew what we were looking for. The large circles of dead vegetation burnt into the ground were easy to miss if you weren't looking for them. They seemed to be added at random in our realm and this one. I had no idea who created them, and I was always thinking about it, conscious or not. Who was it, and why? Seeing the image of the Horned One burnt onto the ground meant nothing good.

At that moment, Laurel came to mind, and with it, a wave of helplessness I didn't like. I had to solve the mystery of her disappearance. She was my employee and someone I respected and valued, and there was a responsibility to keep them safe, and I had failed. That sort of thing weighed heavily on me.

"Shit."

My head snapped up, and my anger evaporated, replaced with confusion and curiosity. Looking up, I wondered if I really had heard someone say that out loud. I tuned out the sounds of the night animals and insects that seemed to have woken in the last few minutes.

"Shit, shit, shit," I heard someone say quietly.

I moved towards the sound, wondering who could be out here when it was getting dark. I let my power build in my hands, not knowing what to expect. I knew the people of the nearby town did not venture out here in the dark. I had done my job well, and the creatures of the forest kept them out. I walked on silent feet as I used my power to move the forest out of my way so I could creep with ease.

Eventually, I stood at the edge of a clearing and saw a young woman tied to a large pole stuck in the ground. I knew this pole was used for the sacrifices the village left for us, but this was the first time I had ever seen a human tied up there. She looked like she was in her twenties with a short blonde pixie cut hairstyle. I could see from here she was too thin, her face hollow and lips cracked, and I wondered why. The village shouldn't be short of food at this time of year. Was she sick?

I watched her struggle with the rope around her wrists. I turned to leave. This was none of my business. I knew this time of year it was Awe's turn for a sacrifice. If they wanted to leave a human sacrifice to Awe, that was their choice. I'd worry about it when it was my season.

I took a few steps but stopped as I heard a noise coming from her. I could hear a crackling and crunching sound. Curiosity got the better of me, and I turned back to look at her. My breath caught as my throat closed up when I saw a power I hadn't seen in over one hundred and fifty years. The ground around her began to wither and die. The grassy area the post was jammed into turned brown and then grey. A shiver ran down my back as it brought back horrible memories from a lifetime ago. Memories of bargains, devastation, and sadness. Involuntarily, I touched the scar that ran down my face from my left eye to under my jaw.

"No, no, no, no," she whispered. She was breathing heavily and looked in distress. I got the feeling this was not planned, and she was trying to control the magic.

I remained rooted to the spot and watched. As she whispered, the affected plants turned to dust and collapsed onto the ground.

Was she the one leaving the symbols everywhere? I couldn't believe I hadn't made the connection between the symbols and the type of power I was witnessing, especially considering the image of the symbols. I looked behind me to make sure Bilvog was nowhere to be seen and took a step out of the cover of the trees. As soon as I stepped out, she froze, but the rot continued. She turned her head and stared blindly in my direction.

Interesting. She knew I was there even though I had made no sound. The wind picked up, and I caught a scent of lavender tinged with panic in the air. Curiosity took over, and I walked steadily towards her. With each step, her breath quickened, and I could see she had stopped struggling.

I took my time walking to her while I looked at her and the damage she was causing. She was average height and wearing the button-up shirt and long skirt the village of Woodmere seemed to favour. Her skin was tanned, and I could see she spent a bit of time outside. Her hands were rough, and the nails were bitten to the quick. I frowned when I saw there were bruises on her arms. It looked like someone had grabbed her tightly. I examined her for a moment, and something told me she wasn't the one leaving the symbols, but I didn't know why.

I could tell she was terrified, and I also knew I should leave her there. Awe would be here soon to get his sacrifice, and he would love it when he discovered it was a human and not an animal. Anything out of the ordinary excited him.

I turned to go, now hearing Bilvog rummaging through the bush. I took a step, but I stopped. I closed my eyes and shook my head. I slowly turned back to the woman as she was trapped there, breathing heavily. I needed to know where she got that power from, and if Awe got her, there would be no chance he would let me talk to her and investigate. Awe didn't share his toys easily. She still hadn't spoken, but I knew she was aware of me. If she was the one leaving those marks, I needed to know why and who she was working for.

My mind made up, I walked over to her, and she froze. Her head lifted, and she watched me as if she could see through the blindfold. I started to untie her as a thought passed through my mind out of nowhere, *I wonder what colour her eyes are.*

<u>FOUR</u>

Amelia

I hardly dared to breathe. Someone was standing in front of me. Whoever it was, they were quiet, but still, I knew they were there. Were they there to help me or hurt me? I reminded myself to calm down and try to stay aware. The stranger reached up and untied my blindfold. I flinched at the contact and hated myself for doing it. As they were untying it, I could smell them. They smelled like coffee and dust after it had been raining.

The list of people it could be was very short. The most likely was Awe. Panic settled into my chest, cold and terrible. Was I too late? How long had I been here, utterly failing to get out of these bonds?

He was going to take me and do whatever he wanted to me. Out of the six Evers, he was not the nastiest, but he was up there. My body began to tremble as I thought of all the things he could do. I knew what it was like to endure pain, and you never got used to it. The pain always lingered, even if it had healed. Tears leaked out of my eyes as fear took over me when the blindfold was peeled from my face.

Blinking the tears out of my eyes, I looked to see the person who was there to claim me. Standing before me was a man with moss-coloured eyes. He had a square jawline and a light dusting of stubble. His dark brown hair was short and untidy, with streaks of deep green through it. On the top of his head were two small brown horns that peeked out above his hair. Other than the horns, he looked like a normal man wearing a long black jacket and black jeans. Even though I was deep in my fear, he was one of the most beautiful men I had ever seen. The only thing marring his features was a long scar that ran down his face. It looked old and made the outside of his eye crinkle slightly. I knew exactly who this was, and it wasn't the Sun Ever, Awe.

This was Gloom, the Forest Ever. All I knew about him was he was the youngest Ever and the most secretive. We had pictures of him in the temple at Woodmere, but they were vague, and his features were not quite clear. Looking at him now, I could see where the paintings were lacking. Everyone had heard stories about how cruel and unfeeling he could be. He showed no mercy to those who had wronged the forest, and the elders did not speak positively about him. He stared at me intently, and I withered under his gaze. I swallowed and almost wished I was back at Woodmere, and all the excitement I felt at the chance of getting free dried up.

His long fingers pulled back as he looked at me, and I watched him. I swallowed, trying to wet my dry mouth, and wondered what he was going to do with me.

"How did you do this?" he asked. His voice was strong and matter-of-fact, but curiosity peeked through his eyes. Shocked by the tone of his voice, I looked to where he was pointing and saw all around me in a wide circle, grass, bushes, and trees had all withered and died. Some had turned to dust, and everything was coloured brown and grey. My stomach dropped, and I realised what I had done in my panic, and it was as bad as I thought. My grandmother always warned me I needed to keep this part of me hidden, and I was disappointed in myself for allowing my control to slip.

"Well?"

My attention snapped back to his face, fear filling me.

"I don't even know why I am bothering to ask." He sighed and bent over to untie my hands.

I sucked in my breath as his fingers released the ropes, and I felt my skin go with it. The pain of my wrist burning sharpened my focus, and I resolved to take note of what was happening so I could escape if I got the chance. Where I would escape to was something I would think about later.

As he bent down, I saw a glimmer on the inside of his jacket, but it was gone before I could see what it was.

"I'm going to untie you now, and I don't want you to run. You aren't in trouble, but I have some questions I want you to answer," he said, his tone gentling slightly. Even so, I could tell he was used to being listened to, and I blinked, confused. Questions?

I stood still, trying to gather my racing thoughts. Once my hands were untied, I reached straight up to hold the necklace that was always hidden under my shirt. It was a silver tree pendant my grandmother gave me. She always said it was passed on to the girls in her family, and it was a good luck charm. I didn't really believe in luck, but it always gave me comfort when I needed it. If ever I needed it to work, now was the time. I had been in bad situations before, but this was definitely the worst.

As he straightened, I heard footsteps coming from the forest. I took a few steps back to create some distance between me and Gloom's overpowering presence. Gloom was muttering as he turned to look at me.

"Say nothing about the decay. It was never here."

Confused, I wondered how he could say it was never here when we could clearly see it. He lifted his arms, and all the decay reversed. Where it was once brown and grey and reduced back to dirt, green shoots emerged. Before my eyes, grass, bushes, and flowers grew at an alarming speed, and I gasped out loud at the beauty of it. The sound drew his attention, and something in his eyes shifted slightly. I shrunk back and looked at my feet. You would think I would have learned not to draw attention to myself. I risked a glance at him, and he was looking at me, frowning. He turned his attention back to the growth as it finished growing, and it appeared as it had before I lost control, with everything blending seamlessly.

A twig snapped, drawing my attention back to the forest, and I spun around to see a small man stepping out of the forest carrying a staff. He was about as tall as my hip, and he had a large nose and red cheeks. His face was lined with wrinkles, and his long white beard reached his knees and was threaded with green and blue ribbons and bells that tingled as he walked. He was a gnome, and my eyes widened at seeing a creature I had been told about my whole life.

"There you are, Master. I have been looking for you. I didn't find any symbols, so I think we should head back to Toleran if you still desire to." He cleared his throat and noticed me standing near the post. "And who is this?" he said with a frown. I don't know how he managed it, but he actually looked down at me. I could tell by the curl of his lip he didn't like surprises.

Gloom turned to me and stared. I looked between the two of them, and it took me a moment to realise they wanted me to answer them.

"Amelia." I cleared my throat and, with as much confidence as I could, said, "My name is Amelia."

He glanced at me, hesitating for a moment. "This is Amelia, and I think perhaps she should come with us," Gloom said, never taking his eyes off me. I hunched my shoulders and wished the ground would swallow me up. I rubbed my raw wrists and wondered where they were taking me as my heart rate increased.

Finally, he looked away, and I felt like I could breathe again. The gnome was frowning at him as he walked closer to us.

"What do you mean she is coming with us? Back to Toleran? What are we going to do with her? Shouldn't she be going back to her village?" he said, waving his hand in the direction of Woodmere dismissively. "It would not be wise to start kidnapping young women and bringing them to Toleran whenever you like, Master."

Gloom looked at him with ice in his eyes. "I'd like her to come to Toleran for reasons that are none of your business. I have my reasons, and when I believe it is necessary, I will tell you what they are."

I cringed inwardly at the sound of steel in his voice. I dared a glance at the gnome. His face went red, and he clamped his mouth together hard to keep in any more complaints. He turned to me with poison in his eyes. "Well, alright then, Master," he snapped before he whirled around and stomped into the woods.

Gloom turned back to look at me. "Do you know who I am?" he asked.

Many thoughts ran through my head. What was the best answer to give him here? I decided the truth was probably the best choice. "Yes. You are Gloom."

He nodded. "I would like you to come back to Toleran with me so we can discuss...that," he said, gesturing to where my powers had touched. "I'd like to know where you got such powers, and it seems like you have nowhere to go."

My mind scrambled at what he had just told me. Eventually, I found my voice. "I don't know where my powers came from. Please let me go." I didn't want to go and become another prisoner. I had no idea what would happen to me in Toleran.

"You have no idea," he muttered. "All the more reason to come with me, and perhaps I can help you find out about them. At the least, I could help you to control them. I'm afraid you don't have many choices, and I need to get back."

I frowned as I thought about my options. Could this be my chance to escape? I looked towards the village, and a bolt of sadness speared through me. Was I about to leave the only place I had ever known? Even though they had not been the nicest to me, it was still my home. Squaring my shoulders, I turned away from that life and those memories. I looked towards where the gnome had disappeared into the forest. I did want to learn about my powers, and Gloom was right in that I didn't really have anywhere to go. I had no money or clothes.

I ignored Gloom watching me, and I closed my eyes and held my necklace, knowing my life was about to change course in a way I wasn't prepared for. What was going to happen to me in Toleran? I stood there, frozen in uncertainty. If I was honest with myself, I knew there wasn't really a choice here. He was an Ever and had powers he knew how to control. If he wanted to take me with him, there would be no other alternative. With my eyes closed, I tried to come to terms with how my life had just changed in an instant when I felt a touch on my arm.

"Are you all right?" Gloom asked.

I flinched at the touch, and he removed his hand. My body started to sweat, and I wiped my forehead with a shaky hand.

"Yes, I am fine," I said, stepping away slightly. I took a deep breath. "I will come with you. I don't want to, but it is all I can do right now. Can I leave when I want? Will I be a prisoner there?"

He frowned and hesitated, and I felt like I had my answer no matter what he said.

"I want to learn about your powers, and I can only do that while you are in Toleran."

I nodded. Truly, I didn't have a choice, and perhaps I could find a way to escape if I went along with him. I wanted to be free and away from everyone I knew and be able to be exactly who I was without being controlled. As brave as I wanted to be, he was still an Ever, and I didn't want to get on his bad side. Perhaps if I didn't go willingly, he would take me forcibly. A shiver ran down my spine, thinking about how terrible that would be. I forced my feet to move, and I took a few steps out of the clearing and into the Jagged Thorn Forest, hoping I would one day come out again.

FIVE

Amelia

It took a moment for my eyes to adjust to the darkness. The mist swirled around my legs, making it hard to see the ground, and there was a chill under the shade of the canopy. The forest had been my refuge more than once, and I knew how to navigate it and avoid the hard and dark parts of it. The mist was constant, but it added to the otherworldly feeling, and I loved it. Sheltered underneath the tall canopy, it almost felt like you were totally alone and safe. Something I hadn't been for most of my life. There was freedom and escape to the forest I think some people didn't realise.

I followed Gloom while thinking furiously if I could get out of this situation. Maybe I should have said no. Could I have simply walked away?

We caught up to the gnome, and as Gloom walked past, he told me over his shoulder, "This is Bilvog. He is my head advisor."

Bilvog nodded at me and said, "Well, if the master insists on you coming, I advise you to follow closely, as you would not want to get lost in here by yourself. There is no getting away, so stay close." With that, he turned on his heel and powered through the woods. Something overtook my body, and I stuck my tongue out at him.

I smiled to myself, impressed with the small disobedience. I looked to see Gloom had stopped walking and was watching me. My face flushed red immediately at being caught. How could I be so stupid to let myself do that? After all those years of living under the watchful eye of Matthew at Woodmere, I felt a fool at my lack of control. I waited for Gloom to say something as I walked past, my body tense, but he didn't. I kept my head lowered and walked on with Gloom behind me. My whole body was tingling and hyper-aware, waiting for something to happen. Waiting for him to grab me or punish me for sticking my tongue out, but nothing. I didn't know if I should relax or not, and that was somehow worse.

I did my best to not get snagged on everything, but it was hard work. I had spent a lot of time in this forest. Grandmother and I would come out here, and she would tell me stories about when she was younger and escaped the village to go out to the real world for a short while. She would tell me stories about my parents and how they were with me when I was a baby. Being here with her were some of the happiest memories of my life.

The ground was blanketed in soft ferns and flowers, and when stepped on, a beautiful aroma floated up. But underneath, it was cold and sharp and, if you weren't careful, deadly. Despite that, I loved it. The forest had the earthy smell that all forests have, but there was a subtle sweetness mixed in from the flowers, which grew all year round.

My favourite thing, by far, was the mushrooms. I loved all mushrooms. I used to imagine when I was small that fairies lived in them. I would spend a lot of my time looking underneath them, trying to find them. Now, I only admired their cute little shapes and how powerful they could be. The same mushroom could harm or cure you, all depending on how it was prepared. This fascinated me with all plants, and it was one of the only reasons I enjoyed living in the village. I was always close to the forest.

Unfortunately, all the things I loved about it were doing nothing to calm me as I was forced to leave and go to another realm. A realm where the Evers lived. I wondered how long my heart could beat like it was before it would give out. I took a few deep, shaky breaths, trying to calm myself, but it was pointless.

We walked deeper and deeper into the trees. Long past the places I had been. I tried my best to try and keep track of where we were going so I could escape when they weren't paying attention. At some point, Gloom walked beside me.

"So, Amelia, what made them tie you to the pole?"

My guard went up right away, and I looked at him out of the corners of my eyes. "I don't know. You would have to ask them," I said.

"I might just have to do that. Usually, we get a cow or something. Seems like you would have had to do something big. Something like revealing an ability no one else has?" he suggested.

I walked in silence, unsure of what to say. Could I trust him? I wasn't sure. He was an Ever, but these days, that didn't mean much. They were essentially one step above regular humans. I didn't think they held much power anymore. Still, he was more powerful than me.

He ignored my silence. "So, I hope we are not going to have any trouble with you in Toleran. Many people have powers there, and I would hate for them to feel threatened and do something to scare you."

I heard the threat loud and clear, and I didn't like the insinuation that I would try and hurt people on purpose. "You won't have to worry about that. I would never hurt anyone on purpose," I said while watching him. Did he believe me? He had no reason to believe me, but he looked so relaxed.

He stared back, and I thought I saw his lip twitch. "But you would by accident. We will have to keep an eye on you."

He left me and caught up with Bilvog.

I sagged with relief when he left. The tumble of emotions I felt was confusing me. I couldn't help but notice how attractive he was, but I had no idea what was going to happen to me. After that conversation, I knew one thing. I never wanted to get on the bad side of Gloom.

Gloom and Bilvog spoke to each other in harsh whispers, but I was too far back to make out what they were saying. Occasionally, they would glance back at me, and I figured it was me they were discussing. I kept my eyes down and pretended I didn't realise what they were doing. This was something I could do. Not much could bother me these days. I had perfected the art of looking disinterested, but I was paying attention to everything, so when they stopped in their tracks, I hung back, thinking this could be my chance. I tried desperately to think of a plan to get out of here, but nothing smart came to mind. The last thing I wanted to do was be trapped in the Evers world. There was no way I was going to leave one prison for another.

Bilvog pointed over to a patch of ground with his staff. Gloom and Bilvog seemed very focused on something, and as they went towards it, I backed away. Time to go. Once I had convinced my mind to go, I had to do the same with my body. I took a deep breath and tried not to think about the consequences if they caught me. The whole walk, I had been building my courage to make my move, and this was it.

I backed away a few steps to test if they would notice me. When I was sure they were distracted, I turned around. I walked fast in the direction I thought we had come. Once they were out of clear sight, I ran. I pumped my legs as the thorns ripped at my clothes and skin. I could feel the stings on my face and bare arms as they tore at me. My long skirt was a hindrance, but if I lifted it too high, the thorns found my legs. My lungs were bursting, but I knew I must be nearing the edge of the forest. I smiled and had a burst of energy. As my chest heaved and I sucked in deep breaths, I looked into the eyes of Gloom. I was back where I had started. I skidded to a stop. How was this possible?

Gloom looked at me and shook his head. "There is no use trying to escape," and went back to looking at the ground with Bilvog.

In my shock, I was speechless. I wanted to scream and cry and demand they let me go. I wanted to hit and fight and get away, but I could do none of it. My situation seemed hopeless. How did this happen? I was running away from them! I took a minute to catch my breath. I tried to hide my face to mask the tears pooling in my eyes.

For the first time in my life, I was starting to hate this forest. I steeled my body and told myself I could be strong. I would not let this beat me. I would get free, and I would live the life I had dreamed about. Deep inside me, in a place buried so deep that sometimes I forgot about it, I screamed to be free. I wanted to be untethered and unafraid. I wanted to be happy. I just had to bide my time.

When my heart had settled, and my lungs didn't hurt anymore. I lifted my head. They were still engrossed in whatever was on the ground, and curiosity got the better of me. I wiped my eyes and craned my head and neck to try and see what it was they were looking at. I didn't want to get closer to them than I had to, but I couldn't see anything from where I was standing. I took a few hesitant steps forward to see what was so interesting. Gloom looked up and stepped aside, giving me space to see. I walked toward him, looked down, and tried to make sense of what I was seeing.

SIX

Gloom

I knew the moment she tried to run. Turning my head, I watched as her short blonde hair disappeared into the sea of green that was my forest. Shaking my head, I focused back on what Bilvog was saying, confident the forest would lead her back to me. Nothing got past me here.

"Yes, you can see here it is the same as all the other ones I have found. The symbol is withered, and all plant life has died here," Bilvog said, pointing to the symbol imprinted on the forest floor. It was a circle about a meter wide, and inside was the image of the Horned One, a stag skull with large antlers. It looked ominous and sinister and...off. I looked around the surrounding area, but nothing else was disturbed. If you weren't looking for it, it would be easy to miss. Not caring about the dirt on the ground, I knelt and studied it closer. Yes, it was the same damage I had seen earlier around Amelia. Was she involved?

I pictured her bright blue eyes that stared at me when I took the blindfold off. She affected me in a way I hadn't experienced in years. It was dangerous, and I needed to keep it in check. She was an attractive human that was all.

I was also intrigued about her powers and where they had come from. I needed to keep her around until I found out.

My mind flashed to those bruises on her, and anger slithered through my veins again. Who had done it and why? For me, there was no excuse for hurting a woman. I had an idea who it might have been. The man who ran Woodmere was a tyrant, and even the people in Toleran had heard about how cruel he could be. I had let it slide because it didn't really concern me, but maybe I should do something about it. I wondered what she could have possibly done to deserve that treatment. She was so mild and worn down that I couldn't imagine her stepping out of line. The image of her sticking her tongue out at Bilvog flashed through my mind, and I smiled a little inside. Maybe she could cause some trouble.

Bringing my attention back to the symbol, I sobered. I'd kept Amelia's powers from Bilvog because I wanted to get to the bottom of it without him in my ear about what we should do with her. He had no love of humans, and bringing her to Toleran when she could be behind these threats was asking for trouble. And I'd had enough of that.

I cocked my head waiting to hear Amelia coming through the woods, but it was quiet. While Bilvog was looking at the symbol, I turned to where she had disappeared and frowned. She couldn't have gotten too far, because the forest would bring her back, but she had been gone longer than I expected. I took a step towards where she had disappeared and focused my energy on the trees around us.

I sensed her presence just before I heard her running, and Amelia burst out of the trees. She had scratches all over her, leaving her striped in red. Her hair was no longer styled nicely against her head. It was sticking up in all directions with twigs and sticks all through it. Her long brown skirt was scattered with little tears, and her white blouse was no longer white. She had done her best to escape. I looked into her blue eyes and saw the shock she was back here in them, but also a fire I hadn't noticed before. I breathed a quiet sigh of relief. "I told you there was no escape," and I turned away, giving her a chance to compose herself, as I moved back to join Bilvog. After a few moments, I noticed that she was trying to see around us. I stepped aside to see what she would do.

"Well, I think we can safely say this is the same as the other ones we have seen. Note its location, and we will compare it to the others to see if there is a pattern appearing." I said to Bilvog, brushing dirt of my pants.

Bilvog pulled out an electronic tablet, took a photo, and noted the coordinates. By now, Amelia was standing a few feet from us. I stepped back a little bit, so I didn't crowd her. I debated in my mind if we should hide it. If she was the one doing this, was there any reason to conceal it? I decided to risk it and let her see so I could gauge her reaction. The risk would be worth it if it led me any closer to who was doing this to my people.

As she stepped up, I watched her closely. Her face was flushed, and she was still breathing heavily. It took her a minute, but once she saw the symbols, her eyes widened, and her hand covered her mouth. I could see her mind processing what was in front of her and wondering what this meant. She froze and turned toward me, her eyes questioning. I stared right back, trying to read her mind, knowing my gaze made many uncomfortable. I could see a small frown forming between her eyebrows, and I knew she wanted to look away. She held my gaze as she tried to work out what this meant about her power.

"What is this?" she asked.

"These are symbols that have been appearing all over Toleran and the Jagged Thorn Forest. We have had reports of at least twelve, and there are more reported every day. What do you make of them?"

Bilvog straightened and put his tablet away.

"Master, I don't think we need the opinion of this human. It has nothing to do with her. What information could she possibly give us that we don't know already?"

I held up my hand to him, never taking my eyes off Amelia.

"I don't know Bilvog. That's why I am asking. Well, what do you think? Have you ever seen these before?" I couldn't stop myself from stepping closer to her, and the scent of lavender invaded my nostrils.

"I have no idea," she said, looking at the symbol again. "It looks like it has been branded on the plants, and they have all died from it. I don't know what it means, but it seems...evil. Contaminated or something." She glanced at me, and I studied her. If she was lying, she was a good actress.

I nodded at Bilvog and watched as he waved his staff over the symbol. The tip of his staff glowed, and the symbol that was imprinted onto the earth was lifted into the sky. It looked like the ashes of a fire lifting and floating above us. It was beautiful in a way. Amelia's mouth dropped open, and my eyes were drawn to her as the ashes flashed a red colour and disintegrated, leaving nothing behind. I waved my hand over the bare patch of forest floor that was left, and using my power, the plants and vines started to regrow until you couldn't tell what had been there a moment before.

"Time to head back, Master?"

"Yes. Let's go home," I said sighing, glad we could head back now.

Bilvog walked off to go toward the portal that would lead us to Toleran. He turned. "Perhaps the human should walk between us so she can't waste our time again by trying to run away."

Amelia crossed her arms as her face reddened, and she shot a look at Bilvog. So, she did have a fire inside of her. She walked to stand behind Bilvog as he led the way. I followed behind, thinking about the puzzle that was Amelia. Who was she to have this strange power? And why was it now making itself known? Why was she the one to be sacrificed?

What I was going to do with this strange human? I was sure I would have to answer to Awe why I had stolen his sacrifice. That would be a conversation I could do without.

I saw Amelia rub her arm and noticed the temperature in the forest had dropped. I took off my jacket. "Here, take my jacket. It is getting cold, and your clothes have seen better days," I said, looking down and seeing all the little tears the forest had put in her outfit. She hesitated a moment before reaching out and taking it from me. "Thank you," she said as she shrugged into it. I could see the surprise in her eyes. "I am not the heartless creature you think I am, Amelia. It might surprise you to know that I don't want to hurt you."

"Is that why you have kidnapped me?" she asked, a spark igniting.

"I didn't kidnap you. You had a choice. But after seeing what I saw, I need to get to the bottom of your abilities. Things are happening in my realm, and I think you might know more than you are letting on."

"I don't know anything. Just let me go, and I won't tell anyone," she pleaded with me. I could see the desperation and fear in her eyes, and a jab of disappointment speared through me. I hated to let anyone down, and it was my job to protect people. But it was for that reason I needed her. I needed to protect my people, and she might hold the answer. The situation with the symbols was getting away from me, and I needed to work out what was happening. Something was building, and I didn't like it. I didn't want to let my people down, and I didn't want them to see I had no idea what I was doing. Sometimes, it was necessary to do things you might not like for the greater good. I let the conversation drop after that, and we continued.

With my mind going around in circles and churning all this information over, the trip to the portal was fast. We stopped in front of two old pine trees with jet-black trunks. They were so ancient it was hard to see the tops of them. The needles were dark brown instead of green, and they were brittle to the touch. Looking at the ground around them, you would expect it to be littered with needles, but it was strangely clear. Bilvog cleared his throat and said the word *voyant* clearly. The gap between the trees shimmered and turned an emerald-green colour. The magic rippled across the surface, distorting everything behind it.

"Right, time to go home," Bilvog said almost cheerily as he stepped through the portal without looking back and vanished.

I waited for Amelia to step through, but she didn't move. I stepped close to her back and resisted the urge to pick out the twigs stuck in her hair.

"Amelia. Step through the portal," I said, my mouth close to her ear.

She shivered and turned her head towards my face. There was a pause. "No," she said.

SEVEN

Amelia

I stood there, feet rooted to the spot and heart pounding as I looked at the shimmering portal. I knew in my bones I could not go through the portal and become a prisoner again. I had finally got free of the village and Matthew and his punishments; I would not allow myself to be hurt again. I felt Gloom standing over me. I could feel his breath tickling my ear, and his scent seemed to press down around me. There was heat coming from him, and I couldn't help myself. I had to step away from him, crowding me.

"I'm sorry, but I can't step through the portal and become another prisoner in your dungeon. I am finally free from the village. I won't do it again." My hands were trembling, and I was starting to feel lightheaded. That was the most defiant I had been in a long time, and I knew it was foolish to defy an Ever. My face grew hotter, and I clasped my hands in front of me so Gloom wouldn't see them shaking and turned away from him.

Bilvog's head poked through the green, shimmering portal, interrupting us. "Are you coming, Master?"

"You go on ahead, Bilvog. We will be along in a moment. I'll meet you in the war room," said Gloom, hardly taking his eyes off me.

Bilvog frowned and hesitated a moment before giving a sharp nod and disappearing again.

Gloom walked around to the front of me and pinned me with his eyes. An emotion I couldn't recognise rolled off him in waves. Why was he looking at me like that? I had never met a more intense person, and it was unnerving.

"This is the portal to my home, Toleran. I have already told you; you will be safe. I need to know more about your powers, and this is the best way to do that." His voice softened a bit. "You will not be put in a dungeon. You will work for me as my...assistant. I have...misplaced mine recently," he said. It did nothing to comfort me. Did he really think I would believe he wanted me to be his assistant? He held out his arm, ushering me into the portal. I stood my ground.

"What? I can't be a personal assistant! How stupid do you think I am? I don't know the first thing about being an assistant, let alone one for an Ever!"

Embarrassed by my outburst, I froze and waited to hear what he would have to say. He stared at me, stone-faced. Looking into his dark and flinty eyes, I wondered if they had ever danced with laughter. Had his mouth ever tilted into a real smile? I doubted it.

His voice grew hard. "What else are you going to do? Go back to Woodmere, where they offered you as a sacrifice to an Ever? For some reason, I don't think they are going to welcome you with open arms. You might as well come with me, and we can work out your magic together. I need to know you are not a threat. I don't want to force you through. That is not in my nature."

A threat? Did he think I had been laying those symbols? I had never been to Toleran before. How could I be the one laying them?

Although, I had to admit the idea of learning more about this magic that had been a hidden part of me for so long was enticing. If he was telling the truth about not being a prisoner, would it be worth the risk so I could get some answers? Not that I had a choice. I knew I would be going if I wanted to or not, no matter what he said.

I closed my eyes and tried to still my mind and think this through. Fear was still coursing through my body. I was on edge, but I stood there and took a minute to listen to the forest. I let the breeze through the leaves calm me. I scrunched my eyes closed and ignored the moss-green eyes that appeared in my head and tried to think clearly. The rain and coffee smell wound around me and made it very difficult. I waited for him to rush me, but he was silent.

He was right. I couldn't go back to Woodmere. I wouldn't go there even if I thought they would welcome me. This might be the best chance I would have to get some answers to this side of me I had been hiding for so long. Could I push the fear aside and stay and learn about this thing inside me? I had been trying to ignore it and make sure I didn't hurt anyone again, but if I was honest with myself, I knew I wanted to learn how to control it. This might be the best place to gain control over it. But what about my freedom? Earlier I had been thinking about leaving and making a life for myself out in the real world. I knew it would be hard, but I could do it.

I reached up and touched the pendant hanging around my neck. I thought about what my grandmother would want me to do right now. I looked at the portal and back at Gloom. I met his eyes and tried to convince myself I had some control over this situation. He stepped back and again held out an arm to motion me through. I walked to the black trees and tilted my head, trying to see the tops of them. They were enormous, and I felt tiny compared to them. I was leaving behind everything to enter a place I knew nothing about and had only heard about in stories. Walking through this portal would change my life forever. Was I ready for what would happen through this portal? I took a breath and turned to look out at the trees that had protected and hid me from my life for so many years. I remembered playing in here with my grandmother, and the feeling of home I got walking among them. Would I ever see them again? I sent a silent thank you, and goodbye, on the wind as I turned back to the portal.

I stepped through.

EIGHT

Amelia

Light. Light was what greeted me when I stepped through the portal. It was dazzling, and it took a moment to get used to the change. My stomach clenched and released, and if I had eaten today, I knew I would have thrown up from the portal's magic. Even though it was early evening by now, bright light still filtered through the tree leaves above. I looked around, amazed at what I was seeing. It was the same forest as the one near Woodmere, but there was no mist, and the colours were much more vibrant. They were deeper, birdsong sweeter, and the smells of the earth and plants were rich and, in a way, comforting. I stood in wonder and couldn't believe how different it was.

Before we moved on, I looked behind me at the portal and noticed it looked the same as the other side. I repeated the code word *voyant* to myself so I wouldn't forget it and tried to make a mental note of where we were.

Looking ahead, the ground foliage looked like it had grown and created its own path through the woods. The dirt was hard-packed and smooth. The trees were tall, and I could see colourful birds darting in and out. Some of the birds were quite large but still nimble as they wove their way through the branches. Ahead of us, I could see Bilvog walking on the path.

Gloom came to stand next to me. "It's good to be home," he said, looking at me.

"It's beautiful," I breathed.

"Yes, it is." For the first time, Gloom seemed to relax. His shoulders were loose, and the crease between his green eyes was gone. His whole body softened as the wind blew through his slightly green hair, and I wondered what he would look like if he truly smiled. I bet it would be devastating.

We walked along the path, and I took in everything around me. Out of the corner of my eye, I could see creatures of some sort darting in and out of the trees. When I looked closer, the creatures looked unfamiliar, but there was something human about them in a way I couldn't describe. Gloom put his hand on the small of my back and nudged me down the path. My skin warmed when he touched me, but I moved out of his reach, not used to being touched.

"They are the folk of the forest," he said, gesturing to the beings I had seen. "Some people call them the Good Folk. I have found them many things, but not often good. I like to call them the Forest Folk instead."

"Will they hurt us?"

"Not if we stay on the path and respect them. We have a deal, the Forest Folk and me. They will not harm us if we stick to the path and don't venture too deeply into their forest."

"Okay," I agreed and knew that was one request I would abide by.

As we rounded a bend, I could see a clearing with a wall a short distance away. It was made from brambles and the spiky vined bougainvillaea that thrived in my version of the forest. The spikes on this vine were much longer and thicker. It looked cruel and beautiful at the same time.

The thorny vine wasn't wrapped around the other plants here. It appeared to be concentrated on creating this wall. Looking up, it was so tall I could only just make out the top of it amongst the tops of the trees. Why did they need such a wall? Was Gloom keeping people in or out?

As we stepped out of the trees and got closer to the wall, I looked for a door or gate, somewhere we could get through, but I could see none. Gloom led me to an indistinguishable spot and repeated the word *voyant*. Before my eyes, the vines slithered and moved aside as a doorway appeared.

"Who goes there?" someone shouted from above. I looked up and saw two men with glowing staffs looking at us.

"It is me. Why did it take you so long to question my arrival? You should be asking well before I get to the wall." The disapproval in Gloom's voice was like a whip, and I cringed in sympathy. "Get me, Kennock. Send him to the council room. I want to speak to him."

The people on the wall hesitated a moment.

"Now," Gloom barked.

"Yes sir, sorry sir. I will do it immediately, sir, he said scampering as fast as he could.

One of them ran off, leaving the other looking down at us as we walked through the doorway.

Entering the city, the first thing I saw were treehouses. There were houses and businesses all interconnected with bridges and platforms suspended in the trees above. It was a tangle of rope and vines, and the people walking on them seemed to navigate it easily. The ground here was the same as the path outside. It was so well-trodden that the dust that was kicked up left a fine haze in the air. There was a clearing for the town centre, and the trees were thinned out to make moving between houses and businesses easier. All along the edge of the path were wildflowers. It was beautiful, and the smell of them was overwhelming and addictive.

The city was bustling with people walking overhead and on the ground. Voices called out to each other, and I could hear people laughing and chatting. I could smell meat cooking, and it reminded me I hadn't eaten all day, making my mouth water. All through the trees, I could see little lights flickering, like scattered jewels catching the dappled sunlight.

Gloom led me through Toleran to the far end of the city. As we walked, we were stopped by a female gnome with white hair in two braids and freckles covering her face. She smiled up at Gloom and offered him a pastry of some sort. It was golden and flaky, and I couldn't take my eyes off it. I felt like it was the most delicious thing I had ever seen. Gloom thanked the gnome but shook his head and started to walk again.

Reluctantly, I followed, watching as the gnome and the pasty turned and walked the other way. I thought about asking Gloom if we could have something to eat, but it looked like now he was home, he was in a bit of a hurry. I started to follow him, and when I looked up, I could see him watching me. In the sunlight, I could see his small horns were slightly textured, and I wondered what they would feel like.

"Wait here a second," he told me as he walked back the way we had come. I waited as I watched all the different people and creatures mingling and talking. It was such a peaceful scene I wondered what it would have been like to grow up somewhere like here.

"Here, you look hungry," said a voice behind me. I turned and saw Gloom holding out the pastry the Gnome lady had offered him. I was stunned that he would do that for me. I held out my hand and took it from him, noticing it was slightly warm.

"Thank you. I am a little bit," I said, not knowing what else to say. I looked at it and I hoped it was safe to eat. I decided I was too hungry to care, and if he wanted to harm me, he could have left me tied to the post. I was surprised he had even noticed me looking at it in the first place. It seemed enough for him as he nodded and continued. I took a bite, and the taste of cherries flooded my mouth as the flaky pastry stuck to my lips. I ate it hurriedly as I followed behind Gloom, trying to work out why he had done that.

From what I could tell, the outside near the vine wall was mostly houses, and the centre looked like businesses. I started to take closer note of the people around me. Most were humans, which was comforting, but I could also see people that looked like trees. They had bark for skin, and their hair was branches and leaves. I could tell from the leaves and the pattern of the bark they were all different types of trees, and I realised what they were. Dryads. Some of them even had little creatures nesting in their hair, and they dropped leaves and twigs as they moved through the crowd.

There were more gnomes and a few centaurs. I could see little creatures flying around that could only be pixies and tree sprites. They whizzed in and out of people, illuminating things as they went. While walking through the town, all the people and creatures made way for Gloom and bowed reverently. Gloom ignored them all, apart from a smile here and there. I kept my head down and followed closely, but I could feel their questioning eyes boring into my back as I passed.

Eventually, we made it to the base of a huge oak tree. The front door was carved into the trunk, and the rest of the building was scattered through the spreading arms of the tree. At the bottom, the roots spread out, and the canopy let in filtered light that danced on the ground around me. Above me, rooms were dotted through the branches with billowing fabric flowing from the open windows and doors. The branches of the ancient tree reached out wide and seemed to hold the rest of the city at bay.

"This is the aerie. This is where I live and where you'll stay while you are here," Gloom said as we approached.

When we entered through the large doors, my mouth dropped open. The inside seemed to glow amber from all the polished wood. It was decorated with flower bunches on decorative tables or hanging from the ceiling, and the smell of sawdust was faint in the air. Strangely, it all worked together, and I spent most of the walk through the tree with my mouth open, looking around in awe.

Something that caught my eye was the small clusters of mushrooms dotted on all the walls and along the edge of the floors. They were glowing and lighting up the walkways. They were all different colours and sizes and the cutest things I had ever seen. I also noticed there was a heavy presence of guards and soldiers scattered throughout the people who were walking around. They were milling about everywhere. Some were trying to blend in, but they were all alert and looked ready for action.

Gloom led me through doors and corridors until I was so confused there was no way I was getting out, even if I wanted to. Finally, he stopped.

I saw his eyes harden, and he grew serious. "Now. Here are the rules, and I expect them to be followed." Wariness filled me at his tone. "If you break them, there will be punishments, no matter how good you think your reason may be. Number one. You will not leave Toleran. You are not to go beyond the wall. As I said earlier, there are people and things out there that are not so friendly, and you don't want to get caught with them.

"Number two. You are not to tell or show anyone your powers. Until we know where they came from and how to control them, it is to be between you and me.

"Number three. As my new assistant, I expect you to do as I say and do it right. I will not tolerate idiots. I know you are learning, but I expect what I give you to be done fast and correctly."

He looked at me, and I realised he expected an answer. "Yes, sir," I said, even though my head was still reeling.

He appeared satisfied with my answer and said, "I'll see you in the morning."

He turned and walked away. I watched him go, happy to be alone for a bit. I needed time to process this crazy day. I walked into the room and gasped. It was beautiful. All over, there was polished wood and vines. It was like the forest was inside this room. On one side was a large bed hidden behind some privacy screens woven from living wisteria that hung from the ceiling. The beautiful purple flowers filled the room with colour and perfume, and I ran my hand down the length of the vines, marvelling. In the main room was a sitting area with two navy blue velvet armchairs, an artificial fire, and a small dining table with some chairs. It was all very human-like, and I wondered if all the rooms were like this.

I walked over to the window and pulled back the gently billowing yellow curtain. Behind it was a small balcony, and the railing was made from a thick, woody vine covered in white flowers. On the ground in the corner, there were more of the little light mushrooms. I bent over to get a closer look at them. These ones had a long stem with a cute little yellow cap on them.

Now that I had a higher vantage point, I could see more of the city. It was starting to grow dark, but in the distance, the huge wall loomed, and I could just barely make out the shapes of the people patrolling it. Down in the town, I could hear music and loud voices talking over each other. A beautiful breeze carried the scents of night, blooming flowers and roasting meats. I let it blow through my soul to try and banish some of the events of the day. I breathed deeply, feeling the ache of exhaustion in my bones. It had been a long day of strange happenings, and I was worn out.

So many emotions were tumbling through my body. Sadness tugged at me from being discarded and thrown out of my village. These were the people who I thought loved, or at a minimum, liked me. I had never been safe or wanted to be there, but I never in a million years thought I would be thrown out and sacrificed. I thought of my parents and the life we could have had if they weren't killed. A life out in the real world, at school, and getting a job and perhaps even a boyfriend. I had had lovers before but not a boyfriend. Someone to love and trust and know would always be there to help me through the tough times. I had dreamt of it so often.

I hated to admit it to myself, but I was scared. It was a feeling I knew well, but it was not welcome. I didn't know where I was, and I had no idea what I was doing here. My fear sat hot in the pit of my stomach, influencing every thought.

But strangely, I also felt hope. I had got out of the clutches of Matthew and Woodmere. I might finally tame this beast living inside me and learn to live with it. Hope had spent so many years buried in my soul, aching to be free, and perhaps now I could finally let it sprout, grow, breathe.

I went and sat on the bed and touched the soft yellow comforter. Yawning, I felt my thoughts scatter. It had been a day of twists and turns, and my body had had enough. I lay down, thinking of closing my eyes for a few minutes, but sleep took me.

NINE

Amelia

When I woke up, it was still dark outside. I hadn't meant to sleep, but at least I was refreshed. And hungry.

Opening my door, I saw a bundle wrapped in large leaves. I picked it up and unwrapped it inside my new room.

Someone had been to Woodmere and got some of my things. There were a few dresses and pants, underwear, jackets, and an extra pair of shoes. As well as some extra clothing that someone must have found for me. In the bottom was another package with my hairbrush, some pens, a picture of me and my grandmother and my journal. I had no idea how they got it, but I didn't care.

Looking at all these things spread out, I couldn't help myself, and I burst into tears. Someone had gone to get these things for me from the village that had tried to kill me. It was a pitiful amount of belongings, but at that moment, I felt as rich as a queen. Picking up the photo of my grandmother and me, I hugged it to my chest. Not for the first time, I admitted I was lost without her.

Holding that photo, I was reminded of the things she had done for me. Like the time I killed half the corn crop because Lana had dobbed on me for sneaking out of my house at night. Matthew had come and told me I needed to be punished. He had dragged me by the hair to the isolation shed and thrown me in. I was in the shed for four days with only two cups of water a day and some bread. By the time they dragged me out, I could barely stand, and there was no way I could fight back. I was so relieved to feel fresh air on my face. I didn't question why, but I found out later I was only released because my grandmother had refused to leave his house until I was.

Growing up, I hated my powers. Because of that one act, my village had almost starved. I would often daydream about what my life would have been like without them. My grandmother had always told me they were a gift and that I had them for a reason. I couldn't help thinking if I didn't have them, perhaps I would have made a good wife. Maybe I could have wanted to have children and settle down. Maybe then Woodmere would have been a happy place for me.

I pushed aside those thoughts, packed my things away neatly in the wardrobe, and opened the other door in my room. Inside was a bathroom, and it was bathed in moonlight. There was a big copper tub and shower at one end and a toilet and wash basin at the other. Looking up, I saw there was no roof, and I found myself gazing directly at the stars and moon. I smiled and turned on the water for the tub. A quick bath and I would go and find some food. Looking at the clothes I had been wearing, I realised they would need some serious washing and mending after my mad dash through the woods. I put them into the hamper and watched as they disappeared. I stood there for a moment while my brain processed what had just happened.

I walked over and looked in the hamper, and my clothes were definitely gone. Was everything in this place magical? I decided not to use it again until I found out where my clothes were going.

I spent the next twenty minutes soaking in the bath, looking at the stars and moon, trying not to think. The stars winked at me, and I was calm. I allowed my mind to float and switch off.

I was shocked awake by a pounding at the door. I sat up quickly as my heart started to hammer. Water splashed onto the floor as I climbed out, looking around frantically for a towel or robe to cover myself with. I spotted the towels on the back of the door and wrapped one around me as I hurried to the door. Just before I opened it, I realised how crazy this was. Should I open the door to a stranger in a towel? I looked around the room, but there were no easy clothes to put on.

I stood there chewing my lip, knowing I didn't want to see anyone when I was so vulnerable. The banging started again, louder and more insistent. I almost yelped in surprise and then kicked myself that I had given myself away.

"Who is it?" I asked through the door, trying to sound confident.

I heard a heavy sigh come from the other side. "It's Rak. I have your dinner. Gloom sent me, I'm from the kitchen." His voice was high-pitched, and he talked like he had a lisp, and he sounded impatient. The mention of food made my tummy rumble, and knowing he was sent by Gloom made me feel a little better.

"Okay, give me a minute," I said, thinking I could get dressed quickly.

"Look, I haven't got all day. I'll leave it at your door. Some of us must work," he said.

I was a bit surprised at his surly tone, but maybe he was just busy. I took a deep breath and opened the door a crack, positioning myself behind it so he couldn't see my body. He was a creature I hadn't heard about, and I felt my eyes widen slightly. He seemed to be half human, half snake. The top half was human, and I could see he was well-muscled under his shirt. His black hair was long and tied back in a ponytail, and he had slitted eyes. I could see small scales glinting in the light all over his skin. The bottom of him was a long snake tail, dark brown with golden diamond marks down the centre of it. He was standing over me, stretched out on his tail, and I looked up to meet his eyes. He thrust out a platter with a cover, handing me my food. I took it with one hand while the other one clutched my towel, making sure it didn't fall off.

"Here. Leave it outside when you are done," he said and then slithered off.

I managed to say "Thank you" to his back, surprised at his abruptness. He waved a hand over his shoulder to acknowledge me and disappeared behind a corner.

I sighed heavily, getting the feeling I hadn't made a friend there, and took my platter inside. I set it down on the dining table while I put on some fresh pyjamas that had been brought to me.

Opening the cover of the tray, I saw fresh fruits and veg-etables as well as nuts and some cooked lamb. I devoured all the delicious food, and afterwards, I could hardly move. While my food settled. I took a moment to study my room more closely. On one of the walls, there was a small bookcase. I walked over to the soft blue rug, and I ran my finger along the titles. There were a lot of story books and some botany books. I took one down and flipped through the pages. I wasn't a very good reader, but it was beautifully illustrated. I took it and put it near my bed before I took the tray back out and put it back outside my door.

After eating, I was feeling sleepy again, so I laid down and flicked through the book until I couldn't keep my eyes open any longer. Sleep pulled me under.

I paced in my room the next morning while I waited for someone to come and get me. I tried to calm my anxiety by tidying and writing in my journal, but I had too much nervous energy to really focus. I spent some time watching the city come to life. As the light filtered through the leaves, people were out and about setting up their storefronts and having their breakfast. Below my balcony, there was a beautiful little garden, and I made a note to go and find it if I had time.

A knock on the door disrupted my thoughts, and I hesitated to answer it. I hoped it wasn't Rak again from last night. I got up to answer it, realising whoever it was would keep knocking. My anxiety was through the roof by the time I got there, and I twirled my necklace around my finger, trying to calm myself.

On the other side was one of the tree-like people I had seen yesterday. This one looked to be made of birch wood and was a light grey colour striped with black marks. Around her eyes was black, making it look like she was wearing eyeliner. Her eyes were also black but had little flecks of orange through them, and they were warm. Her hair was the colour of autumn leaves, vibrant against the paleness of her skin. They framed her face and created a lion mane of leaves behind her. Standing closer, I could see her skin looked the same as mine but slightly textured. I wondered if it was hard like wood. She wore a simple black dress, and she was stunning. And I could sense the...otherness about her.

"Amelia? Hi, I'm Lilly. I am Gloom's PR Assistant. He sent me here to help you get organised and show you the place. Are you ready to go?" she asked with barely a break in between.

"Umm, yeah. I'm Amelia." I stepped out and closed the door behind me. I followed her as she walked down the hall, and I tried to keep track of where we were.

"So, how much did Gloom tell you yesterday?"

"Not much. He brought me here and told me I was going to be his assistant. That's about it," I said. I clamped my lips, wanting to ask her how I could escape, was Gloom cruel, or could she help me get out of here, but I was worried she would laugh at me. I didn't want to let her know my thoughts before I could trust her, and I didn't trust anyone here yet.

"Pfft. Sounds about right. He is always so busy. He likes to do everything himself, which is fine, but it doesn't make him a very patient person. I'm sure he forgot to fill you in. So, you are in the employee wing now. This is where we all live. I'm going to take you to the informal dining room. It's where his main staff eat and chat about the day ahead and stuff."

I followed behind her, not saying anything, but she didn't seem to mind. I wondered what Gloom would think about her talking about him like that. She seemed to know him pretty well.

At the end of the hall, we turned left at the split and kept going. While we walked, we passed more soldiers and staff of the aerie. Gnomes, humans and sprites hurried and flew past. Some looked busy and rushed while others chatted. I wasn't sure I would ever get used to seeing these fantasy creatures, and I tried not to stare. Lilly nodded and said "good morning" to everyone, and she seemed like she knew everyone.

After a few twists and turns, we made it to a large room with a big round table in the middle. Around the table were eight chairs and more small light mushrooms, casting the room in a warm glow. The room had three other doors that were pointed at the top, and there was a red and orange plush carpet on the ground. It was one of the nicest rooms I had ever seen. I wondered what the formal dining room looked like if this was the informal one.

The table was covered with all kinds of food. There were fruit and vegetables, eggs, bread, and different coloured juices. I had never seen so much food, and I didn't know where to start. Lilly directed me to sit, and she sat next to me. She loaded her plate with nuts and fruit and poured us both a glass of water. I got some bread and fruit and tried to eat, knowing it was going to be a big day, but my stomach was in too many knots to take advantage of what was spread before me. I pushed the food around my plate.

"So, this is where you will take most of your meals. The table has food on it most of the day, and you are free to eat here whenever you want. I'll show you where Gloom's quarters are after so you can get your jobs for the day, then I will take you around and help you get started," she said between mouthfuls.

I was trying to remember everything she was saying. What jobs would I be doing? I had never even had a job before. What if I stuffed everything up like usual? What would happen to me? As I started to spiral, the coldness rose. I looked at my hands and tried to keep my emotions under control. I took a steadying breath and managed to hold it off, but it was still there, waiting.

Lilly continued, not noticing my distress. She pulled out a tablet device and handed it over. "This is your schedule. It works the same as the ones from the human world, so it shouldn't take too long for you to get used to it. We find it makes it easier on the humans who work here. And hey, if it isn't broken, why fix it? Am I right?" She didn't wait for an answer. "On here will be Gloom's schedule and all the things you need to remind him of, like where to be and who he is meeting with. That sort of stuff. Also, what he wants to eat and where and any errands he needs you to run. He is pretty good about remembering all these things, but he does need a hand sometimes, so it is better to remind him. He can add things on here whenever, so make sure you are checking it regularly." She paused long enough to see the confusion on my face. "Are you okay? Do you understand all this?" she asked, looking concerned.

I looked into her black eyes and grew hotter. I was so out of my depth. If I told her, would she help me or laugh at me? She seemed kind, and I didn't think she would be mean. I opened my mouth to reply when the door at the end of the room swung open, and more people arrived.

First was Bilvog with his staff and long white beard. He was followed by a centaur man. Now I understood why all the rooms and doors were so big in this place. His body was a beautiful piebald black and white with a long black tail braided with bells and ribbons that jingled when he moved. The man half was a very tanned, handsome man with the glossiest hair that reached past the small of his back. He was wearing a black T-shirt and rings on every finger. As he approached the table, he spotted me.

"Good morning, Lilly. How did you sleep?" he asked before he noticed me. "Hello there. You must be the new girl I am hearing about. I'm Mezz, the master's personal shopper. What's your name? He had a deep, smooth voice, and I felt myself relaxing listening to it. He extended his hand, and I stood to shake it. His smile showed the whitest teeth I had ever seen.

"A-Amelia," I stammered out.

"Amelia. That's a lovely name. Now, if you need any clothes or anything for your room, you let me know, and I can get it for you." He smiled and started filling a plate with food as he started chatting to one of the humans who had come in with him.

Bilvog filled two plates in silence while ignoring everyone. Once they were full, he started to walk towards the door while the rest of us ate and chatted quietly about the day. I kept to myself and tried to anticipate what my day would look like. A few of the staff came and went, replacing food and taking away the empty plates. Rak was one of them, and I looked away, so I didn't have to talk to him.

The sound of bells shattered the air around us. They were loud, and I looked to the roof for the source but couldn't see anything. I covered my ears, looking around at the others to see what was happening. Everyone stopped eating, and after a moment's hesitation, the room erupted into movement as I sat there staring. All the people in the room stopped what they were doing and bolted for the far door. Lilly turned back and called out to me, motioning me to follow.

My body got over the shock, and I stood, knocking over my chair and followed them out. After winding through more corridors, we arrived at the front door of the aerie. Looking out over the town, we could see people in huddles everywhere, panic in the air.

"What is going on?" I asked Lilly, trying to stay calm in all the chaos, but the atmosphere was starting to scare me a little.

"The bells mean an attack of some sort," Lilly said absently as she studied the scene in front of us, trying to find the source of the chaos. Leaves fluttered everywhere as she whipped her head back and forth surveying the scene.

"Although looking at this, whatever it was, has gone now." I followed her down the steps to the ground, where some people from the city were gathering. As I got closer, I noticed Gloom had beaten us there. He was at the bottom of the steps, dressed in what looked like the same outfit he had on yesterday. I watched as he talked to the people of the town calmly and reassuringly. Even though I could see the panic and worry on their faces, I could tell they were comfortable around him. I always thought people would be scared of the Evers. They were like Gods, after all.

But here, they were comfortable with no barrier between them.

As we neared, the people were telling Gloom what had happened. Gloom frowned as we approached, but I could see he was taking everything in. Next to him was a large satyr. He had goat legs covered in light brown fur and a human top half. His little ears stuck through his brown hair, which was long on the sides and short at the front to keep it out of his eyes. His eyes were chocolate brown, and they looked alert and ready for anything. He was wearing some kind of metal armour, and he was a lot larger than I thought satyrs usually were.

"Sir, my people have been through the town, and it seems like the enemy is gone. It was a fast-targeted attack. They stole four people last night when everyone was sleeping," he reported, short and to the point.

Lilly covered her mouth and shook her head, making orange leaves flutter all around her. "How did they get in, Kennock?"

"We are still investigating. Security of the wall has been increased since this all began, so we are trying to sort it out," Kennock replied with a frown on his face.

I took a step back and looked around. People were still rushing around, and I could see a few families huddled together, crying. They must be the families of the ones who were taken. What a terrible thing to have happened. Everyone was still in shock, but up the back, I heard raised voices.

"What is Ever Gloom going to do about this? How is he going to protect us? And don't say stay inside the wall because obviously, that isn't helping!"

"Yeah, that's true! Why isn't he protecting us?" I couldn't see the people who were talking, but a murmur spread through the people gathered.

A wave of anger, confusion, and desperation rolled through the crowd. Gloom turned to everyone and spoke over the noise.

"I have protocols in place, but now is not the time to be discussing this. Things are being done."

"Well, clearly not enough! People are being taken from their beds in their homes! How are we meant to sleep at night knowing they could get in and take our children?"

The mood of the city was turning, and I saw Kennock step in front of Gloom and the others. I took another step back and, looking around, realised this could be my chance. Everyone here was preoccupied with the discussion; I could slip off, and no one would notice. I took a few more steps away until I was sure no one was watching me. I thought about when I tried to escape in the forest. Would he chase me down? I hesitated a moment then my decision was made.

I turned and calmly walked away.

TEN

Amelia

Walking through the town, I tried my best to keep out of peoples' way as they streamed past me, trying to hear what Gloom had to say. My heart was pounding, but I couldn't turn back now. This might be my only chance to get out of here.

Walking to the wall, I tried to be as unobtrusive as I could and repeated the code word in my head, hoping I had it right and this part of the wall would open. What if the word didn't work for me? Maybe they change it every day? I pushed these worries from my mind and kept going. I stopped behind a building and looked up, hoping I could avoid the eyes of the guards on top of the wall. I was lucky. Most were looking at what was happening near Gloom's aerie and weren't paying attention to where I was. I walked to the closest section and said *voyant*. After a beat, I watched as the branches slithered and moved to form a door perfectly my size. Relief flooded through me. Now, I had to hope the portal was the same.

I took one more look at Toleran and thought about the things I had left in my room. Things could be replaced, but I was upset about my photo. I reached up to touch my necklace and was glad I still had it around my neck. I would be taking my grandmother with me. I smiled to think she would believe I was crazy to be trying to escape Toleran. She would have loved to come here and see all the beings and have crazy stories to tell. I differed from her in that way. She wanted adventure. I want peace and freedom, and I didn't think I was going to get it here. I stilled my nerves and stepped outside the walls.

I could see the path into the woods, and I hurried along it. The forest had a thin layer of mist from the night before, but the sun was gentle and strong enough I could see. Birdsong and other animal noises filled the air as they greeted the morning. I walked quickly, hoping no guards on the wall would turn and see me.

From memory, the walk was only about fifteen minutes to the portal, and I hoped, coming out of the wall where I did, did not add too much time. My shoes and bottoms of my clothes were soon wet from the dew, but I kept on. As I walked deeper into the forest, it got darker, the sun not strong enough to pierce through the canopy yet. I pulled my hands into my sleeves to try and keep them warm and sped up. Not long into the forest, I was uneasy. It took me a minute, but eventually, I noticed the birdsong had stopped. I paused where I was and listened but couldn't hear any noises. My belly fluttered, and my focus became hyper-aware. Why did the birds stop?

I continued walking, picking up my pace. The portal should be up ahead if I remembered correctly. I heard a twig snap behind me. I froze. I heard footsteps. I managed to unlock my muscles long enough to turn and look. I couldn't see anything behind me. There was only the path and the trunks of the tall trees lifting to the sky. The ferns on the ground waved lazily in the morning breeze. While scanning the area, I noticed a dead tree with branches sticking out. That's odd. I couldn't remember seeing any dead trees or plants on my walk from the portal to Toleran the day before. Looking at it closer, my heart jumped in my chest when it moved.

I didn't waste a single second. I turned around and sprinted to the portal, knowing it couldn't be too far ahead. My heart pounded, and it felt like my whole body was tingling. I couldn't look behind me, but I could see a shadow running alongside me. It was too fast to see what it was properly, but it was big, and it was keeping up.

Cold spread through me hard and fast as my power punched through my body and shrivelled all the plant life around me. At this point, I didn't care about my power. I just needed to get to the portal before whatever it was caught up to me.

Rounding a bend, I saw in the distance the two black pine trees, and I whimpered as I ran towards them. I noticed the shadow was no longer running beside me, but I didn't slow down. As I was about to shout *voyant*, a figure stepped out from behind a nearby tree. I screamed and stopped running.

My chest heaving, I held out my hand, shooting my power at whatever it was in front of me. I let the coldness and the wildness of my power surge through my hands. The forest became distorted as I looked at it through my power. Closing my eyes, I hoped I hit the target and could get through the portal. After what seemed like an eternity, my power drained out of me. My head spun, and I had to hold onto the nearest tree for support. I missed and fell to the ground in a heap. Seeing double, I looked up to see if I had got whoever, or whatever, had been waiting for me.

With my funny vision, I saw someone rush towards me. Hands touched my arms and guided me to the relatively dry path. I screwed my eyes closed, hoping for a quick and painless death, when a voice spoke to me.

"Amelia. Open your eyes. Are you alright?" They snapped open at the demand, and I recognised who it was.

"Take some deep breaths. You will feel better soon. You used too much power. Just breathe."

I did what he said, and he was right. Within a few minutes, my vision had returned to normal, and I could sit without support. I glanced into the forest around me but couldn't see the thing chasing me. Had I imagined that horned creature? I didn't think so, but maybe. All I could see was a wide strip of dead forest along each side of the path. Some of the plants had disintegrated altogether. The rest were grey and wilted over. In front of me, to the side of the portal, thirty or so trees were leafless, twisted, and dead. I couldn't believe my power had done that. I had never been so out of control before.

"What are you looking for?" Gloom asked with a frown.

"I thought I saw...Nothing, it was nothing." I looked at the dead grass around me. I didn't want to tell him what I thought I saw. I was already in enough trouble that I didn't want to add to it.

"Were you going to go back to Woodmere?" He seemed surprised and annoyed that I had run, and I couldn't blame him. "The people who wanted to kill you? I was in that village last night, and I can tell you no one is mourning you."

I flinched at his hard words. Why did he have to be so cruel? I lifted my head and looked him right in the eyes. Fear and relief overtook me, and for the first time in a long time, I spoke without thinking.

"Do you think I want to go back there? I hated it! And now my parents and grandmother are gone. There is nothing there for me anymore. I want to be free. Why can't anyone understand that? I want to be free to do what I want and be myself. I am so sick of having people tell me what to do all the time." I held his eye contact and refused to be intimidated. He looked back at me steadily, but I saw a flicker of sympathy there. I hoped my passionate outburst would sway him or make him let me go, but I could see it hadn't worked.

When he spoke, his voice was gentler, "I know you want to be free, but it can't happen right now. Look around you. You are dangerous. You could kill someone with this power. Things are happening here, and looking at the power you just exhibited, you could be an asset in the fight to come. I can help you get some control. Someone is trying to take over Toleran. People were taken last night, and I'm pretty sure it wasn't for a tea party. Dark symbols have been showing up all over the forest, and we need to work out how and why. You could help us destroy whoever this is. I need to protect my people, and I'm sorry, but I won't let you go until it is done." He spoke with such passion it dawned on me he really did love his people and would do anything for them. No matter my feelings about it.

A pit formed in my belly, and all my hope seemed to fall into it. I knew it was no use. There was no way I was going to get out of here. It was time to accept that. I should stay and get some help with my powers. Clearly, I wasn't doing so well on my own on that front. Tears threatened to spill out of my eyes, but I held them back. I gave him a tight nod. I could cry later.

Gloom nodded and held out his arm to help me get up. I ignored it and hauled myself up and dusted off my skirt. The world spun for a moment but quickly settled. He dropped his arm, and I saw...approval...flash in his eyes. It was gone too fast for me to know what it was. He turned and strode back down the path towards Toleran, leaving me to catch up.

"All this time wasted. I should be helping to coordinate the search for the missing people," he muttered under his breath.

Guilt washed over me, and I thought of the people crying earlier who were missing their loved ones. I couldn't imagine how it would feel to have a loved one stolen from you in the middle of the night. To not know where they had gone and if they would see them again. "How did you know I was gone? How did you beat me here?"

"One of the guards saw you going through the wall. I know almost everything that happens in Toleran."

Before I could stop myself, I snorted. "Well, clearly not everything, or you wouldn't be having this problem."

Gloom stopped dead in his tracks for a moment. I waited to hear what he was going to say, but he started walking again. Maybe I had surprised him? I was surprised myself. The rest of the walk was silent, and I went straight to my room when we got back, feeling sorry for myself.

ELEVEN

Amelia

The next day, the aerie and Toleran were a hive of activity. I spent the day doing anything I could think of to help that would take my mind off my escape attempt. I helped pack food and supplies for the constant search parties, and I took food and anything else the families needed for the people who had lost their family members. Seeing their faces droop in worry made my stomach knot, and I couldn't shake it. Seeing them so worried made me forget about my own problems, and I felt the need to help the people who needed it. Growing up, I had often wished for kindness, and now I could give that to them.

At some point last night, I had decided that if I was going to stay here, I wanted to change. My whole life, I had wanted to be part of a community and voice my opinions and thoughts without the fear of being punished or locked up. Something inside of me decided this was my chance, and I was going to take it. No more timid and shy Amelia. I wasn't going to let things happen to me. I wanted to participate in my life, and now was my chance.

By the time I made my way to the war room for a meeting, my feet ached from walking back and forth to town all day. Inside the war room were a few smaller meeting rooms. As I was walking past one of the doors, I could hear people talking. A word caught my ear, and I slowed. I looked around the room, knowing this was a private conversation, but I was unable to back away.

"I don't want to sacrifice anything, but we have come up with nothing. It is time to seek her out."

"But what about the payment? It's such a high price."

It was Gloom and Kennock talking, and I could tell they didn't want anyone to hear what they were talking about. I couldn't move away now. What were they sacrificing?

Gloom replied, "I know the price is high, but what else can we do? I need to know who has taken these people. It is escalating, and I'm not just going to sit around and let it happen. I need answers. I will take the guilt and live with it somehow."

There was a pause, and someone sighed. "Go Kennock. Find our payment for Vivian. I have made my decision. We will leave in the morning."

I jumped back from the door as Kennock stormed out. He looked at me and scowled, his face red and ears pointed back. He didn't say anything to me and instead stalked off, his hooves clopping against the wood flooring. I waited a moment, wondering what the payment could possibly be that would cause him to be so angry.

"Amelia," Gloom called from inside.

I jumped, annoyed with myself that I had been caught eavesdropping. I stepped into the room. Gloom was sitting behind a desk on the other side of the small room, and I could see his face looked troubled.

"How much did you hear?" he asked.

"Not much. Something about a payment. Who are you paying?"

Gloom sighed heavily as he slumped in his chair for a moment, "Vivian Calerook. She is the most powerful mystic in Toleran. She is known as the Prickly Hag, but don't call her that to her face. We haven't found anything in the searches, and I think it is time to see her and see if she has got some answers. Her answers come at a high price."

I could see from his expression this decision was weighing on him. I wondered what it could possibly be that would affect him so much.

"Have you used her before for information?"

"Yes, but it was many years ago. I do not see her lightly." His eyes refocused and his attention came back to the room. "You will stay here. We will be gone for a day at least. When I return, we will discuss what I expect of you while you are here. I have already added items to your task list that should keep you busy until I get back. Lilly can help if you need."

"So, what exactly is she? Some sort of seer or something?" I asked, trying to sound normal while my mind raced with a plan, I was sure was crazy.

"Of a sort. She is an ancient hag or witch. She was here long before me, and she and her coven have proved to be useful and dangerous in equal parts."

"Can I go with you?" I asked, not really expecting to get permission, but I had to ask.

"It is much too dangerous. We need to travel fast, and I can't risk that she will take a liking to you. The less she knows of you and your power, the better." He stood and shuffled some papers and started to walk around the desk. "Bilvog will be here if you need anything while we are gone. Now it is time for our meeting. I need to go and get some paperwork. You can wait in the war room. I won't be long." He brushed past me, and the smell of coffee invaded my senses. I stood for a moment and wondered if I had imagined the worry I saw on his face. Now, he was composed and business-like. I sighed and walked out the door behind him, thinking I might get out of here after all.

I sat in the chair at the back of the room behind Gloom's chair and looked around. On the walls, there were large maps. They were old, yellowed and curled around the edges. Since there was no one else here yet, I walked over to them and looked at what was marked on them. They were maps of the region, and on them were black circles all around the wall that surrounded Toleran.

Looking at the next map, it looked similar but without the city marked. It took me a minute to realise I was looking at a map of my world. On that map, there were some black circles, but fewer of them. They must be the spots where the decayed symbols were found. Who could be leaving these and what did they mean? Judging by the circles on the map, there had been a few symbols quite close to Woodmere. I shivered, knowing evil had been so close without us knowing. There was no question these symbols were evil. So, what did that say about my powers? I tried to make out some patterns, but I couldn't work them out. They looked completely random.

I turned away and looked around the rest of the room. There was a bookshelf with old leather-bound tomes and a small refreshments area. It seemed like they spent a lot of time here. I looked out the window and at the ground. Here, we were only up one story, and I could see the little details of the garden space below me. I missed walking around the forest barefoot and wondered if I would get the chance anytime soon. I poured myself a goblet of water from the refreshments table and made my way back to my chair. I settled in and wondered how much longer they would be.

As if I had summoned them, the door swung open, and people and creatures started filing in. Bilvog was first, carrying his staff. He walked to the seat next to the head chair and arranged himself for a moment. He leaned his staff against the table and smoothed his beard, not sparing me a glance. I wondered why he didn't like humans.

"Hello, Bilvog. How are you today?" I asked, hoping to break the ice.

He looked over at me, bored. "I am tired, Amelia. People have been stolen from this town, and it is up to me to help find them. I am busy and tired." He looked back down at his beard and rearranged some of the bells that were woven in it.

I looked down at my lap, regretting saying anything. Luckily, I was spared any more awkwardness by more people arriving. Next to arrive was Kennock, and you would never know he was so angry just a few moments before. He came in with three others of the city guard. They all looked human and wore dark purple cloaks and had a green tree sewn onto the front of their shirts. Behind them came another group of people I didn't know, but they all wore robes of varying colours. By now, there were eight people in the room, and everyone talked amongst themselves. As they sat down, they all smiled my way politely, and I smiled back.

"Kennock. Any news on the poor souls that were kidnapped?" Bilvog asked.

Kennock sighed heavily. "No. We have sent out multiple search parties, but nothing. No tracks or signs of how they came to be inside the wall. It is a total mystery. I know Gloom has an idea he is going to discuss when he arrives. Perhaps we will have more luck with that.

"Oh, he does, does he? He didn't mention anything to me," Bilvog replied, frowning and shifting in his seat.

Kennock opened his mouth to reply, but at that moment, the door swung open, and Gloom entered. All talk stopped immediately as everyone stood up. He sat and was as still as the stone table he was sitting in front of. We all took our seats, and anxiety hung in the air as the gravity of the meeting sank in. How were they going to find these people?

"I am sorry for the late start. We are here to discuss the kidnapping that happened in Toleran. It is unacceptable that this has happened, and even worse, we have no leads. I am implementing an emergency protocol. I am having the local magic guild," he gestured to the group wearing the robes, "install a magical binding that will entwine in the wall."

He nodded at an older gnome, even older than Bilvog. What little hair he had on top of his head was wispy and bright white. He was wearing long robes of a deep red colour, and he walked with a bent-up bit of wood.

He nodded at the gathering, and Gloom continued, "Any time someone enters or exits the wall, certain people will be alerted, and it is to be investigated immediately. Also, no one is to enter or leave Toleran without first notifying a senior member of the leaders. I've been told this will take about twenty-four hours, but we are going to stop them coming in and taking our people if it is the last thing we do. Kennock." Kennock sat up straighter if that was even possible. "I want the soldiers and guards training as often as possible. Rounds are to be more frequent. I want every inch of this place guarded, twenty-four-seven."

Gloom stopped for a moment, and everyone waited to hear what he would say next. The silence seemed to drag, and a few people shuffled in their chairs, waiting. Bilvog was watching him closely, and finally, when Bilvog opened his mouth to speak, Gloom looked up. "I have made a decision." He cleared his throat. "I have decided to seek help. I will be taking a group of people, and we will be travelling to Nightshadow Grove to seek help from the Prickly Hag." People started muttering together, and I could tell that her reputation was well-known among these people. Bilvog looked shocked, but he tried to hide it.

"Are you sure that is a good idea? Surely, it hasn't come to that yet. I am positive that if we search and use our collective minds, we will find these people. Vivian cannot be trusted," Bilvog said.

"If I am right, things are only going to escalate from here. We need to stop it before it goes too far. I will do anything to stop the people of this town from being a target. Even if it means visiting...her. We will be going, and we will pay whatever price she demands. Kennock, select a handful of troops to come with us. I know you are busy, but I will need them in case things get bad in the forest."

Kennock looked a bit overwhelmed but nodded. I had a feeling his troops were already spread thin, and I wasn't sure how he was going to accomplish this increase in security and a trip to the forest. After his announcement, the meeting continued for another half an hour or so, and no matter what was suggested, Gloom did not waver. He was going, and nothing would change his mind. I diligently took notes and made no noise as I formulated my own plan. At the end, everyone filed out, and all that remained were Gloom, Bilvog, and I.

"Master, are you sure this is a good idea?" He asked as he shuffled closer to us.

"Yes Bilvog, I am sure," he sighed, sounding like he had had this conversation before.

"I don't mean to overstep, Master, but I really think you should take my advice and continue to search—"

Gloom looked at him with ice in his eyes. "Who is the Ever here?"

"You are, Master," Bilvog replied, his face turning red as he ran a hand over his beard, making the bells tinkle.

"That's right. Now, *you* are an advisor, which allows you some grace, but I have made my decision, and I will hear no more about it. While I am gone, you will be in charge, so I suggest you organise yourself."

Bilvog's brow furrowed, and I watched as the red spread on his neck. "Yes, Master." He turned on his heel and marched out, his staff slamming on the ground as he walked.

I stood there awkwardly waiting for Gloom to tell me what he wanted me to do now the meeting was over. Finally, after a pause in which he took a deep breath, he turned to me.

"Tristan will find you soon. He is going to guard you and make sure you are safe. With this attack, we need to take extra precautions. Now, go to Lilly and see how she is going with the damage control. We will meet again tonight for dinner with the group to go over the day."

I couldn't help but think Tristan was there for more reasons than he was letting on. Did he not trust me? Probably not. I hadn't given him any reason to, but it still annoyed me, knowing he thought I needed a guard.

I nodded, and he left, leaving me to find Lilly. My brain was processing everything that had been mentioned in the meeting, and I was wondering if I was safer in Woodmere. It seemed impossible that I had stumbled into more danger here, but I was beginning to expect danger at every corner.

After making a few wrong turns, I found the Comms Room and entered. It looked exactly how you would think it would look. TV screens and monitors were mounted everywhere. Control boards with lights and switches sat under them, and there were keyboards scattered around. It looked just like what I imagined a Comms Room would look like in my world, except that there were crystals emitting light scattered around. I could see little strands of light emanating from them and into the computer systems. It seemed like they were run by magic.

I found Lilly reading on a screen and typing. It looked like she had created a nest all around her workstation. There were jackets, plates, bowls and cutlery all over the bench. She must have seen me looking at it.

She smiled shyly and a blush spread across her cheeks, "Oh yeah, sorry about the mess. These days, I never seem to leave my desk, and it gets sort of...messy."

I smiled at her, secretly glad to see she wasn't as perfect as she looked. "No worries. Gloom was wondering how the damage control is going?"

She spun around back to the screen and furrowed her brow. "The damage control is going as well as expected. With so many incidents happening lately, people are not happy. Let Gloom know we have about a sixty per cent happiness rating, which is pretty good considering. But it looks like the people want to hear from him, so he better decide what he wants to tell them."

I got out my comms device Lilly had given me and worked out the messenger service. I sent what Lilly had said through to Gloom. I didn't get a reply, and I wasn't surprised. While I was there, I found my schedule of jobs needing to get done. It was a huge list, and I knew I didn't know how to do most of these things. With every item on the list, my stomach dropped. How would I ever get these things done? I groaned out loud, and Lilly looked at me.

"That bad? He is a hard master, but there is a heart of gold buried deep."

"It must be very deep," I muttered while scrolling the list. "I have no idea how to do most of these things. How am I going to get it done?"

Lilly laughed and took my tablet. She read my chores for the day. "Well, I can help you with this. There are a few things we can do here. Then we are going to have to go out and finish."

A wave of relief and gratitude for this beautiful tree woman crashed over me. "Aren't you too busy for this right now? By the way, if it isn't rude...what are you?"

She laughed and confirmed what I thought. "I'm a dryad." She shook out the leaves on her head, and a few fluttered to the floor. "We are bonded to a tree, and we look after it with all we have. My tree is close by, and I can go and visit it whenever I want, too. And yes, I'm busy, but I can't do too much more until Gloom speaks to the people. I have a bit of time to help."

"Wow, that is so cool. I would love to see your tree sometime. And thank you for helping me. I have no idea what I am doing. I don't know the first thing about being an assistant. What is all this stuff anyway?" I asked, gesturing to the computers.

"Oh, these are like mega computers. We have a whole social media network set up where we can monitor the people of Toleran, and they can give us feedback and any problems they have. The human world does have some amazing technologies. Did you use social media out there?"

"Not a lot. At Woodmere, it is all pretty controlled. The whole thing there is going back to the time before technology took over. Matthew liked us to do things the simple way, but we did have access to some stuff."

"I don't mean to offend you, but Woodmere is a bit weird. I am always asking Gloom why he doesn't move them on. It creeps me out how they are always prowling through the woods and stuff. And don't get me started on leaving the sacrifices. Like the Evers care about if they get a sacrifice. Awe and Ashes are the ones who care the most, and it's all their ego talking."

"Don't worry, I totally agree. I always thought the Evers didn't care, but when I mentioned it to Matthew, well, he didn't take it so well." I rubbed my wrists with the old memory. "Anyway, I will take all the help I can get. Thank you."

"You're welcome," she said. "Here, let's make a few calls."

For the rest of the day, we went through my list, starting with some calls to people Gloom wanted to see. We booked all the appointments and went on to errands. We walked outside the huge tree that served as Gloom's aerie and out into Toleran. My eyes were drawn upwards to the many tree houses and bridges spanning the trees. They blended in and fit the surroundings so nicely that it was like they were part of the branches. It looked like they belonged there, and if they were gone, the forest would be bare. Walking around, I saw all the small flowers dotting the edge of the walkways and scattered all over the ground. It was a beautiful place, and I was excited to spend more time exploring.

People nodded to us as Lilly and I walked past, and it was like she knew everyone. People stopped and chatted with her, and she was always kind and considerate. I was happy I had met Lilly. She was a genuinely nice person who could help me here. The people of the town seemed normal, but there was a taste of worry in the air. People had been stolen, and the street seemed a little less busy than it had when I arrived.

We ticked the errands off one by one, and Lilly introduced me to the people I needed to know. I tried to be a bit more outspoken, but after years of conditioning to stay in the background, it was hard work. I also tried to recall all the things I needed to do daily and remember everyone's names. It was overwhelming, and I wondered if I would ever work it out. This looked like a much larger job than I first thought.

Unfortunately, there wasn't much time to explore, but just being out in the lively, bustling town seemed to fill me. I noted anywhere that looked interesting, so if I got the chance, I could visit.

The rest of the day passed in a bit of a blur, where I took many notes and did my best to remember all the elements of my job. By the end, I was overwhelmed and feeling like I could never keep up.

By the time dinner came around, I was ready for a sleep. It had been a full day, and I thanked whoever was listening for sending me someone like Lilly to help. Toleran was even more beautiful at night. All the treehouses were lit with a blue and golden glow, and they sparkled against the darkness of the tree canopy. We went to the more formal dining room in the aerie and took our seats.

We were the first there, and it gave me a chance to look around and soak it all in. On the walls were great big curtains in deep green and gold. They outlined the many paintings and portraits around. Most of the paintings were of trees and plants found in Toleran, with one being a big portrait of Gloom. He was standing regally in a doorway, looking bored. I hated to think how long he had to stand there for.

Hanging off all the walls were the glowing mushrooms found all throughout the city, but these ones were bigger and brighter. It was a warm and inviting room, and some-one had decorated it well. The view was beautiful, and I could see the city lit up and shining below us. Above us was a chandelier carved from wood with candles to throw off light. The table itself must have been from a tree the size of the one we were sitting in. It was the biggest continuous slab of wood I had ever seen. It was so polished I could see my reflection in it, and it looked like it didn't have a scratch on it. I sat and stared at the whirls and circles in the wood while Lilly chatted on the phone with someone.

This was the fanciest room I had been in, and it made me feel insignificant.

Eventually, the doors opened, and people started filing in. I was worried I was going to be underdressed in my skirt and top, but the people coming in were not dressed up, and I relaxed a bit.

Bilvog, Kennock and Mezz came in. There were a few others, including Tristan, but it was a small group. Mezz gave me a wink, and I couldn't help but smile back in return. When Gloom arrived, we all stood and sat with him.

Throughout the dinner, people spoke about the progress they had made on various projects and updated everyone on what they would be working on next. A lot of it was about the security of Toleran, but also ways they were going to improve the place while all this disruption was happening.

When dinner was over, I said goodnight and went straight back to my room to prepare. If I was going to pull off what I had planned, I needed to be ready.

TWELVE

Gloom

We had been walking through the forest for a few hours, and the trees were starting to blend together. The forest outside Toleran was wild and unruly, and I loved it. Under our feet, there were no pathways, and branches tried to trip us up with every step. Out here, the birds were singing and darting through the trees, as well as sprites and pixies, but even though I loved the forest, I still made sure I was aware of what was around me.

Further in the trees, I could hear something large moving through the bushes, and I was keeping a mental track of it. The sun didn't touch the forest floor, and it was dark and misty. Still, I could feel a slight sheen of sweat on my body from the tough terrain. Of course, all of this couldn't distract me from my thoughts turning around and around inside my head.

I could hear the others following behind me, and I shook my head, trying to focus on what I was doing. I could hear Tristan and Caleb talking quietly in the middle of our group while Bran hung back a little, carrying the payment we would need for Vivian. My troubled mind turned back to the Prickly Hag and how I was going to get what I wanted without giving too much. She was part of the fey and had lived long enough to know all the tricks she could play to get what she wanted. I would need to be careful. However, if things were as bad as I thought they were, she might be more inclined to help. It would affect her and her continued life at Nightshadow Grove as much as Toleran.

My thoughts were interrupted by Kennock approaching me.

"Master, we should be arriving soon. Do you have any orders for us?" he asked as his ears twitched atop his head, alert and ready for anything.

"Yes, but I think I'll wait until we are a little closer."

"Yes, Master." He fell back, leaving me alone again with my thoughts. Immediately, my mind turned to the fact we still hadn't found the people that were taken from us. How could four people just disappear from a fortified city with no trace? I thought I knew how, but I pushed that thought from my mind. I didn't want to believe it was true, and like a child, I thought if I didn't think about it, it would go away. I had failed my people, and I didn't know how to fix it.

Since seeing the symbols burnt into the ground a few weeks ago, a pit had formed in my stomach, and nothing seemed to be able to fill it. My skin felt too tight, and I had lived in a constant state of anxiety.

I looked up and saw beings moving alongside us. So far, they had stayed away, but I could see they were starting to edge in on us. They were too fast to see what they were, but they had been following us for a while. Another problem to deal with. My problems seemed to be multiplying.

Leaving Amelia back to Toleran had been the right choice, but I was annoyed to say my mind had turned to her more than once on this trip. I wondered if I had treated the situation correctly. Making her come to Toleran did not sit well with me. I liked to think I was more civilised than kidnapping young women and forcing them to come with me, but I needed her. Her power was something I couldn't have out in the world unchecked.

Seeing it in action, it looked like it was at the peak of settling in her body. If someone else had seen her power, they might have made the connection I did, and that would be dangerous for everyone, including her. No, I think it was best that she came to Toleran. If I could work out a way to train her and have her use her powers *for* us, then all the better. The only fly in the ointment would be if she knew about where she got her powers. That is something I needed to keep from her. No one would be happy if they received that news.

I was broken out of my musings by Tristan. In this dark forest, his normally shining blond hair looked dull and lifeless. I could see just poking out two slightly pointed ears. Tristan must have had some elf ancestry, which was what made him such a good tracker. There weren't many full-blood elves anymore, but you would occasionally see ones like Tristan.

"Sir, Kennock has told me I am to watch over Amelia while she is staying in Toleran. Is there anything else I need to know about that?" he asked.

He had a focused look on his face, and I was impressed. I had always tried to be someone people could approach, but being an Ever, some people were intimidated. I was impressed that Tristan was straightforward and just wanted to do his job to the best of his ability. He was fast rising through the ranks, and I could see him one day being Kennock's second.

"It is fairly straightforward. She has tried to escape, and I don't want her to do that. She may be useful in the times to come, and I want to know where she is. I just want you to watch her. She is allowed her freedom within Toleran, and if you see anything suspicious, I want you to report it directly to me. Don't chase after her, just let me know, and I will deal with it." The last thing we needed was her hurting Tristan if he tried to stop her.

"Yes, sir. I did have one other question. Is she a danger to us? It is not often you put guards on the people who come here for refuge. I'm sorry if that was too forward, but with Mary and my son, I would like to know if I will be in any danger."

In my mind I saw the small family as they shopped in Toleran, and a tiny spear of jealousy stabbed at my heart. Seeing the joy on their faces was truly something to behold, and I wished I could also feel that, even though I knew it was unlikely. "You should be fine, Tristan. Just be sure to let me deal with her if she runs. I'm afraid you might be in more danger today than you will be with Amelia." I smiled at him and hoped my words were true. I did not want to leave Tristan's baby without a father.

He smiled at me and dropped back to talk to Kennock.

Up ahead, I could see a small clearing and the entrance to Nightshadow Grove and goosebumps raised on my arms. I turned and faced the others with me and told them all to stop.

"We will have a break here. Past these trees, we will be entering Nightshadow Grove, so be prepared." I sat on a fallen log, took a drink from my bottle, and ate a bit of the food I had brought with me. The others did the same, and from the outside, I'm sure we all looked relaxed, but I could feel the tension in the air. My eyes kept straying to the tall birch trees that almost formed a wall in front of us. We would have to get through their tall white bodies before we made it to the cottage.

From out of nowhere, a crashing noise shattered the calmness of the forest around us. I leapt to my feet a second before the others and whipped out my sword. My heart pounded in my chest, and all of my awareness got sharp as I waited, alert and ready for the creature to come thundering from the trees. The noise grew closer, and I ran through the list of creatures that could be out here – redcaps, banshees, even an ogre had been spotted once or twice. This was the last thing we needed right before visiting the hag. The rest of the forest had grown silent and even the beings that had been following us seemed to have gone into hiding.

I braced myself as the creature drew nearer to us. When it finally did emerge, nothing could hide our shock.

"Amelia!"

THIRTEEN

Amelia

I tripped on a branch that had fallen and fell flat on my face in a small clearing. "Shit," I said as I heard my name ring out.

"Amelia!"

I cringed inside as I stood and brushed off the leaves that had stuck to my jeans and ignored the new cuts on my hands. I had so many after tramping through this damn forest I hardly felt them anymore. I looked up to see Caleb and Tristan looking at me with their mouths open and weapons at their side. Bran was at the back with a bundle tied to his back and a small smile on his face. His dark brown eyes that matched his skin had a sparkle of amusement in them, and I wondered if his quiet nature hid a bit of mischief.

I looked at Kennock and Gloom, both of whom showed *no* amusement. Both stood with their weapons at the ready and a fierceness in their eyes. Gloom stepped forward. "What are you doing here?" He didn't yell, but his voice was intense, and I knew he was trying to keep himself under control in front of the others.

I took a deep breath and tried to ignore the effect it was having on me. All I wanted to do was run back home and hide in my room. My heart was thudding, and my palms had started sweating, making all the little cuts sting. I balled them up and put them behind my back.

"I wanted to come and see the hag. I thought she might be able to help me."

"Help you? Help you with what?" Gloom demanded as he strode forward. Kennock and the others, realising there was no danger, had hung back, happy to let Gloom deal with me. They tried to look uninterested, but I could tell they were listening to every word. Gloom came so close that eventually, everything else was obstructed, and all there was, was him. His coffee and rain smell invaded my nostrils and my personal space, but I didn't back down.

I said in a voice loud enough that only he could hear me, "I wanted to see if she could help me with my powers. You said she was a powerful being. Maybe she would know where they came from and how to control them."

Gloom ran a hand through his dark green hair and looked towards the sky, taking deep breaths while I took the opportunity to step back slightly.

"Look, my powers have been flaring up more than usual lately, and I thought she might have some answers. I promise I won't get in the way, and I'll let you ask if you don't want me to talk to her." I waited for Gloom to say something, but he seemed at a loss for words.

Not for the first time, I wondered if perhaps I should have listened to him about staying at Toleran. Actually, standing in front of him now, I could see I had made a fatal mistake in coming here. I had no idea what this witch could be capable of, and for all I know, she would vanquish us on sight. I started to feel clammy as the enormity of what I had done started to settle in. What did I think I was doing? I had never seen a magical being in my life, and now I thought I was ready to stroll into some ancient witch's house and start asking her for training?

Gloom looked down at me, his face a mask of control. "Well, it is too late to send you back now. You will have to come with us." He rubbed his eyes with his hand and said in a quieter voice, "Do you know what you have done? This is the last place I want your powers to show themselves. Vivian is the last being *on this earth* that I want knowing you have this power. I would argue she is the most powerful being in this realm, and the things she could do with your power scares even me, but there is nothing we can do now. You will have to come with us."

He turned and walked away, and I held back the tears that were pushing behind my eyes. I took a second to compose myself, then followed him over to the group. I stood awkwardly to the side, not really knowing what would happen.

"Right. Amelia is here now, and it is too late to take her back. We still need to see Vivian, so here are the rules. You don't speak unless she directly speaks to you. Let me do the talking. We are going into her home, so be polite. We should be safe there as the fey have rules of hospitality and reciprocity, but do not be rude. Lastly, don't touch anything or take anything. Now that Amelia is here, our plans will have to change. Bran, I want you outside until we are done. We don't want her distracted by what we have brought," he said, looking at Bran. For a moment, a haunted look came over his face, and he hesitated a moment before shaking his head and continuing, "Amelia will stay by me. As much as I don't want her to notice you,

I also want you close to protect you. You are by far the most vulnerable here. Kennock, I want you on the other side of Amelia with Tristan and Caleb in the middle. I need everybody to appear relaxed but be on your guard. No sudden movements and following the rules I gave, we should be okay." He sighed heavily. "Let's go."

We walked over to the birch trees that were tall and branchless. They grew so close together that it was hard to fit through them, which made walking difficult. By the time we came out the other side, I had even more cuts and bruises from squeezing through them, and a layer of sweat sat on top of my skin.

On the other side of the trees, there was an archway. A tunnel of dead branches and trees that had grown lying over. It looked like it went on forever. They were all leaning over and resting at the top against each other, and I wondered what could have caused this. Magic. Someone had used magic to create this little walkway to get to their land. The forest here was quiet, and there was no question we were entering the hag's domain. Gloom looked back to make sure we were all together before we stepped through.

Inside the tunnel was darkness with little slivers of light that penetrated the branch tunnel, blocking everything else out. Instead of being protected, I felt vulnerable, like there was something watching us that we now couldn't see. We walked slowly but with purpose, careful not to kick or knock the branches in any way. They were sharp, and I was scared if one fell, they would all fall, and we would be stuck under an avalanche of sticks and branches.

The air was cool inside the archway, but there were strange pockets of warmth. I wondered where they came from but tried not to think about it too much. I had the feeling that being distracted here would be very bad. However, not being able to see what was happening outside meant we couldn't prepare ourselves, and we all jumped. I yelped in surprise when something on the outside started to bounce on the archway. It rattled and clicked together, and the whole tunnel appeared to move and roll like a wave on an ocean.

Sweat broke out all over my body, my heart in my throat. I was breathing so heavily I could see it coming out in short puffs of mist. I was sure whatever it was, they were trying to break in and attack us. There was more than one, and I could hear them shrieking and yelling in a strange, garbled language. Tristan drew his sword and pushed me behind him, waiting for them to come bursting through the sticks. I could sense my power building, and I shook out my arms, trying to calm myself so it wouldn't be unleashed.

The others had all formed a circle, and I looked at Gloom. He was crouched, ready to attack. His mouth was set in a straight line, and I could see the sweat on his brow. The fear was building, and just as I had reached my limit and my power was ready to burst forth, the creatures stopped. We strained, trying to hear what they were doing and where they were. Silence. Nothing moved or made a noise. In some ways, this was worse than before. We relaxed a fraction and continued on slightly faster, hoping we would reach the end soon. Eventually, we made it.

Emerging from the tunnel of sticks was a relief. I took in deep breaths of the fresh air and cast a wary eye to make sure nothing was going to jump out at us. That was when I saw where we were. We were standing in front of an old wooden two-story house. The forest around it was dark, and fog and mist clung to everything, including us. The house was built on eight stilts with rotted steps leading to the veranda surrounding it. It was in the middle of a small clearing, and the trees surrounding it were all leaning away like they were trying to get as far away as possible from the house. I could see the railings were covered in moss and mushrooms, and there were holes in the veranda. On the left was an old stone well, which was collapsing on one side. Any sane person would have turned back when they first laid eyes on it.

Looking up, I saw pointed roofs with a broken weather-vane on the tallest peak of the second story. Some of the tiles of the roof had slid off long ago, and there were bird nests and moss covering what remained. Coming out of the brick chimney was a curl of smoke. Someone was inside.

We walked onto the veranda, every step creaking, announcing our arrival. I saw round windows with no glass in them, and they looked to be covered with a curtain on the inside, which did nothing to prevent the wind and fog that howled through. I shivered, thinking about how cold it must be inside.

As Gloom reached up to knock on the door, it creaked open before he could touch the rusted knocker that had seen better days. We stepped inside.

Unbelievably, it was warm as I entered the room. Looking at the broken windows, I could see the curtains fluttering, but there was no cold wind blowing through them. Every surface was dusty, and there were cobwebs everywhere. Looking up, I gripped the back of Gloom's shirt in shock. Cages hung from the ceiling. About twenty of them, all different sizes. Some of them were empty and open, but some had bones sticking out of them, and a few others had animals trapped in them. Birds and rodents ran around, thin and starving. Amongst the cages were drying herbs and plants. Hearing their screeching put my teeth on edge, and I wondered how she could stand the sound of it all day and night.

There were shelves lining the walls, all overflowing with bits and pieces, including jars of liquid and things I didn't want to identify. Books, cooking utensils, shoes, clothes, dried food, and jewellery were among the items. Under it was a workbench that looked to be the only place to ever be cleaned. It was scarred with all sorts of stains and burns and covered in scratches, and there was a bowl and knife placed neatly in the centre next to a large book.

At the back of the room was a staircase leading up to a pile of small clothing and a stack of children's wooden toys. There couldn't possibly be children living here, could there? Next to these items was a small bed with blankets piled on top of it that was much too small for an adult, and I wondered who had been sleeping in it.

Looking to the centre of the room, there was a large fire pit with purple flames dancing in it. Hanging over the fire by a chain that disappeared into the cages hanging from the roof was a huge black cauldron. I could smell food cooking, and despite the disgust and unease I felt being in this room, my stomach grumbled. I put a hand on my belly, hoping no one heard, and wondered what was in the cauldron. I would not be eating it, that was for sure.

Standing next to it and stirring whatever foul brew was in the cauldron was the hag. She didn't look anything like I thought she would. She was tall and willowy. She had long black hair reaching to her knees that was wavy and shiny. Around her head, she wore a silver circlet. She wore a long, tight blue dress with large bell sleeves that showed off her pale skin and thin wrists. When she looked up, her eyes were a golden brown, almost yellow, and turned up at the end. Her beauty looked so out of place in this hut, full of filth and despair. She gave a sweet smile with her full pink lips and looked at Gloom.

"Hello, Destin. It has been a long time since you have graced me with your presence. Please come in," she said with a sweet, clear voice. For a moment, I wondered who Destin was, then Gloom nodded and took a step further into the room, with us following behind.

As we entered, I stayed behind Gloom—or Destin, whatever his name was—trying not to be noticed. I saw that Bran had stayed outside the door, and I was surprised at the look on his face. It had paled, and his face had a sweat sheen covering it. What could cause such a reaction? I knew it wasn't pleasant being here, but it seemed like it was more than that. He turned and looked into the forest, his back straight as a board, and I could feel the tension rolling off him in waves. What was going on?

She walked away from the cauldron and left the large wooden spoon to stir itself. She sat on one of the chairs that encircled a small wooden table. Now that she was closer, I could feel the magic rippling through the air, making it thick like soup and leaving a sharp taste on my tongue.

"Please sit. It has been so long since I have had company." She let out a trill of a giggle, and Gloom sat, leaving me exposed. I stepped back to stand near Tristan when her eyes landed on me. "Destin, this is new. Is this a gift for me?" Her eyes lit up, and I drew back, trying to make myself appear smaller. "You are too kind." She outstretched her arm to take my hand, but Gloom's hand shot out faster. I felt a bolt of electricity travel up my arm. And I shivered before I could stop myself. Gloom's hand tightened, but he kept his eyes on the hag.

She turned to him, and her eyes turned flinty. It was clear she was used to getting what she wanted.

"I'm sorry, Vivian, but Amelia is mine." He ushered me behind his chair. I stood there looking at Vivian, waiting to see what she would do while I rubbed the spot he had gripped me. Rising suddenly from my memories was Matthew gripping my arm tightly. I scrunched my eyes closed and tried to separate the experiences. Matthew was cruel, and Gloom was yet to display any cruelness towards me. I felt the coldness start to trickle down my spine, and my stomach dropped as I worked hard at keeping my powers back. I looked back at Vivian in time to see her image flicker.

For a moment, she took the form of someone else entirely. Her hair grew matted and streaked with grey. She was hunched, and her beautiful skin sagged, deep lines appearing. Her eyes sunk into her head, and her long, dainty fingers grew swollen and cracked. As soon as I saw it, it vanished. She was disguising herself. Gloom was right. Nothing was as it seemed.

She glared at Gloom a moment longer than visibly got herself under control, although her hands remained clenched in her lap. "Well, if you are refusing me this gift, your *guest* must sit with us. Come, girl. Sit," she said to me. I hesitated a moment but, realising I had no choice, took the seat she offered. It was hard, and the wood was cold. I sat as still as I could and tried not to look her in the eyes.

"Much better." She smiled sweetly at us both, but we both knew the smile concealed sharp teeth.

"Oh, where are my manners? You must be starved walking all this way! Here. Have some stew." She stood gracefully and ladled out what was brewing in the cauldron. I swallowed the bile rising in the back of my throat. There was no way I was going to eat that stew. She sat the bowls on the table in front of us. Neither of us picked up a spoon to eat. She smiled at us and sat daintily on her chair again.

"So now we are settled. Let me introduce myself to my new guests." She turned to me and offered me her smile again. "I am Vivian Calerook. I am an all-powerful mage, and I prefer to live out here in the woods, where I am free to do what I like when I like. Where did you come from, human girl?"

I swallowed again because my mouth had gone dry. I glanced at Gloom and then back to Vivian. "My name is Amelia. I'm staying in Toleran with Gloom."

"Gloom. I hate that name." She sniffed. "Why you chose that one, I will never know. In this house, we use real names, dear. And where are you from?"

I didn't want to tell her where I was from. If she found out, it would not be good for me or the people of my village. Even though not all the people were kind in Woodmere,

I couldn't let an ancient hag loose on them. "I am from a small town, a few days' travel from here." A lie and yet not a lie. She looked at me, and a bead of sweat dripped down my back. She knew I was lying. She likely already knew where Woodmere was, and I didn't think she would appreciate me lying to her.

"Lovely, dear. And what is it about you that is so...different?" She took a deep breath, smelling me. "There is an element in you that is *very* interesting. Something I could use. Are you sure you don't want to leave her here with me, Destin? I think we would both benefit from it."

I shrank back in my chair even though this could be my opportunity to ask her about my powers, but I knew better. Now that I was here, I knew why Gloom didn't want her to know about me. She was the last person I would tell, and I realised what a bad mistake I had made by coming here. She laughed lightly. "Well, it looks like she has chosen. Shame. I could do amazing things with you. Perhaps you will change your mind once things begin to happen. It might be hard to believe, but this might be the safest place for you soon. I assume that's why you are here?"

Gloom leaned forward in his chair. "Yes. So, you know what has been happening?"

Another tinkling laugh. Although beautiful, it was hollow and grated against my nerves.

"Of course, I know. I know everything that goes on in this forest."

"Who is terrorising my city? Who is leaving the symbols?"

She smiled knowingly, "come now, Destin. Why waste time asking when you already know?"

Gloom's shoulders sagged slightly, "so, it is Dread. Is he back?"

"No, not yet, but somehow, he is gathering his power back." She sniffed again, and I knew she wasn't happy about it. Who was Dread? I filed the name away to ask about later. "Someone is working for him. He has a nice little band of followers now that are doing his bidding until he has his power. They are doing quite a good job, but he is not free yet."

"Who released the Horned One? He was bound along with Dread."

Another laugh. "So many questions, Destin. Is this the only reason you have visited me today? I think I have been quite generous. If you don't have anything else to offer me, I think you have used all your hospitality for one day." She stood as if to leave.

"I have your payment. Can you not smell it? You will be paid after I have the answers I need. It will be sufficient, I assure you." He grimaced and looked a little sick.

She sniffed the air and closed her eyes. After a few sniffs, her eyes snapped open, and she looked at Gloom. "Yes, I can smell it now. My, how you must want your answers. It must have killed you to offer me *that*." She sat back down with the grace of a cat, and my worry spiked about what Gloom had offered. "Go on. Ask your questions before my patience wears out." She bent over to a basket near the chair, took out some strings, and started to plait them. It took a moment for me to realise it wasn't a string but human hair. My scalp tingled, and my body grew colder. I grimaced and moved closer to Gloom, hoping he would hurry so we could get out of here.

"Who released the Horned One? Who is working with Dread?"

"Now, there is a question I cannot answer. They are cloaked. I would like to know how because it is rare someone can get around my magic, and I don't like it one bit. I do know it is someone in Toleran, but his followers are scattered throughout all the realms. I imagine your siblings might be having a bit of trouble with them soon, also. They have a hideout in the forest. That is all I have been able to discover. As for the Horned One," she turned and looked directly at me, "well, he is hunting...you."

FOURTEEN

Amelia

I straightened in my seat at the intensity of her gaze. Again, her image flickered to her true image of the hag.

"Me? What could he possibly want with me?" I squeaked. Fear filled me and my thoughts focused on ways I could possibly try and hide from him, but my mind was blank.

"Maybe he can sense what is inside of you. Maybe he wants it." She leaned forward, and I looked into her intensifying gaze. "I wonder what he will do with your pretty little body when he gets you. I can't imagine it would be anything good." My heart sped up and sweat beaded above my top lip. My legs and hands were getting cold now, and it was intensifying. I tried to lengthen my breaths, which had turned short and choppy. "He will likely give you to his followers. They would have a field day with someone like you. I imagine the torture would last for hours. It has been quite a long time since he had a plaything, all those years locked away," she mused.

The cold spread until I could feel it in my fingertips. I was so terrified; I couldn't control it, and my power began to leach out of me. The herbs above us started to dry, and flakes of them drifted down on top of us. I closed my eyes and tried to find the calm in me to stop my magic from rotting everything in this place. I tried not to think about where I was now.

Tried not to think of the creatures who had been trapped above us in the cages for so long they had turned to dust and bones.

Tried not to think about the fact there had been children in his house.

Tried not to think about the magic vibrating in the air.

Instead, I thought about my grandmother, Hazel. How she would bring me to the woods and teach me all about the different types of mushrooms and plants. I thought about the day she gave me my necklace and told me a story about how her great-grandmother had received it from a beautiful fairy man who had been her best friend. I thought about my parents before they died and the love that had been between us before it was ripped away.

I lifted my hand and held onto my necklace. It worked. My body started to return to normal, and the cold dissipated. My powers settled, and I had control again. It had only been a few seconds, but I was drained. I opened my eyes and sagged in my chair. Vivian was staring at me with hunger in her gaze.

"There it is. That's what I was looking for. How extraordinary would it be if you could control it? You could defeat anyone. No one would stand a chance against you. We could do great things."

I was startled when Gloom jumped out of his seat. "That's enough, Vivian." He moved to stand in front of me. I could see his body shaking slightly, and he looked ready to attack. I had the urge to see what his eyes looked like, but I couldn't move.

They stared intently at each other, their powers crackling in the air. After a tense moment when I wasn't sure if we would be walking out of there, Vivian smiled. Her tinkling laugh rang out and bounced off the walls of the room.

"Ah, Destin. Careful now. Don't do something you will regret." I heard the wind pick up and rattle the house. I turned to see anxiety in everyone's eyes. Tristan's hand travelled to his weapon, but it stayed in his belt. Gloom and Vivian were in a death stare, but Gloom was the first one to break the stare. Vivan smiled, and the wind died down outside again.

Gloom took a moment before he sat. "How can we trap him again?" he asked, and I could hear how forced his polite tone was.

"How? Well, now that would need a very large payment. Larger than what it was before, I would expect. Without your items, it would be very difficult."

"Do you know where the items are?" Gloom asked.

"I know where one is. Speak to Awe about that. I would have to scry to find the rest, and you know how busy I am. I don't think I would have the time," she said innocently.

The roof above us creaked. My heart skipped a beat as I looked up and could hear someone walking above us. I followed the sound as they walked back and forth. Vivian looked up with a frown and muttered something quietly that none of us could hear. There was a loud thump, and it went silent upstairs again. I hoped whoever it was, was still alive.

"It sounds like you have plenty of help here, Vivian."

"Oh yes, well, nothing gets by you, Destin. I shall try and see what I can find. I will send word when I have your answers. But I think it best you speak to my sisters in the coven. They might have more light to shed on their location," she said, dismissing us.

"It would be appreciated." He stood, keeping me behind him, and bowed his head and ushered us out. Before he walked out the door, he turned to face Vivian. "A pleasure as always. Thank you."

"No, thank *you*, Destin. Always a pleasure to have you in my home." She gave him a wave, and another girlish giggle followed us out.

I felt exposed, and my whole body was in flight mode as I turned my back on her and walked toward the door. As we walked out the door, I could see Bran waiting to enter the room. He was holding something in his arms, which I realised was the bag he had slung across his back. Now that I was closer, I could see it was a bundle of blankets, and it was moving. A tiny fist appeared out of the bundle, and all the blood seemed to drain from my body.

I stopped and tried to get a closer look, but Gloom's hands clamped down on my shoulders as he leaned in. "Keep walking, Amelia."

"Wait. He has a baby! You can't give her a baby!" I hissed at Gloom. When he didn't react, I cried out, "No, Bran, stop!" Gloom kept a firm hold of me and continued to drag me away. Bran's eyes were wet with unshed tears, and he was taking small breaths as he took the baby out of the sling. Gloom was practically pushing me by now. "Amelia, stop. It's the payment. Come on."

I struggled and yelled and pleaded and begged, but they kept dragging me away. Eventually, I was struggling so hard Gloom flung me over his shoulder. How could they leave a baby there? She was evil.

I kicked and hit him with my fists like a crazy person. I knew what it was like to grow up with someone evil, and there was no way I was going to let them leave a baby there. None of it seemed to affect Gloom, and he walked with me like that until we were back in the tunnel, and I couldn't see the house anymore. The last thing I saw of the evil house was Bran walking out empty-handed with a face carved of stone and a haunted look in his eyes. We made it to the stick tunnel, and Gloom set me down.

"How could you?" I asked softly. "How could you go in there knowing you would leave a baby in her care? What is she going to do with it? Eat them? Train them to be exactly like her?" I was shocked that anyone would do such a thing.

"It's the price we must pay to get her help." He sighed, and I could see it weighed heavily on his conscience, but I didn't care. I ran back, planning to go in there and take the baby back. I would do whatever it took. I was stopped in my tracks as vines lashed out and tied my hands and feet. I struggled against them, knowing I couldn't get free. I sagged in my bindings. Defeat washed over me. I was pathetic. The reality settled in, and I knew I could never get that baby back. The hag would kill me the moment I touched the child. Gloom approached as the others walked further into the tunnel, giving us some privacy. Did they know about the deal?

"She asks for a female. The baby will grow and learn and eventually join her coven. She will care for it in her way. I have seen the children, and they all look healthy. This is why it is a last resort to ask her," Gloom said softly while he released me.

"Where did you get the baby from?" My stomach twisted thinking about the poor mother who had to give up her child.

"She was an orphan. Her father died in an accident at work, and her mother died during childbirth. We keep track of when girls are orphaned. It is surprisingly common. Then we glamour the foster parents looking after them and take them. Most of the time, they are in orphanages, although they don't call them that anymore. It is rare that we need to do it. We only go and see the hags if it is really important."

"Well, I hope whatever information you got from her was worth it," I spat, turning my back to him and stomping off to follow Tristan and the others, leaving Gloom behind me in the gathering dark.

FIFTEEN

Gloom

By the time we returned to Toleran, it was full dark. The stars were bright in the sky, and it was nice to not be covered by trees. The lights shining out from the tree houses filled Toleran with a warm, inviting glow, but it didn't improve my mood. The trip back was quiet and tense, and I watched as Tristan led Amelia to her room. The unease in my stomach didn't lessen as I walked into my office.

I closed and locked my office door behind me and leaned my head on the door, trying to calm the emotions that were raging inside of me. Visiting Vivian was one of the worst things I had done in a long time. Leaving that child there made me physically sick, but I needed answers. Something was coming, and if she was right, Dread was rising. That would mean danger for both worlds, and we needed to do anything we could to stop it from happening.

I closed my eyes, and all I could see was the betrayal and horror in Amelia's eyes when we were in that tunnel. She would never understand why I did that, and I knew why. I had seen the bruises on her arms and how thin she was. She had not had an easy or good life at Woodmere. I walked to my bathroom and washed my hands, hoping to wash away the guilt of what I had just done, and what I had just subjected that poor little baby too. I knew the life they would have. While they would gain a lifespan almost four times that of a human, to be in the hag's coven meant pain and bargains and hard training. Nothing would be soft for her any longer. Love would be a difficult thing to feel and receive, and I had done that. No wonder Amelia hated me. After washing my hands, I went to my desk and breathed in the scent of cedarwood, pouring myself a drink. I went over to my bookshelf and took out a book I hadn't read in an extremely long time. It was a history of the Evers. My family were not the first, and there were Evers before us. In the book, it listed all the Evers, their powers, domains, and bits about the time of their rule.

I flipped through the pages. There weren't a lot of Evers as we tended to live a long time. Looking at all the entries, no one else had the withering or power of death. I had hoped it had been passed on to Amelia from someone else, but no. It was the Shadow One.

I took a drink as I read the familiar entry. The Shadow One was an Ever who wanted to rule all the humans. When he couldn't get the others to go along with his little plan, he decided to do it himself. He killed thousands of humans all because they didn't want to worship him. What followed was a dark time. A time of war, blood, and betrayal. The humans had tried to rise up and stop the killing, but the Shadow One was too powerful and annihilated them all. A small group of devoted followers did everything he asked of them, no matter how evil and depraved. Those humans he kept.

The other Evers devised a plan, and the powerful hags from each realm bound him to a sliver in the dimensions.

He would be locked there forever. Never being able to use his powers or rise again.

These days, no one really thought of him. He had been locked away for over a hundred and fifty years. What threat could he possibly be now?

I took out my tablet and brought up the image of the symbol that had been placed around the forest. It was an image of the Horned One, the Shadow One's most loyal subject. He hadn't been seen for centuries. It was concerning that his image had been appearing all throughout the forest. I did not like the idea of it being near my home. I put the tablet away and thought of the Shadow One. If it was him, we would need all the help we could get. More than the power we currently had. I rubbed my temples as I thought about all the things we would have to do, to get help. There weren't many beings left that would have the power we needed to defeat him. Even us Ever's were not at full power anymore, and without the artefacts we used the first time to bind him, I was at a loss about what, and how, we could do it. While sitting there, another thought troubled me.

How would I tell the other Evers about Amelia's powers? They would know immediately who they could have originated from. I didn't think they would be too pleased about having a descendant, if that's what she was, of the greatest evil in our history running around in our houses. This was going to be difficult to explain. I needed to think fast. Because if what Vivian said was true, I needed to talk to them soon. We would have a lot to deal with. Our family did not get on well, and I couldn't imagine what it was going to be like when I brought up the Shadow one.

Dread.
Our adopted brother.

SIXTEEN

Gloom

"**M**aster, search parties have been deployed constantly, and the families are being well taken care of. We have increased the guard on the wall, and people in neighbouring houses have been questioned if they saw anything," Kennock reported.

"Good. I would also like a guard posted in the staff wing of the aerie. Bilvog, do we have any more information on the people taken? Do we have a reason why they were selected?"

"Uh, um, four people were taken, sir. Caroline Willis, Nud Dak, Abalise Ash and Borys Hollier. Caroline and Nud work at the children's school, Abalise is old and retired, and Borys runs one of the local clothing stores. From what we can tell and from interviews, they lived normal lives. We have no idea why they were taken."

"Well, keep looking. There must be a reason why. Otherwise, why break into four different houses on opposite sides of the city? Why not take all the people in one household?"

I sat in my chair in the war room and thought over this attack. Four people taken from the safety of my walls. All without anyone seeing or hearing a thing. There had to be some connection. What were they doing with them?

Was it a power play to show they could come in at any time, or were they taking these people for a reason? There had been no communication from the enemy to explain or demand ransom. I knew it had to do with Dread, but why? How many followers did he have? There must have been a few to accomplish the abductions.

Kennock, Bilvog and I strategised for a bit longer, trying to work out what the enemy was doing, and got nowhere. I sent them out to do their tasks but asked Kennock to stay.

"Kennock, I have spoken to Tristan, and I want him to shadow Amelia while she is here. She is...hesitant to stay here, and I doubt her experience yesterday will improve that."

"That's true, sir. Tristan is kind. Perhaps he can change her mind. If I may ask, how did she escape Woodmere? They don't let people go so easily."

A fissure of anger ran through my body, thinking about how they had thrown her away. "They offered her as a sacrifice to Awe. She was tied to a post when I found her." I could never imagine doing that to people I had sworn to protect.

Kennock frowned and shook his head. "Poor thing, to treat one of your people like that." Hesitantly, he looked at me. "Awe, won't like that you took his sacrifice, sir. He is bound to work it out. You know he has spies everywhere."

"Yes. I will deal with *that* when it knocks on my door," I said, rubbing my eyes. I was not looking forward to it.

"Right, well, I'll get on with the day." He nodded as he left, leaving me in the quiet to think. Four of my people. Gone. How did this happen? Most people thought Evers were Gods, but they were only half right. We were half God and half human. It is only by fluke that we became Evers. There were many half-breeds out there like us that don't ever become Evers. Granted, my family were *more* God than human, but we weren't all-powerful. We might live a long time and have some powers, but we aren't immortal. I made a point to never forget all this could be taken away. Some of my other siblings needed to remember that, too, sometimes.

My mind turned back to Amelia. I hadn't seen her yet today, but I could imagine the mood she would be in. Yesterday was traumatic for all of us. I could only wonder what it was like for her. I was worried about what Vivian would do with the knowledge of her power. All it would take would be for her to decide she wanted it, and she could click her fingers and get Amelia. I had a feeling she would bide her time. If Dread was rising, it would be bad for Vivian as well. She would likely want us to finish him off before targeting Amelia. I couldn't believe she had followed us like that.

A small smile tugged at my lips. She had more strength than I thought. Did she know that? It was likely why her powers were so powerful. I needed those powers if we were going to defeat Dread and his minions. I was unsettled, but she brought feelings I hadn't had in a long time to my attention, and I didn't like that. I needed to focus on the problem in front of me and not think about her, even if she did make my blood hum and curiosity override my brain.

Standing, I stretched and headed back to my quarters. Along the way, I noted everything. The guards were vigilant, and people were running around busy. Good. On the way, I stopped one of the kitchen staff, a young gnome who was carrying a basket with food. "Hello, Leena. Are those for the people in town?" I asked her. She curtseyed to me and nodded her head, her bright red curls bouncing around her freckled face. "Yes, Master. The poor things."

I nodded. "Good, keep them fed for a few more days. I don't want them worrying about what they are going to eat."

"Yes, sir." She turned, and I continued on my way.

Waiting in my room was a plate of food I ate without tasting. I did my best to not think about what was going on and instead read my book. Not many people knew, but I loved to read pirate romance novels. The older, the better. There was a surprising amount of them out there, and something about sailing called to me. Maybe because I had spent most of my life in the middle of a forest.

Not long after I started reading, there was a knock at my door, and for the rest of the night, people came and went with reports and information on what they had found out. It wasn't much. The groups Kennock had sent out to track them returned with nothing but a few scratches and bruises from fighting off the creatures that lived outside the walls. No trace had been left by these people travelling through the forest. They had hidden their tracks well.

All night, I lived off coffee, which was one of the things the people of Toleran had accepted from the outside realm. I sat in my room and watched people coming and going while I grew more worried about what was happening. I hadn't forgotten what the hag had said about it being someone in Toleran, and suspicion was starting to creep in. Who was it that was betraying the good people of this town? It left a sour taste in my mouth, thinking about it. By the time the sun had broken the horizon, I was tired but jittery from all the coffee. I locked my door and took a break for an hour. I paced my quarters, trying to calm my racing mind.

The wood from the inside of the tree was carved and polished, and I could see my reflection in every wall. There was an eco-fire which had no real flame on one side, but it still threw out heat with no chance of burning the whole tree to ash. Vines and ivy covered the wall, breaking up the polished wood. I usually decided what colour flowers I would like, and today it was a bright periwinkle blue.

My bed was in another room and was covered in a rich green quilt. Candles and mushrooms glowed all over, and the sitting room was open and airy. I walked into the bathroom, took off my clothes and had a hot shower. The water poured like warm rain, and I let it wash some of the stress away from the previous night. When I was as refreshed as I was going to get, I wrapped the towel around my hips and walked out to get a change of clothes. I put on the same black pants and white shirt I wore every day. It was like a uniform and one less thing I had to decide on. After getting dressed, I brushed my hair and shook it out.

Picking up my jacket from yesterday, I took out the tree-shaped pin I always wore on the inside of my jacket. It reminded me of who I am and of the good people I had met. For them, I would be the best I could be. As I was about to open the door, there was a knock. Opening it, I saw Lilly and Amelia behind her.

Amelia was dressed in a long orange skirt with a white blouse. The white of her shirt made her skin look brown and her eyes bright. I noticed the leather cord wrapped around her neck but couldn't see the pendant that hung off it. Like she was reading my mind, she reached up and held it through her shirt. I tried to see her eyes and how she was feeling today, but she kept her head down, avoiding my gaze.

"Hi, sir. Amelia is here reporting for duty. I have given her a brief rundown of what to expect. I will be a bit busy today doing damage control, but I will help her out when I can. Is there anything you want me to say about the abductions or just the usual like we are taking care of it?" She took out her magic tablet and started writing hurriedly.

"I think the normal statement is enough for now. But it's not going to last long. Think of a new update and get back to me. I want to know how everyone is feeling and what they are talking about. Tristan will be with Amelia today to help her if she has any trouble, too, but I am sure she would appreciate you helping."

"Righto, I'll get straight on it." She looked at me strangely for a minute and saluted with a smile, and I had to work hard to keep my smile from showing. I appreciated that Lilly knew how far she could push me and knew how to walk that fine line. She could read me like a book and knew when I was laughing on the inside.

She turned to Amelia. "Come and find me when you are done here, and I'll help you with your tasks if you need me. Do you remember how to get back to the Comms Room?" Amelia bobbed her blonde head. "Okay. I will see you later, and I will do my best at damage control today, but I think they are going to need to hear from you at some point."

"Yes, I think you're right," I said, wondering how I was going to reassure the people of my city when I had no new information.

With that, she walked away, the leaves of her hair rustling and dropping a few as she walked.

I looked at Amelia. Again, she was looking down, and I felt uncomfortable knowing my actions had caused her to withdraw. I had brought her here against her will, exposed her to an all-powerful hag and disappointed her by giving a child to the hag. I cleared my throat, and she looked up. Her eyes were guarded and cold, and something shrunk a little inside of me. I didn't like letting people down. I pushed feelings aside and decided business-like would be best.

"First thing, we have a meeting in the war room to discuss how the searches are going and fill everyone in on our visit. I want you to sit in the back and take notes and record what happens." I cringed inside at the stiffness of my voice, but I knew that I had to put some distance between us. Her eyes still held a hardness as she nodded, not saying anything. I tried to ignore my disappointment. An attraction was building, and I didn't have time for that. I could try and make her life easier here and avoid my attraction to her at the same time. I made a mental note to find out if there was anything I could bring her to make her stay more comfortable.

I closed the door to my rooms behind me and walked the short distance to the war room. I could hear her following, and I didn't look back. I checked my watch and noticed I was running early, and it was likely no one else would be there. It would give me time to settle in and try and think about what our next step would be.

I opened the door to the war room, expecting it to be empty. Instead, all I saw was fire.

SEVENTEEN

Gloom

I jumped in front of Amelia, knowing the fireball would likely kill her while only injuring me. I took the full force of it right in my chest as it exploded. I winced as my clothing smouldered and burnt away, leaving a large hole in my shirt. Amelia screamed, and I pushed her further back. I stood up tall, the skin on my chest pulling and stretching. I could smell my skin burning, and it was not pleasant. I tried not to let it show how much it hurt as I looked at my brother Awe.

"Awe. What an unpleasant surprise. What are you doing here, throwing fireballs in my very flammable house?"

"You have something of mine, brother, and I want it back. You know I don't share."

Awe stood at the head of the table. His skin glowed slightly all the time, and his golden hair and beard were neatly groomed as always. His yellow eyes blazed, and I could see he was furious.

"Now, Awe, let's take a minute and talk this over before we all get too angry." Amelia was standing pushed against my back, and I could feel her breaths coming short and sharp. I let my magic pool in my hands in case I had to restrain him. I didn't want to do it if I could help it. Awe was quick to anger and would not take it well.

"I think it's a bit late to be worrying about if I am angry. How would you feel if you went to collect the annual sacrifice that you are *owed* and it wasn't there? Then you were to find out it wasn't the usual cow or sheep those idiots left me, but an actual woman. Finally, a change in this predictable world, then to find out someone had taken her. My own brother, no less. What did you do with her brother? Finally decided to break your self-imposed celibacy and couldn't do better than a human?" he said, his mouth turning into a sneer. With every question, he stalked closer until he was standing in front of me, his large body imposing and intimidating. I needed to cool him down, or the next time he unleashed, it would be much more painful. I didn't *think* he would kill me.

I held my hands in front of me. "Yes, I did take her. I knew she was a sacrifice for you, but for reasons I can't tell you, I need her." As I said it, I knew it was a poor explanation and would do nothing to calm him.

Amelia stiffened behind me, and Awe zoomed in on the movement. "Ah, so is this her?" He smiled, and before I could react, he pushed me aside and stood in front of her. "Well, here she is. Why, I wonder, did they leave me you and not the usual animal?" He took her chin in his hand and turned her face side to side. Seeing him touch her face disturbed me inside, and I wanted to tear his hands away. Him touching her was wrong somehow. I schooled my features and held onto the control I was famous for. I could see Amelia was terrified but trying to appear calm. Strong girl.

"Thank you, brother, for retrieving her, but I am afraid I will be taking her back now. My kitchen is in need of more staff. After all, she was given to me and not you. Perhaps when your time comes, they will sacrifice something more interesting." He gripped her upper arm and went to walk away. Amelia flinched, and fear flooded her face as it paled, appearances forgotten.

Vines shot out of my hand and wrapped around his legs, stopping him from moving. They stretched up over his knees, rooting him to the spot. This time, they were thornless.

"No Awe. You will not take her anywhere," I said with steel in my voice. I tensed and waited to see what his next move would be.

He let go of Amelia, and flames shot up his arm. Being the Ever of the Sun, he had control over fire. I was at a disadvantage here. Fire consumed plants. I wished my sister Enduring was here. She would have him watered down in no time.

"I told you I need her. She has gifts that could help to save Toleran."

The fire died down. "I had heard you were having a bit of trouble in this little garden here. People disappearing and whatnot. What could she possibly have that will help you with that?"

I looked at Amelia as she shrunk away from Awe. When she looked at me, I could see the fear there, but also the curiosity of what I might reveal to Awe about what we had learnt.

"I can't tell you now, but old things, long forgotten, seem to be waking, and I need her to help stop it. This could help you in the long run, brother. If I am right about who is rising, they will not stop at controlling Toleran. They will move on to Ceplar. If we can stop them here, we might be able to save Ceplar and the others as well. I don't have time to get into it now, but it is serious."

My tone and words must have convinced him. The fire disappeared altogether, and I dropped the vines that were holding him. I knew the threat to Ceplar would have an impact. Awe loved his realm. Not for the people but because it made him feel important to rule over them, and it gave him power.

"Well. If you are to keep her, what am I to take as sacrifice? Perhaps I will go back to Woodmere and find someone else. Or take someone from here." Turning to Amelia, he said, "Is there anyone there you are particularly fond of?" Without hesitation, Amelia met his gaze. "Matthew would be my choice."

Awe laughed. "The leader? Well, I suppose I am not surprised. I have heard some stories about him, and he is the one who chose you, I assume. You may keep her, brother, for now. I'll be waiting to hear about this dire news, so don't leave me waiting, or I might change my mind. I bristled at the threat and moved to stand in front of Amelia again. Awe noticed, and a grin spread across his face. "Interesting." He paused for a moment as I stared at him.

"Well, I will be going. Don't worry. I will make sure to fill everyone in on the trouble you are having here, Gloomy. You must have forgotten to let us know in all the fuss." Again, he gave a sarcastic smile, knowing I had been keeping this all to myself. "Until we meet again, lovely Amelia."

He walked past us both and strode down the hall with the confidence and power of someone who knew there was no threat at his back.

After he had gone, I slumped into the closest chair and leaned on the large stone rectangle table that was the focal piece of the room. "Well, that wasn't as bad as I thought it was going to be."

"Really, you think it went well? You have a burn the size of a dinner plate on your chest, and I was threatened. I can't see how it could have gone worse," Amelia said as she sat in the chair next to me. "Is he always like that?"

"Unfortunately, yes. He is the oldest and the strongest of us, and he knows it. He likes to throw his weight around. He is the last person I wanted to know about our troubles here. He will rub it in any chance he gets. I'm sure the version he will tell my brothers and sisters is that I'm incompetent and allude to me mismanaging Toleran. Maybe he is right." I sighed. I was the youngest and weakest of us. Maybe I wasn't cut out to be an Ever.

Amelia was watching me, so I made myself sit up. She reached out hesitantly and put a hand on my arm that was resting on the table. "I don't think it's you. It is clear your people respect you, and you have proved you would do anything for them," she said with a small frown forming between her eyebrows.

"While I don't approve of what you did yesterday, I know you did it for a reason, but really, is there no way to get the child back?" Her eyes pleaded with me, and for some reason, a bolt of anger shot through my body.

"Do you think I would have done it if there was another way? Dread is no joke, and he will destroy this world if he is released." I stood and looked down at my singed shirt and skin. "Wait here. The meeting will start in a minute." I stalked out the door, trying not to look at the shock on her face.

EIGHTEEN

Amelia

The next day, my head was still reeling with the fact I could have been going home with Awe if I wasn't so lucky yesterday. The Sun Ever was intimidating and awe-filling. He had chosen his name well. I hated to admit it after what had happened after seeing the hag, but by the time I left the meeting, I was feeling a little bit grateful towards Gloom.

He had managed to convince Awe to leave me here, and when telling the story to the people in the meeting of what we had learnt at the hag's house, he had pretty much left me out of it. I didn't have the annoying questions, and I didn't have to relive anything there if I didn't want to. There was one person who kept their eye on me, however. Bilvog. He knew I was there, and he kept a close eye on me during the meeting. By the end, I was happy to flee and get to work and put a little distance between me and everyone there.

Over the next few days, Tristan was a constant shadow. As I did my errands, we got a chance to speak a bit, and he told me about his family. He had a wife and child living in the town, and he showed me pictures of the three of them, and they made an adorable little family. Every time he spoke of them, his chest puffed out, and he couldn't wipe the smile off his face. He helped me with tasks, and I could see us becoming friends. I knew he was likely going back and reporting everything to Gloom and Bilvog, but I couldn't help but like his easy attitude.

It took a few days, but I was beginning to enjoy other aspects of the town. The people of Toleran were so nice and patient with me, and I came to get to know a few of them quite well. I loved to spend time walking the alleys and streets and seeing what people had for sale. I spent a bit of time in the sewing section. There were all kinds of fabrics. Some looked like starlight, and others were stiff and unyielding. I loved to touch the different textures and imagine what clothes and items would be made with them.

At Woodmere, everything was so boring and practical, but here, I could make anything I wanted. I made a mental note to ask Mezz about getting a sewing machine. Designs filled my head, and Tristan nodded along good-naturedly with every outfit I imagined. He practically had to drag me out of that street, but I vowed to return. The clothes I had wouldn't last for long, and I needed new ones anyway. Maybe Lilly could come shopping with me?

I didn't seem to be improving at my job as an assistant, but most people were happy to help me out. Unfortunately, it seemed Bilvog's opinion had not improved. Every time I got something wrong, he was there to point it out and make sarcastic comments. If I was late for a meeting, he would sigh loudly and whisper to whoever was sitting next to him.

Even though I was trying my hardest, I still did poorly at some tasks. In the meetings, it was my job to take notes. Most of the time, they talked so fast, and I was still learning everyone's names, so it was hard to keep up. I kept missing things, and the reports always came out with holes in them, where I had missed bits of information.

Another job I took on was ordering supplies from around the town for Gloom. I struggled to keep on top of the list of things he needed, so not everything was at the aerie when it should be. In those first few days, nothing arrived when it should have. It was either too early or too late.

The worst things were when I would forget appointments and lose messages. That really made Bilvog and the others mad. I don't know what they expected of me. I told them I was bad at things and had never been an assistant before. They should have known I would be terrible.

One thing I hadn't counted on was how much time I would be spending with Gloom. Every time we had to work together, there was tension, and I couldn't help but see the small baby he had let go into that hag's terrible house. I knew it was something I would need to get over. Things were happening here I had no idea about, and maybe he was right, and it was necessary, but it was hard.

He always spoke to me with respect and even asked if there was anything I needed to make my stay more comfortable. I mentioned I would like to talk to Mezz and see if he had a sewing machine I could borrow and that night, there was a brand new magic-powered one in my room with instructions on how to use it. There was also a note that said I could go and pick out any fabric I wanted, and it would be added to the aeries expense. Even though I was so excited, something felt off. Like he was trying to buy my favour, but I pushed that thought down. I was too excited about being able to create what I wanted.

I was also getting impatient. We hadn't spoken once about him training me in how to use my powers. That was one of the reasons I wanted to stay, and I had heard nothing about it. I desperately wanted to learn how to use my powers, but every time I went to ask about it, someone would come in, or he would walk away, not giving me the chance to talk. I tried hard to find the right moment, but it was getting clear there might not be one with Gloom.

At the end of the first week, I checked my schedule and noticed it was my day off. I hadn't thought about a day off. I was hoping I would get one, but I wasn't holding my breath. Relief washed through my body. Even though no one else thought so, I had been working so hard and trying to keep out of everyone's way. I was excited at the chance to explore and do whatever I wanted. I decided I would ask Lilly if she wanted to come shopping with me, and I could pick up some clothes and fabric to sew with. My stomach danced in anticipation.

While in the shower, I realised this could be my chance to go and do some practice with my magic. I knew my way around town fairly well now, and I knew of a place near the wall where no one really went, and the guards didn't seem to patrol. I could go there and practice and get ahead on what Gloom had promised me but never delivered. I got dressed, grabbed a bag for my purchases, and made sure I had Gloom's note about the fabric. I headed out to the Comms room to see Lilly.

When I walked in, she was at her desk, and I wondered if she ever left. "Hi, Lilly."

"Oh, hi, Amelia. What are you up to today?" she asked, turning her head and dropping autumn leaves all around her.

"It's my day off. Do you want to come shopping with me? I need some new clothes and fabric."

"Shopping? Sure. Just give me a few minutes till Grum is here, and I'll fill him in on what to do." She shook her head, and a rustling sound filled the room. "Here's hoping he does a better job than last time," she said with an eye roll.

We chatted for a few minutes until Grum arrived. It was the first time I had met him, and I was surprised to see he was a satyr-like Kennock but shorter. His goat-like legs were covered in thick black fur that was long and sort of curled at the ends. He was wearing a button-down business shirt, and his black hair was combed neatly and laid flat against his head. He had a pair of glasses perched on the end of his nose, covering his gold-coloured eyes. Horns jutted out of his head and pointed straight back in a perfect line. He was middle-aged and would have been attractive if he was smiling. He was currently frowning and looked very out of sorts.

"I'm sorry I'm late, Lilly. Something...came up..." He trailed off as he saw me standing there.

"Grum, this is Amelia. She is Gloom's new assistant," Lilly explained as she stood and tidied her desk. I gave him a small wave as he nodded curtly at me.

"I am going out, so I expect you to keep an eye on things here. Please don't make a mess like last time. That took me hours to fix, and I don't have time today."

"Well, that wasn't really my fault," he blustered. "The computers were malfunctioning. I explained this to you before."

"I know, but I don't have time for that today. Just do your job, and we will be fine," Lilly said as she left. I followed her, keeping my head down. As I closed the door, I heard Grum talking to himself, complaining about Lilly.

"Agh. Sorry about that. He is an okay worker, but man, when he makes mistakes, they are big," Lilly said. "So, what do you want to buy?"

I was glad I had thought about my response to this before-hand. It technically wasn't a lie either. "I was just thinking some clothes. I am running out of the ones that were given to me when I arrived. I also would love to get some fabric to sew with."

"Oh, you sew? That's so cool. I don't have time to do that sort of stuff, but I would love to learn one day. Maybe you could teach me?" she said with a big smile. I blushed slightly and nodded. It was nice to be appreciated and to be valued for something I could do rather than demanded and expected.

"Sure, sounds good. I was the seamstress at Woodmere. I made all their clothes, but I would love to make something nicer and more...me.

"Well. that sounds great. Here comes Tristan." She waved him down, and he joined us.

"Hi, Tristan. We are going into town to do some shopping. Do you want to come?" I asked.

He grimaced slightly. "Sure. I have to get something for Oak anyway. He will be one in a few weeks," he said with a small smile.

"Wow, one already! It only seems like yesterday he was born," Lilly exclaimed. We continued on, Lilly and Tristan chatting, and I smiled to myself. This is what I had always wanted. Friends to talk about my life with and people who would laugh and joke with me. At Woodmere, I had been an outcast because of my powers and, as a result, had never really had friends apart from my grandmother, but she had been dead for years. I soaked up the companionship and contributed when I could to the conversation. For the first time in what felt like a long time, I was completely at ease and relaxed.

Once we had made it to the fabric district, Lilly took over. Within an hour, I had more clothes than I knew what to do with. Pants in every fabric from cotton to leather, and shirts to go with them. I had some nicer dresses for dinners and comfortable pyjamas for sleeping. Tristen was a good sport throughout the whole thing and chatted along with us as Lilly took over. Despite that, he did keep a watchful eye. It had only been a week since the people were taken, and there was still an air of fear and unease among the crowd. Some stores were still closed, and I could see more than one had a guard at the front door while others patrolled the streets.

My arms were full by the time we made it to the fabric area, and I wondered how we were going to take all this stuff back to the aerie when Tristan flagged down Caleb in the street. He stopped and spoke to Tristan and Lilly for a minute, wearing an easy smile, his red hair glinting in the sunbeams, turning it flame-coloured.

"Hey Caleb, you couldn't do us a favour, could you? Can you take these parcels back to the aerie? Just leave them in the guard house, and we will grab them on the way in," Lilly asked, smiling sweetly at him.

"Oh well, anything for you, Lilly, you know that." He winked at her. Lilly blushed a little, turning the white skin on her face a dark brown.

"Thanks," she said before turning around and heading into the closest store. I smiled at him, and he winked at me as well before turning back to Tristan. I followed Lilly inside.

"So, what was all that about?" I asked her, browsing the many bolts of fabric on display.

"Oh, nothing. Caleb and I just like to flirt," she said, trying to sound offhand.

"Is that right? Well, it looked a little more than flirting to me," I said and wiggled my eyebrows at her.

She stared at me and eventually couldn't keep her smile in anymore. She grinned. "Well, maybe there is something else there, but we haven't found it yet. Anyway, changing the subject, how are you going? Coping alright with all the changes?"

My mood deflated a little at the reminder of where I was and what I had seen a few days ago. "I'm okay. Going to see the hag was terrible, and it just reminded me that it wasn't only confined to Woodmere. I thought I was free of that sort of stuff or would at least get a break from it." I touched some beautiful deep purple chiffon fabric and felt it run through my hands like water.

"Yeah. I don't blame you. I have never been to see the prickly hag, but I can imagine it is terrible. I had a question," she said, not looking me in the eyes. My stomach tightened, and I wondered what she was going to ask me. "I have always known Woodmere was strange, but what was it like living there?"

"Well, where to start?" I took a breath, knowing if I was going to tell anyone my story, it would be her. I turned to the next stand of fabric and ran my hands over the soft material.

"I was born there. My family have lived there for generations, and from what I was told, it was an okay place to live before. Lots of communities and people could come and go. It was a nice place where people could live and be closer to nature, worship the Evers, and be happy, you know?" My heart had started pounding, and my mouth was dry, but I continued.

"Before I was born, things had changed. There was a new leader, Matthew, and he did things differently. Now the people couldn't leave. He said the outside world was mean and cruel and wouldn't understand us. He told us if we went out, we would go to hell and disappoint our ancestors. He built a school and forbade the kids to go to an outside school. Any broken rules would be punished.

At this point, we are so insular half the people there have never left. When my mum was pregnant with me, she and Dad decided they had had enough and didn't want to raise a baby in that environment. They took what they could carry and, with the help of my grandmother, snuck out one night and got away." I stopped for another drink. Every time I thought about it, it gave me chills to think about how brave they all were to defy Matthew like that.

"Did your grandmother go as well?"

"No, she wasn't well enough. They wanted to take her knowing she would be blamed, but she didn't want to slow them down." I smiled, thinking of her. "She was always a rebel. I don't know why she stayed there. All she ever wanted was for us to get away, but she stayed. Anyway, we lived out in the real world for a few years. We were happy, and Mum and Dad had put it all behind them. I knew pretty much nothing of Woodmere growing up, and we were good." I paused for a moment to gather my thoughts. I didn't think I had ever told anyone this part. Everyone at Woodmere already knew, so I hadn't needed to tell anyone.

"One night, when we were in bed, someone broke into the house. They tried to attack my mum, and my dad fought the attacker. The guy shot him and killed him. I heard the shot and ran out of the room. Mum managed to get away and hide me in the linen closet. But she didn't get a chance to get away herself and was also shot and killed. I stayed in the closet, knowing what I would see if I went out. I didn't want my last image of them to be...that." A tear ran down my face, and I brushed it away. Lilly took my hand and squeezed it.

"Luckily, the neighbours heard the shots and called the police. They arrived and took me out. After looking through the house, they found an emergency contact phone number in Mum's wallet. It was a number for Woodmere. Grandma was the only family they had. They called, and Matthew sent people to come and get me, and I was taken there. I was five years old, and I lived with my grandmother until she died a few years ago.

It is a terrible place. Matthew and the elders would always say my parents had died because they left the community, and it was their own fault. If I defended them, I would be beaten. I was...different from the other kids, too," I said, being careful not to mention my powers. "I knew if I let it show, I would be beaten as well. They are big on beating there. Anyway, it was terrible, but now I am here, and I'm glad to be out of there." I wiped my eyes. It was hard to talk about my past, but I trusted her, and I knew she would understand. I finally lifted my eyes. She looked at me with sympathy but not pity.

"I am so sorry you have had such a hard life. I can't imagine the strength it took to get up every day and live there, knowing how cruel Matthew was. That was so brave. At least you are out now, even if it isn't exactly where you wanted to go." She gave me a sad smile.

I had never thought of myself as brave, but I guess she was right. I had endured it all and survived. Not everyone who had lived there could say that. We moved around the store in silence for a while in our own thoughts. I picked out a lovely floral linen fabric and some accessories and took it to the counter where another dryad was waiting. He was tall, and his skin was dark brown and lined. His hair stood up in a large green burst that looked like it had been pruned and trimmed regularly. I showed him the slip of paper from Gloom, and he smiled as he passed over my fabric.

As we left the store, we caught up with Tristan, who had bought a wooden train toy for Oak, and Lilly told me a bit about her childhood. The way she said it was so normal, but I thought it sounded amazing. Her parents were still alive but lived on the other side of Toleran. They lived in a little grove with their trees. Growing up, they had supported her love of technology even though it was strange for them being dryads. Usually, their job was to protect the forest and trees, not post on social media.

"One day, there was a job offer from the castle to be the PR rep for Gloom. My parents suggested I go for it, so I did. I was lucky and got it. I was so nervous on my first day. I mean, my first job was working for a God. No pressure! But it was fine. We knew Gloom was a fair Ever, and he has been great to work for. He trusts me and lets me do my own thing. I love my job. Not everyone can say that."

"I love my job," Tristan piped up, and we laughed, walking back to the aerie.

After lunch, I was in my room putting my things away when I decided now would be a good time to go and try out my magic. Nervousness built in my stomach as I made my way out of my room. I had told Tristan earlier I was going to spend the rest of the day in my room sewing, hoping he wouldn't be around when I snuck out. I couldn't see him outside my room, and guilt twisted in my chest. I hated lying to him, and I didn't want to get him in trouble, but this was important. I needed to learn how to control these powers, and sitting in my room and waiting wasn't going to do it.

I had promised Gloom I wouldn't tell anyone about my powers, and I knew it was a risk practising here, even if no one could see me. The memory of Awe was still in my mind. I had to do this. Gloom had said I could be helpful. I liked the city and the people in it so much that my mind changed, and I wanted to help them in any way I could.

These innocent people didn't deserve to live in fear, and if I could make their lives easier and safer, why wouldn't I?

I made my way to the spot near the wall, ducking and weaving and taking the long way in case I was being followed. When I got there, I hid to see if anyone had arrived. When no one did, I stepped out and looked at the area. It was as I remembered it. It was large and open, about twenty feet across. It was mostly surrounded by the wall and a few other small houses that didn't have anyone living in them. I poked my head out and went and picked a few of the flowers growing along the pathways and roads. I put two flowers a few feet in front of me and sat. For this first attempt, I wanted to try and discolour the flowers in front of me and none of the others.

I took a deep breath and tried to block everything else out. I had no idea what I was doing, but clearing my mind seemed like a good start. After a few moments, I felt calm and centred. I reached out my hand and willed my power to the surface. I waited for the cold to spread to my arm and to my outstretched finger, but nothing happened. I concentrated harder and puffed out my cheeks, but nothing.

I centred myself again. Maybe doing one or two flowers was too hard. I put down the rest of the flowers I had picked. All up, there was a pile of about ten. Again, I tried to direct my power and had no results. I stood and stretched. I should have known it would be difficult the first time, but deep inside, I thought it would be as simple as thinking and willing it.

I thought about the times I had used my power. It was always when I was under stress. When I was running from that thing I thought I saw in the woods. When I was getting overwhelmed at the breakfast table my first day, and the countless times I was in pain and scared at Woodmere. I needed to tap into that, without actually surrendering to the panic, and try and replicate it. I sighed and sat again. I stared at the plants, feeling like they were mocking me with their bright colours.

Eventually, I straightened and focused again. This would be the last chance I would have to practise for a while. I couldn't see Gloom living up to his promise anytime soon. I needed to make the most of it. And what better place than somewhere magic was relatively commonplace? For the next hour or so, I worked and tried and pushed and sighed in frustration with no results. By the end, I was exhausted and sweaty. I gathered the perfect-looking plants and put them in my bag. I might as well press them in my plant book. They were a beautiful fuchsia colour with big fat petals, and I didn't want them to go to waste.

I gathered my things and poked my head out to make sure there was no one there. Convinced the coast was clear, I stepped out and headed towards the aerie. On the walk, a small flash of light caught my eye, and I looked at a section of the wall. Something was glinting in the vines. Approaching it, I caught a glimpse of what looked like a black stone before the vines moved, and it was swallowed up. I moved in closer to see if I could find it again, but all there was, was a cold spot. Touching the wall, it was cold. Strange.

Something moved at the edge of my vision, and I whipped my head around. Moving behind a house, I caught a glimpse of Rak, the snake man from the kitchens. What was he doing out here? Did he see me practising? My stomach dropped, thinking I had just been caught, when I realised, he would have just seen me staring and pointing at some flowers. Not ideal, but not incriminating. Just weird.

Had he been here? I frowned and looked at the spot again, but the gem was gone.

I heard someone clear their throat behind me, and my stomach fell further into my feet. I knew that voice.

"You know it doesn't look very good, a stranger in the city standing and staring at the wall that was breached a week ago. What are you doing here?"

NINETEEN

Amelia

I spun around and saw Bilvog standing there, running his hand through his beard and holding his wooden staff in the other.

I stood back from the wall like I had been burnt. I opened my mouth to tell him about what I had discovered and who I had seen but stopped. I knew if I told him, he would take the credit, and I didn't want to give him the satisfaction of being the one to find this anomaly. I held my head high and walked to stand in front of him, trying to look much more confident than I felt. I stood close enough that he had to look up at me because I knew he would hate it. I was right. He looked up and scowled.

"I was just looking at the wall. It's amazing how it works. It's my day off, so I thought I could spend my time however I liked. Is that not true?" I did my best Diana voice and tried to mimic the way she would speak to me at Woodmere.

"Yes, that is true. But you must admit it's a little strange you are standing there, hiding in the shadows, looking at the main protection of our town. Especially when the wall has been breached in unknown ways recently. No, no, no, this will not do. I think you will have to come with me and explain yourself to Master Gloom." He heaved a sigh like it was the last thing he wanted to do. He was a great actor.

I sighed and followed, thinking it would likely be faster to see Gloom and get it over with. The sun was starting to set anyway, and soon it would be dinner time.

Bilvog led me to Gloom's study, where he was sitting at a big wooden desk writing in a large leather-bound book. This room reflected Gloom the most. Everything was bathed in a soft golden glow, and the deep blue curtains were flung open. There was a mantle over the fake fireplace, which held strange knick-knacks and things collected from the forest. He looked up when we entered, impatience written on his face.

"Master, I'm very sorry to disturb you, but I saw some concerning behaviour from our new guest here." His voice sounded sweet, like honey, and it made me want to throw up. It was so fake I hoped Gloom would see right through it. Looking at Gloom's face, it looked like he did. He turned his green eyes to me.

"Well, what was this concerning behaviour, Amelia?"

"It's my day off, and I was out exploring the city. I'd been shopping, and on my way back, I noticed something glinting in the vines of the wall."

Out of the corner of my eye, I saw Bilvog's head snap around and glare at me. This was news to him. I smirked, proud of the fact I surprised him.

"I moved closer to see what it was, and it was a strange black gem or stone. Before I could get a good look at it, the vines wrapped around it, and it was absorbed into the wall. I noticed, too, there was a cold patch. It was strange. It wasn't cold anywhere else but where the stone was, and it was cold to the touch."

"This is very strange. Did you see anyone else there?"

I shook my head, thinking about Rak. I didn't want to get him in trouble if he was just in the area. Also, if he had seen me, I didn't want him to tell Gloom what I was doing.

"Right. Bilvog, go and get a few mages and guards and lead them to the place on the wall. I want them to find that stone and guard the area. Perhaps this is a way they got through the wall. Thank you, Amelia, for your information."

Before anyone could speak, he sat back down and began working again. Bilvog looked at me, his face bright red, and I could tell he was furious. I knew my suspicion of him taking the credit would have been true, and I was glad I followed my instincts in not telling him. He stormed out ahead of me. As I was reaching the door to leave, Gloom put his head up. "Amelia. Can you stay for a moment?"

Bilvog spun around to go back in the room as well, but Gloom stopped him. "Just Amelia. Bilvog, attend to the tasks I gave you." Bilvog smiled tightly and inclined his head, but I could see how much he resented not being in the room with us.

I walked to stand in front of the desk and waited for him to finish writing. His dark hair fell forward and hung in his eyes. He pushed it out of the way absently.

"So, it was your day off today?"

I paused, not knowing what answer he wanted but knowing I was walking into something.

"I was sitting here earlier, and I thought I could sense some kind of magic use near the wall behind the old Flutterby house. Do you have any idea what that would be about?"

I waited a moment. I hoped he would continue talking so I could think of an excuse. It was obvious he knew it was me. Luck was not on my side. He stared at me until I got uncomfortable. I stared back as long as I could, but eventually, I broke under his piercing gaze.

"It was me. I had the day off and thought this would be a good time to try and control the magic you promised you would help with. I found the spot the other day when I was running errands, and it was the perfect spot to hide and try to get some control. I double-checked I wasn't followed, and no one saw me. I was careful."

His brow furrowed, "well, as careful as you were, being close to the wall, magic will raise a flag now. You were lucky I was able to stop anyone from going out there and catching you. We need to keep your magic a secret, and you being out there throwing it around is not going to do."

I felt my face redden, "hang on a minute. I wasn't out there *throwing it around*. I was trying to wilt a few flowers. I hardly think anyone would have known what I was doing. As it is, I didn't manage to get any wilted, so I don't know how you felt it. You promised to help me, but I have heard nothing further on that."

Gloom looked at me calmly after my outburst. Did I see his lips twitch?

"You are correct. I did promise to help you, and I haven't followed through. There has been so much going on I have barely had time to sleep and keep up with my regular duties." He looked at the paperwork in front of him and thought for a minute. "The only way out of this I can see is if we get up early in the morning and train. It is making more and more sense to me. We may need your help to get through this sooner rather than later. I need to be making the time to use your power so it is an asset and not a liability when we need it."

Even though I had decided to help the city, I didn't want to become someone's weapon. I wanted to master my power mostly so it didn't get out of control. I didn't know how I would react to using my magic to hurt someone on purpose. I pushed my thoughts aside and decided the most important thing was to get the training and control, and I could decide how to use my power later.

"It will have to be at five AM. Meet me out the front of the aerie and wear some warm clothes. Don't put it in the planner. It is to be a secret."

I nodded, some excitement beginning to stir. Finally, I was going to get the help I desperately wanted. I left, hopeful I would finally have some control over my life. I wouldn't have to worry about hurting people anymore.

The rest of the night, I could hardly keep the smile off my face. At dinner, in my excitement, I may have had a bit too much wine, and Lilly had to walk me back to my room. I crawled into bed. This was it. Something I had dreamt about since my powers had shown themselves. I was finally going to master them and not the other way around. Finally, I couldn't keep my eyes open, and I went to sleep with the room spinning around me.

TWENTY

Amelia

Too soon, I could hear the birds chirping in the trees. It sounded like they were sitting on my pillow and screaming into my head. I rolled over and opened my eyes. The sun was rising, and it was already too bright. My mouth felt like cotton wool, and I had a throbbing headache. I sat up, regretting the wine I had drank at dinner. I sat in bed for a minute, trying to get my brain to catch up, when a memory niggled on the edge of it.

Looking at the time, it was 5:15 AM. I sat there looking at it for a few more seconds. Shit. I was meant to be training with Gloom. I groaned and threw off the covers of the bed, as I staggered to the bathroom, brushed my teeth, and splashed my face with water, hoping it would make me feel better. It didn't. I ran out the door, cursing myself. I couldn't believe I was going to be late when I had made a big song and dance about starting my lessons.

On the way, I went past the kitchens and got a bottle of water. I tried to drink it, but it threatened to come back up. If this is what it felt like after a night of drinking, I was never drinking again! I rushed out the door and saw Gloom leaning against the railing at the bottom of the steps. He had his eyes closed, and face tilted towards the sun. He was bathed in a golden glow of the rising sun, looking every bit the Ever he was.

"I'm so sorry, Gloom. I can't believe I am late. It will never happen again, I promise."

He looked me over, and one side of his mouth lifted into what looked a lot like a smile. I patted down my hair and straightened my clothes.

"I was wondering how you would be feeling this morning," he said with a smile. "No excuses, but. You will still be training, and I will still expect your best." He turned, walking through the town.

I followed after him, glad I wasn't in trouble but confused about his chipper attitude. I was expecting to get in at least a little trouble, but he seemed amused. I took another sip of water and kept my head down so the sunlight peeking through the trees didn't blind me. My headache was no better, and I dreaded trying to cast magic while feeling like this.

He led us out of the wall and into the forest a short way. It was strange to be outside of the wall and in the wild. I kept my eyes open for anything strange but saw nothing. After about five minutes, we walked into a clearing. It was a beautiful grassy circle. There was no question it was made by magic. There was electricity in the air, and it was too perfect. Dotted around the edges were different kinds of plants growing in groups of ones and twos. There were small trees, ferns, flowers, shrubs and long vines hanging off nothing. The sun was bright, and I shielded my eyes so they could adjust. In the middle of the circle, there were two figures. Gloom stopped suddenly and held out his hand to try and shield me.

"Good morning, Lord and Lady," he said, bowing his head but never taking his eyes off them. I did the same as tingles spread over my skin and cold filled my body. I gritted my teeth and willed my power in as I took a small step behind Gloom. Was it power I could feel skimming my skin? If it was, these were very powerful beings.

"And good morning to you, Gloom. How are you on this fine day?" the Lord boomed out. He was about seven feet tall and was wearing a suit made out of deep green velvet. It had gold buttons and piping and gold embroidered vines all over the coat. His black hair was long and touched his shoulders. He had purple eyes and a long, straight nose. Every inch of him radiated power and command. I could tell Gloom was wary, and I wondered where they had come from.

"I am fine, thank you. What brings you and your beautiful wife here today?" he asked.

"Well, we were about to ask you the same thing, weren't we, dear? He held out his arm, and the Lady took it. If he was night, she was day. Her yellow hair glowed and flowed down her back in soft waves. Bright green eyes stared out of her long lashes, and her lips were painted a striking red colour. Her dress was tight at the bodice and flared out at her feet. It was the colour of autumn leaves, and she appeared to radiate light.

"Yes, dear. We were wondering who had created this little pocket dimension in our lands and thought it best to come and investigate," she said, her voice tinkling like little bells. There was no mistaking they were from the Forest Folk Gloom had spoken about when I had arrived in Toleran.

"Forgive me, but I thought because we were still so close to the wall and in a pocket dimension, we would have permission," Gloom said to the lady.

"You may be correct, but a simple request would have been appreciated," she replied.

"And what *are* you doing in here, Gloom?" the Lord asked, stepping forward. I could sense the power pulsing off him, and I trembled, but Gloom stood firm.

"We are here to do some training, which is to be kept private and from prying eyes. I thought this was the best way."

"Ah yes, I see. Well, you are right, and this is an excellent way to ensure privacy, but I am sure you won't mind if we take a peek now and then. We like to know what is happening on our land. Speaking of that, perhaps you should deal with...the other things on your land. Things we would rather not deal with but are still causing us trouble," the Lord said.

There was no mistaking it was a command. Standing there, a presence brushed against my mind. I had not gone unnoticed standing behind Gloom. I shuddered at the intrusion, and the scope of their power hit me again. These are beings I would not want to mess with.

I saw Gloom's shoulders stiffen at the threat, but there was no trace of annoyance when he spoke.

"Of course. It is being handled. There may be a reason to seek you out about this matter soon, but we will do our best to put a stop to it."

"See that you do." The Lord turned to join his Lady, and they linked arms. For the first time since she spoke, I looked at the Lady and was surprised she was looking right at me with a small smile on her face. I looked back but did not smile. Her lips quirked, and her gaze shifted to Gloom, and I was relieved to be out of her scrutiny.

"Come along, darling, we have many things to tend to today," she said to the Lord. "Gloom. We will speak again soon, I think."

Gloom bowed again to them, and they turned and walked into the trees until they disappeared. Once they were gone, Gloom stepped away from me and relaxed a little.

"Well, that was a bit unexpected. We will need to keep this visit in mind, I think," he said with a frown between his eyes.

"Were they from the Forest Folk?" I asked.

"Yes. That was the Lord and Lady of the forest. They lead the Forest Folk here and are not to be messed with. They have more power than all the Evers put together. We may need their help soon."

"I could feel their power. Something brushed my mind."

"Yes, that would be the Lady. She is as dangerous as the Lord. I had hoped you would never encounter them, but it looks like they have taken an interest in us. We will have to be aware of them." He paused for a moment, thinking. "Right, well, time to get to some training. We have some time left."

He led me to the middle of the clearing and turned around. "I have created this little clearing for us to practise. Very few people will be able to find it, so it should be safe, and our magic won't be sensed outside of it. Here, we can train in private."

I nodded, and butterflies built in my stomach, the unease from the encounter with the Lord and Lady fading. I hoped it wasn't from the drinking last night. He sat cross-legged and invited me to do the same. I sat and was relieved to get off my feet.

"Now, these first few sessions, we won't be using any magic. I know it's not what you want to hear, but we need to lay a foundation. You need to be in control when you use it. This is how we get control. Close your eyes and take a deep breath. Do that ten times and try to meditate and empty your mind. It will be hard at first, but try to focus on the things around you. We will also practise some basic self-defence. It is important to be able to fight physically if your powers are empty or you can't use them."

I did as he told me and tried to focus on what was around me and not think. It was a lot harder than I thought it would be. In my current state, all I could think about was the pounding of my head and if we were being watched right now.

I must have sat there for half an hour. All my concentration was on how sore my legs were getting and the full day of work waiting for me when we returned. Gloom tried to give me instructions and help, but by the end, it was pointless.

"Okay, that's enough for today. How about a little bit of jogging, and then we will call it a day." He took off his jacket and laid it over a vine that had just snaked down from an above tree.

I stood and tried to build up any enthusiasm but failed. Gloom started to jog around the clearing, and I followed. It didn't take long for my legs to stretch and free up and also for me to be puffing and panting with my head feeling like it was about to crack. Thankfully, we only did a few laps before we stopped.

"Let's get back to Toleran," Gloom said as he put his jacket back on not even breathing hard. I nodded as I sucked in deep breaths, and I was sure I saw a twinkle in his eye that wasn't there before.

"Well, what a waste of time. I couldn't stop thinking," I said when my breath had come back.

"It wasn't a waste. This is only the beginning. Soon, you will be able to centre yourself in the most chaotic of places. You will be able to control your magic and do what *you* want, not what *it* wants. You did well. Especially considering the condition you are in and the interruption from earlier."

I nodded and readied myself to ask the question that had plagued me for years. It seemed as good a time as any. "Gloom, do you know where my powers come from? My grandma said they were passed down from generation to generation. Is that true? Have you ever seen a withering power like this?"

I had wanted to know the answers to these questions for so long. My heart started beating faster as anticipation rose in me, waiting to hear the answer.

He looked at me with a strange look in his eye. I waited.

"I don't specifically know. I would assume it was an Ever that bred into your family, but I don't know who. It is not uncommon. You would be surprised how many half-human, half-Evers are out there. I wouldn't worry about it." He walked off and headed back to Toleran.

I stood frozen to the spot. Annoyance crawled through me at the way he had brushed me off. I had a feeling he knew where these powers came from. Why wouldn't he tell me? Disappointment crashed into me, and my heart sank. We walked back to Toleran in silence.

The city was starting to wake as we walked through it. Merchants were setting up their shops, and food and drinks were being delivered to the local inns and restaurants. As Gloom walked past, everyone stopped and nodded or bowed. I was worried about all these people seeing us and wondering what we were doing. We were supposed to be keeping a low profile. Gloom didn't seem to care, but I hoped no one stopped and asked me later.

By the time we got to the aerie, my headache was worse than ever. I had finished my bottle of water earlier, but I was still thirsty.

"I'm going to go to the kitchens, then get changed, and I will be ready for the first meeting." Gloom looked at me, and I wondered what I must look like for him to say, "Amelia, why don't you have the morning off? Go to the kitchens and get them to deliver you some food and have a sleep. I will expect you at lunch. Take advantage of this because if you do this again, I won't let it slide. You have worked hard today. Have a rest and get better."

"Oh well, if you are sure. I promise it will never happen again. I never want to feel like this again, believe me. Thank you."

"Okay, well, rest well," he said, giving me a small smile before he walked off.

I went to the kitchens, grabbed some more water and asked them to deliver some breakfast in a few hours.

Martha, the lady who ran the kitchens, was more than happy to do it, but as I was walking out, I heard a muttering. I paused and listened at the door to the cool room where the meat was stored.

"Oh yes, don't worry, we love being your slave. If the human says jump, we say how high. God, I hate everyone in this place. Everyone expects me to do exactly what they want when they want. Well, they will see. Things are going to change around here."

I peeked my head around the door to see who was talking to themselves. It was Rak. I was shocked to hear someone complaining. For the week I had been here, everyone appeared to like it despite Gloom's moods. I wondered where he had come from. I hadn't seen any other snake people around Toleran. I made a mental note to ask about him. Hopefully, he was just having a bad day because his mutterings were a bit creepy.

I headed off to my room, had a drink, and crawled back into bed. Heaven.

TWENTY-ONE

Amelia

The next few days passed in a blur of meetings, errands, and training. My body ached in places I didn't know it could, but I kept telling myself I was getting stronger, even if it didn't feel like it. Gloom had me learning all-new fighting stances and taught me how to throw a punch. Plus, the running. So much running. I was actually enjoying it, and even though I was tired and sore most of the time, it was good to feel like I was a little more capable if something happened. However, the morning training and being Gloom's assistant, it did mean I didn't have a chance to scratch myself.

I had found my footing with most of my daily tasks, but some of them still gave me trouble. Bilvog never failed to remind me when I had missed or forgotten a job. Gloom was too distracted to notice most days. He spent more and more time in his office or the War room, and we had a lot of meetings. There was anxiety in the air as we waited for the next attack to happen. It had been a few weeks since the townspeople were taken, and with no new leads, the mood of the town was starting to turn. We all knew there was another attack coming. We just didn't know when or where. Plus, it didn't help that we were no closer to finding out who it was.

Any spare time I had was spent in the library. I stumbled upon it one day while running errands, and it had taken my breath away. It was a huge room surrounded on all sides with bookshelves carved into the walls. Light filled the room; it was almost like being outside. Looking up, there was no ceiling. It had been enchanted to let no weather in, like my bathroom, and the light flooded the whole library. At night you could see the stars and the other trees, it was magical.

Luckily, my grandmother had taught me to read at night when no one else was around when I was growing up, but I was still slow. I loved to scan the titles and pick out books to flick through and read. I would lounge in the comfy sofas or sit at the desks dotted around the room. My reading was improving the more I read, and I wished I had more time to sit and indulge. Plus, I was looking for something.

I didn't believe for a minute Gloom didn't know who my powers came from, and I was determined to find out what he was hiding. Something had opened in me that day when he had lied and said he didn't know. The only reason to lie was because he was hiding something. I needed to know what it was. Since my powers had started a few years ago, it was always at the back of my mind to know who it was that had passed them down. Had they been good? Did they use it to help people in some way? Judging by the nature of my powers, Maybe I didn't want to know.

I read through all the titles I could find on the Evers, but nothing stood out as what I was looking for. I picked out a couple of books at random and flicked through. There was a book about the history of the region. A book about imports and exports. A lot of information on a lot of different things. This was looking impossible. But there was someone else who would know about this stuff.

The only person I could think of was Bilvog, but I didn't think he would be overly forthcoming. I needed to butter him up a bit. My eyes rolled involuntarily in my head at the thought of it. He was one of the last people I wanted to ask, but he was one of the only ones who had been around long enough to know. I needed to try with him, and I resolved to do so over the next few days.

I was hoping I could get a chance to talk to Lilly as well. It had been days since I had hung out with her, and I missed it. I wanted to ask her about Rak. I wanted to know where he came from and why he hated living here so much. There was never enough time in the day, and the list of things I wanted to do was getting longer every minute. Every night, I went to bed exhausted, and every morning I woke up tired.

Despite that, I did enjoy what I was doing. It was nice to be needed, and like I was making a difference. In Wood-mere, I was shunned and invisible. Here, I had friends and contacts, and what I was doing was helping people in a small way. It was nice.

Making my way to a morning meeting, I saw Bilvog up ahead. I rushed to catch up with him, planning to butter him up a bit.

"Good morning, Bilvog. How is your day going?"

He looked at me suspiciously. "Fine. It is fine."

"That's great. I have a bit of spare time in my schedule today, so if there is anything you need done, I can try and get to it if you like."

After a pause, Bilvog replied, "Yes, well, there is one thing you can do. You can go and see old man Hucket. He has a few things I need. If you could see to that, it would be most helpful." He smirked, but I didn't let him see how much I dreaded doing the job.

Old man Hucket was one of the local jewellery makers. He made beautiful jewellery but never stopped talking. Once, I had gotten stuck with him for over an hour and only managed to get away because he had a coughing fit, and I ran out before he could stop. Picking an item up from him was one of the worst jobs he could have thought of for me. I already didn't have enough time in the day. This would only slow me down more.

I plastered a smile on my face. "Okay, no worries. I'll make a note." I smiled and sped into the meeting room. I took my seat, and when he entered, he looked at me strangely. I smirked inside, hoping my plan would work.

After the meeting, I went to see Lilly for an update on all things PR for Gloom. It would be so good to see her and have a chat while we were working. Luckily, we were the only ones in the Comms Room, so we could talk freely.

"Hi Lilly, how's it going? I haven't seen you for ages!" I said, before I noticed her mood. Her mouth was in a hard line, and she was glaring at the screen in front of her.

"Yeah, well, I've been better."

I was surprised at her tone. I had never seen Lilly be anything but good and cheery, but something was wrong.

"What's wrong? Are you okay?"

"Ugh. Bilvog was just in here. Man, that little guy has some issues. He was in here carrying on about whatever it was I didn't do because I ran out of time yesterday. He comes in here on such a power trip sometimes. It's like he thinks he is an Ever. Half of them don't even like him," she whispered. "He has been all their advisors, but he can't stay with one for long because they kick him out. Sometimes, he is so annoying." She sighed heavily. "Sorry to winge. He gets under my skin." She gave me a forced smile.

"That's okay. He certainly likes power. He's sending me to see old man Hucket today."

She cringed. "Ooh, that sucks. Good luck."

"I know. Hey, I've been meaning to ask you. What do you know about Rak? What's his deal? He doesn't look like he comes from here, and he's always so sour."

"Oh yeah." She screwed up her face. "He comes from The Bleak Wilds. That's the desert where Ashes rules. There was some skirmish on the border, and a small war broke out. It is always happening there. Ashes loves to fight." She rolled her eyes. "Anyway, the mage lost, and Ashes took his son to make sure he did not attack them again. I don't know how, but he ended up here with us. He's a bit weird and always cranky, but harmless anyway. He's been here a few months, and if you keep out of his way, he seems okay."

"Oh, so he hasn't been here long? No wonder I heard him winging about Gloom and me. It didn't seem like he was very keen on humans, either. I'll stay away."

"Probably for the best."

We chatted a while longer until I had to move on. A comment Lilly had made about Rak was nagging me. That night, after reading through more books, it finally clicked. He had been here for a few months. That was around the time the symbols started appearing. Could he be the one behind it? I needed to learn more about the symbols and what they meant. I knew what it looked like, so I needed to work out who the image was. I wondered if Gloom would tell me. With training in the morning, I would have the perfect opportunity to ask without anyone else around. I went to sleep thinking of a plan.

TWENTY-TWO

Amelia

As we made our way to the clearing, I rubbed my hands up and down my arms. The weather was definitely getting cooler, and I needed to get some more warm clothes off Mezz. I had tried to put my old jacket from Woodmere on, and it barely fit me anymore. I looked in the mirror and could see I was not so gaunt and hollow. It dawned on me I hadn't been hungry in weeks, and it was changing my body. I smiled, liking the effect and feeling it was giving me.

On the walk, I was trying to work out how to bring up the symbols and what they meant, but I was having trouble. I knew the chances of him telling me were slim, but it was worth a try.

I went and sat in the usual spot and prepared for more meditation. I settled my mind and body and relaxed. Gloom was right. After a few weeks of this, it was definitely getting easier. I had also noticed there were fewer times when I felt my magic building when I didn't want it to.

"Well done, Amelia. I think today it is time to see what you can do."

I opened my eyes, and he was standing next to the small sapling. I walked over with a mix of anxiety and excitement building in my belly.

"Now, I want you to look at the tree and imagine exactly what you want to happen. When you have visualised that, find where your power is inside of you. Deep down, you should feel it in the pit of your stomach. Call forth a small tendril and direct it at the sapling."

The way he said it made it sound so easy, so I tried...and nothing. I stood there imagining the sapling withering and dying. Thinking about my magic that way made my anxiety kick up a notch. Not a lot of good had ever come from my magic. I pushed it down and found my Zen place. I focused on what my body felt like and tried to find my power in me.

Deep in my stomach, I could feel something swirling and writhing. It made me think of black smoke twisting in the air. I reached for a tendril, and the length of my arm got cold. I pointed at the tree, and the magic shot from my arm. Black smoke shot out, barely visible, but unfortunately, it veered off and hit another tree, but the result was what we wanted. The tree's leaves started to brown and fall from the tree. It was dying. It worked. I could get control of this power inside of me.

"Good job, Amelia. Try a few more times, but not too many. We don't want to tire you out too much."

We practised a couple more times, and I managed to hit the tree once. Better than nothing. By the time we had finished, it felt like the smoke inside me was all gone. I had never really taken much notice of where my magic was and how it felt when it was gone, but now I felt almost empty. We finished up our training and headed back to Toleran. I was fast losing my chance to ask him about the symbols. Now was the time.

"Gloom, I was thinking about those symbols in the forest. What do they mean, like represent? I saw it was an image of stag antlers, but where does that come from?" There was a long pause. So long, I didn't think he was going to answer me.

"A long time ago, there was an Ever, Dread, who went rogue," he said quietly. "He didn't agree with living peacefully in our own dimensions, and he didn't like the idea of humans living alongside us like you are now. He wanted to enslave humans and ended up killing a lot. The other Evers did not agree with his plan and were disgusted by what he had done, so they bound his powers and locked him away. He used to have a very loyal servant, and that is his image you see in the seals."

"And he is trying to get free? Can he do that?"

I didn't think so," he said, worry lacing his voice. "But now I am not so sure. When the symbols first appeared, I hoped it was a prank, but I know it isn't. I worry about what he is going to do with the people he took." He paused, and we were both lost in thought.

I asked the question that had been on my mind since seeing Vivian the hag, "Who do you think is helping him?"

There was a longer pause, and I could see he was struggling with the answer. "I don't know. I can't think of anyone who would want to bring back such an evil person. Not many people would even know the details of Dread's imprisonment. It was over a hundred and fifty years ago. I have no idea, and it scares me."

I looked away from him, and we continued walking. I didn't want to say anything, knowing how he reacted last time in the war room. In my mind, one thing was circling. I had an idea of who it might be.

My plan to befriend Bilvog was slowly working. I had fetched him drinks, done errands for him and anything else I thought would make him like me better. Today was the day I was going to ask him a bit about himself. I needed to start slow, and if there was anything I had picked up the last few weeks here, it was that he loved feeling important and telling you about himself. After talking to Lilly, I wanted to find out a bit more about Bilvog and his opinion about why he had moved around a lot.

I found him out in one of the courtyards surrounding the castle, reading a book. There was no one else around, so it was perfect. I took a deep breath and approached him.

"Hello, Bilvog."

He jumped and slammed his book closed. "Oh, Amelia! Why would you scare me like that? Are you trying to give me a heart attack?"

"I'm sorry Bilvog. I didn't mean to scare you; I was wondering if I could ask you a question? You appear to know a lot about this place and Gl...the Master. Have you worked for him long?"

He looked at me suspiciously. "Yes. I have known them all for a *very* long time. I'm over three hundred years old, you know. Not many people know because I look so good, but I have known them for an astonishingly long time. I have worked for them all. I am probably one of the only people who knows them as well as they know themselves! Why?"

I ignored his question. "Oh wow, you really have known them a long time. Between us, who was your favourite to work for, if you have a favourite?" I wondered if he would actually answer.

He seemed to warm up to the question, "Ah well, that's like asking me to pick my favourite child. I don't know. The boys are always a bit harder than the girls. A bit stubborn, I think. Not as willing to take my advice. I have been around a long time, you know. I do know a few things. Sometimes, it is easier with the girls to talk some sense into them. I think Gentle is the most reasonable one who listens to my advice."

"And out of curiosity, why do you move around so much?"

He gave me a sharp look. I wasn't as subtle as I thought. Talking was not my strong suit.

"Well, they don't fire me if that's what you mean. They all want my advice and counsel. Sometimes, it is just time to move on and be of assistance elsewhere."

"Of course, I didn't mean to offend you. I was curious, but that makes sense. So much wisdom should be shared." I couldn't believe the words coming out of my mouth. But Bilvog did, and that was the most important thing. Now, he was on a roll. I couldn't stop him talking.

He filled me in on all the Evers and what they were like to work with. Ashes was arrogant, Crescent was wise, Gentle was kind, Enduring was passionate, and Awe was vain. I took notes in my head in case I ever met them so I would have the upper hand. Eventually, he ran out of things to talk about.

"Right, well, thanks, Bilvog. You know so much! I will see you later."

"Yes, well. Thank you. It's nice to be appreciated around here. So many people take me for granted, you know." He turned back to his book with a small smile on his face, and I hurried off to my next appointment. I hoped our little chat had made him a bit kinder towards me. I needed to quiz him about my powers, and I couldn't do it if he still hated me.

I headed into our next meeting. This one was different from the others. People from the town could come in and have an audience with Gloom and discuss any problems they were having. Some of the complaints were about people stealing or land disputes. Gloom listened to them all carefully and was often the one to suggest how the problems were to be dealt with. He was considerate and weighed all the sides fairly. I saw the kind side to him, and it was obvious he cared about the people he ruled over.

Only one disturbance was had from the husband of Caroline Willis, one of the people who were taken. He came in accusing Gloom and his people of not doing enough. Gloom let him rant and rave and get it all out. I worried for him, expecting him to get thrown out by the guards scattered around the room, but that didn't happen.

Watching from behind Gloom, I could see the man's face was ravaged by grief. In a few weeks, Caroline's husband had lost weight, and his face was hollow. Deep lines covered his forehead, and the smell of alcohol was strong. His clothes and body looked like they hadn't been washed since she disappeared, and there was something missing in his eyes, like his soul had winked out. It was devastating to see, and I felt so sorry for him.

When he was finished, Gloom stood and walked to him. The room was silent, apart from the heavy breathing of the husband. Gloom reached out a hand and laid it on his shoulder.

"I'm sorry. I am doing everything I can to bring them back. I know it doesn't make you feel any better, so if you need to be angry at me, that is fine. I want you to know anything you need will be provided. At any time, approach one of my people, and you will have whatever you want. Clean clothes and food will be delivered after this meeting. Let us help you." Gloom squeezed his shoulder, and I saw the man crumble. His face collapsed, and he cried in great, heaving sobs. Gloom pulled him in and motioned for everyone to leave the room. I couldn't leave. The sorrow that filled the air rooted me to the spot, and all I could do was watch as Gloom held the man while he cried.

When he was all cried out, he straightened and wiped his eyes, looked at Gloom and nodded his thanks. He shuffled out of the hall while I watched silently.

"Amelia, see to it he has food delivered every few days, a laundress to wash his clothes once a week and someone to tidy the house for him. It is the least we can do. While you're at it, make sure all the others have what they need as well. We have failed them. It is time we look after them better."

"Okay. I will," I said, looking at his back.

He squared his shoulders and came to sit back on his chair. I took it as a dismissal and got up to leave. Before I could take a few steps, the doors flung open.

We looked up and saw Awe stride in. His presence filled the room. He was as imposing as the last time I saw him, and I was thankful again it was Gloom and not him who found me. He was big and attractive, but there was an undercurrent about him, and after talking to Bilvog, I knew what it was. Pride. He thought he was the most powerful in the room, and he was probably right.

"Hello," he boomed. "Just in time, am I? I don't want to miss you. I was coming to check on the current status of my little brother's kingdom. Have you found who is responsible?" He looked at Gloom, and I saw his jaw tighten. Whatever softness had been there a moment ago was firmly behind a mask now. There was a look in his eyes I couldn't quite put my finger on. Awe was looking right back, smirking, and I knew they knew something I didn't. It was tense for a few minutes. I took a few steps closer to the door, wanting to get out of Awe's way. He was so overpowering, and I felt myself shrinking in his presence. The last time I had seen him he had thrown a fire ball, and I didn't want to be around if he did that again. Having been through that once, I felt my own mortality strongly around him this time.

"Awe. We have everything under control. There is no need for your assistance, though we are grateful you offered it. Time to go, big brother."

Awe laughed. "That's no way to greet your brother! I thought we might spend the day together before everyone else arrives. Our siblings should be here soon to catch up."

"It's unnecessary. Remember the last time we were all together? It did not end well. If you insist on staying, how about we go to my rooms where we can have a proper conversation." Gloom stepped forward, and Awe followed. He took a few steps, turned around, looked at me and said, "Don't worry, dear. I haven't forgotten about you. I didn't end up going back to the village. I thought I would wait and see if you changed your mind first." He gave me a wink, and it took everything I had not to shudder. I could see Gloom watching closely. Awe walked out, and Gloom followed. As Gloom walked past, he stopped.

"Amelia, deal with the things we spoke about. Then I want you to go back to your rooms for a bit. You will have the rest of the day off. It's almost the end of the day anyway." He looked up and glared at Awe's back. "I don't want you wandering around. Could take some reading back to your rooms?"

I looked at Awe as well and realised Gloom didn't want me in sight of him while he was here. I tended to agree with him. I didn't want to see Awe if I didn't need to, especially by myself and without the protection of Gloom.

"Okay, I think there are a few books I haven't read in the sitting room. I'll head back there now. Thank you."

Gloom smiled at me and hesitated. I thought he was going to say something, but then he nodded and caught up to Awe. I went to my room with some books and settled in for the night, trying to keep my thoughts at bay.

TWENTY-THREE

Amelia

I awoke with a jolt. My brain struggled to untangle from my dreams of being locked away in the shed at Woodmere. I had dreamt I was right back there being starved, in the hot, dark shed again. The hot air sawed in and out of my throat, leaving it dry and brittle. Someone opened the door, and I was afraid of seeing Matthew in his bright white robes and cold eyes. But it wasn't him. It was a tall, dark-haired man wearing a long black coat.

There were alarms going off. The same ones I heard on my first day. My mind cleared, and I leapt out of bed. My heart started hammering, and dread filled me, but I knew I had to help. The people of this town had burrowed into me, and the thought of them being in more pain was unthinkable.

With my heart racing, I got dressed as fast as I could and headed down the stairs. I could see people running past the front door. When I got there, I could hear others in the town yelling "Fire!" and there was an orange glow against the darkness of the sky. If the fire got out of control, the whole forest would burn. On the streets, it was chaos. Noise flooded my ears, people shouting, fire crackling, and others screaming. All around me, there was soot and embers flying in the air, creating a beautiful but devastating light show. It was dark and confusing, and I could see clusters of children and adults bundled together, terrified and unsure of where to go.

As I got closer to the fire, I realised it wasn't one blaze. There were at least four fires I could see. The flames leapt and bounded, catching hold of anything they could. One of the houses had already collapsed, and a woman was trying to run back into it. Others were holding her back as she screamed. The heat was intense, and it was consuming whole houses in its fiery jaws. The crackling of the wood and the woosh of the flames was overpowering.

Even though it was scary and there was panic, I soon noticed the people of Toleran knew what to do and were dealing with it well. It was pretty clear people had been trained for this. There were wells scattered around every-where and people were hauling water out of them light-ning-fast and getting it where it was needed.

I ran to the nearest house, joined in, and helped as much as I could with my skinny arms. My arms and body were soon like jelly, but I kept going, gritting my teeth and rubbing my stinging eyes. The smoke was in my nose and eyes, and the air burned all the way down to my lungs. It was a struggle, but we kept going.

The heat from the flames was unbelievable, and I could have kissed the person who put a cold towel over my head and neck. Through the haze, I could see people from the aerie helping, and somewhere could hear Gloom's commanding voice directing people and organising them. I could see many people were burned, and some of them looked bad. Healers and mages were busy tending to them while we worked on getting the flames out.

I don't know how long we worked for, but after a while, someone came and took over so my group could have a rest. I got out of the way and sank to the ground. The fires looked fairly under control, and I nodded at the people walking past, who looked as exhausted as me but still said thank you. I stumbled up and went to the spot that had been made into a rest area and drank greedily from a cup of water that was pushed into my hand. Gulping down the water reminded me of when I was released from the hot box at Woodmere. I pushed that uncomfortable thought from my head and looked around to see if there was any-one else that needed my help.

I surveyed the damage and was sad to see about ten or so homes were destroyed, as well as the surrounding trees. Their black and burning branches simmering with coals were ugly in this normally vibrant town. I could hear peo-ple calling out to their family members who were missing, and I worried there would be more devastation to come in the next few hours.

I wandered around, looking at the damage and if there was anywhere needing my help until I found myself stand-ing near where I had felt the cold patch that day, when I was practising my magic. My eyes were drawn to the spot on the wall where the gem had been. Something wasn't quite right about it, and I cocked my head and tried to make out what I was looking at in the gathering dark. It moved. My eyes widened, and I dropped the cup I was holding, water splashing all over my shoes, and the singed hair on my legs.

Standing against the wall was a creature that had blended in with the branches of the wall. It was taller than any man

I had seen, with long arms ending in sharp claws. It had tall, strong legs and big feet, and it was black in colour, but the worst bit was its head. Instead of one, there was one huge skull with long antlers poking out the top of it. It was the creature I had seen in the symbols in the forest. The creature loyal to Dread. Where did it come from, and what did it want? It was watching the chaos going on behind me.

Before I could yell or scream or draw attention to it in any way, it looked at me. As I looked back, I felt cold, and I knew it was looking into me with those empty, soulless sockets. For a moment, I was transfixed and couldn't move. Some instinct kicked in, and I raised my hand and summoned my power like Gloom had taught me. I pushed it out and tried to hit the Horned One. Unfortunately, my aim was off in my panic, and I hit the fence to the left of him. He looked at the mark my magic had left. A stillness seemed to come over him, and he stared at the spot I had hit for a beat like he was letting it sink in.

It turned back to me a moment later, and a coldness tiptoed down my spine. Suddenly, my brain seemed to freeze, and I felt like I had been branded or marked in some way. I waited for it to charge me or attack me in some way. I was scared, but I didn't want to show it. If this was it, I was going down bravely. Instead, it took a step back, blended into the wall, and vanished. I waited a second, my feet not wanting to move.

When I was sure he wasn't coming back, I whirled around and went to find Gloom.

TWENTY-FOUR

Gloom

The people of Toleran were tired and drained as I helped the last group put out the final fire. Standing there in the street, I looked around me at my people. They were singed and covered in black soot. Some had tracks running down the soot on their faces from crying. Amidst the exhaustion and anger, I also felt pride. My people had done an amazing job putting out the fires and helping with the injured. Everyone had come together, and as a result, the damage was nowhere near as bad as it could have been. Overriding most of my emotions was devastation. How much more could this community take? There was a big job ahead of us now. There were people missing and a mess to clean up.

I sat on a stump and shared a small, sad smile with the others who had perched there for a break. I had stripped off my jacket when I got here, and I could see the little hairs on my arms were singed from being so close to the fire.

Someone came around with a jug of water, and we all drank deeply. Wiping my mouth, I looked up and saw Amelia walking hastily through the streets, looking around frantically. I frowned and forced my body to stand. She was also dirty and looked like she had played her part in saving the rest of the town.

When she finally saw me, she sagged with relief. A thrill zipped through me. Was she worried about my safety? It had been so long since someone had worried about me. I smiled and walked towards her.

"Thank the Evers I found you." Her eyes were wide, and she swallowed trying to speak. "I saw it. I saw the thing."

I reached out and held her shoulders, worried she might collapse where she was standing. "What thing did you see? Are you alright?

"The thing. The thing from the symbols was there. The Horned One or whatever."

My head snapped up, and I looked where she pointed. I took off at a run, sprinting through the crowd. I could hear her running behind me, trying to keep up, but I was fast. I was a blur weaving in and out of people, but when I made it to the spot, I couldn't see anything. I paced and prowled, waiting for Amelia to catch up. Was she right? If that thing was back, it would be very bad for everyone. How the hell had it got inside the wall? I thought about what it was like all those years ago, and I hated the idea that time would repeat. Touching my scar, I thought about the night I had received it and anger boiled through me. Anger and a bit of fear.

Finally, Amelia caught up. She was puffing hard, and a twinge of guilt hit me. I had made her run so fast after all the drama of the night. I waited for her to catch her breath to tell me what she had seen, seeing how it was clear the creature was gone now.

"There. It was right there. I thought I was imagining it because I am so tired from tonight, but it looked at me." She steadied herself. "It was awful. It looked at me with those eyes, and it was like it was looking right through me. Then it vanished into the wall and disappeared." She shuddered.

I knew exactly what she was talking about. The Shadow One seemed like it could stare into your very soul and suck out all of your deepest darkest secrets.

I walked closer to the wall to see if there was any evidence left behind. All that was different was there was a cold patch. It wasn't lost on me that it was the same spot Amelia had alerted me to before. I could see another mark on the wall.

"Did it say anything to you?"

"Say anything? That thing can talk! No, it was standing there looking around at the fires, and it saw me, snorted, and melded into the wall. Then I went to find you."

"Yes, it can talk. And it is extremely good at following orders." I closed my eyes to think for a moment. This was definitely not good. There was only one person who had ever successfully tamed the creature, and it was Dread. I rubbed my eyes as a headache began to sink its claws into my head. As soon as I saw a soldier run past, I called him over and organised them to do a full perimeter search of both sides of the wall. I wanted anything and everything they could find. Once they were gone and Amelia and I were alone again, I pointed out a patch on the wall where it looked like it had been injured in some way.

"What is this, Amelia? Did it do this, too?"

"Uh, no. That was me. I tried to hit it with my power. I had poor aim and missed."

"I see. Well, you did well to control your power enough to try and get it. Well done."

I could see how my compliment affected her. She smiled a small, soft smile and appeared to unfurl a bit. Warmth seemed to trickle down my body, and looking at the small smile on her lips, I wondered what it would be like to kiss them. I found myself stepping closer to her. From the moment I saw her, I had been drawn to her spark. She hid it well under the layers of quiet, hesitation and invisibility she tried to portray, but it was there. I had grown to love seeing that flame come through. I watched her as I stepped closer.

She froze and looked at me. I stared at her, and she stared back unflinchingly. I raised a hand to brush the soot off her face. She closed her eyes. Before I could do whatever it was my body wanted, we were interrupted. I pulled my hand away quickly. What was I thinking? We had just survived an attack, and here I was, thinking about kissing someone in the middle of the disaster. I needed to get a handle on myself.

"Master, the fires are all out, and there are three people unaccounted for. We have set up a search party to go through some of the wreckage when it has cooled down. Is there anything else you need from us?" Kennock asked.

"We will find a place for people to stay. Make a list of the missing people. Make sure there is food and drink and any clothing you can find available for the people who have lost their houses. I'm coming now."

Kennock left, and I looked at Amelia. Whatever spell we were under had been broken, and her eyes were downcast. I cleared my throat.

"Amelia, it's going to be a long night. We will need your help tomorrow, so why not go and rest now while you can."

"I would like to stay and help if I could. These poor people need all the help they can get."

I looked at her. She looked exhausted and ready to collapse, but if she wanted to keep going, it was her choice. I nodded.

She turned and managed to take four steps before she swayed on her feet and collapsed. I grabbed her before she hit the ground.

"I'm sorry. I don't know what's wrong. I'm weak all of a sudden."

"It's probably from the long night and the use of your power. Here, lean on me, and I'll walk you to the castle."

She stood. "No, no, no, I'm okay. I can manage." She pulled away and went to take a step but stumbled again.

"I will walk with you. That thing could be out here, and it will only take a few minutes. They will manage without me. Please." I held my arm out to her. She hesitated, then put her hand on it, leaning heavily. I tried to ignore the warm weight of her body leaning against my arm. The scent of ash and water and fire was in the air, but I could still smell the lavender that seemed to seep from her pores.

We were silent on the walk. Too many thoughts were swirling around my head to make any sense of them. Finally, I spoke, "I will send Tristan to your door when all this is sorted. I think it would be a good idea to have a few guards around tonight."

"Tristan! What about his family? Where do they live?" Her hand had tightened on my arm, and she was twisting around to look at the destroyed homes frantically. I stopped walking and put my hand on hers.

"It's okay. Tristan and his family are on the other side of the town. They are fine." She sagged in relief, and we continued onto the aerie. Just as we made it to the guest wing, her legs gave out.

"I'm sorry. I'm just so weak," she said with a frown on her face.

"Don't worry, there isn't long to go."

Before she could object, I scooped her up and carried her in my arms. She let out a little squeal, and I tried to keep the smile off my face. Her arms came around to wrap around my neck, and they brushed my hair, making me shiver.

"You don't have to carry me, you know. I will be fine in a minute. You should get back down to the town."

"Here we are," I said, ignoring her and opening her door. I set her down on the floor and hoped she couldn't hear my heart beating like a drum. As I put her down, I noticed she winced a bit.

"Are you hurt?" I asked, leading her to a chair. Her brow furrowed.

"My ankle. I dropped a bucket on it earlier. I didn't realise it was so sore till now," she said as she rubbed the spot.

"I can help," I said while I hovered my hand a centimetre away, kneeling before her. Her skin grew hot, and the bruise that was starting to form faded slightly. I looked up at her as she leaned closer for a look. For a moment, our breath mingled, and I became acutely aware of her, and the air changed between us. We looked at each other for a moment, and my eyes dipped to look at her mouth. My body warmed, and my lips parted and tingled. Her gaze intensified, and she licked her lips. I held back a moan at seeing this reaction.

Slowly, our mouths drifted towards each other. I was practically vibrating, waiting for our lips to touch, when coming down the hall, I heard a voice call out, "Master Gloom. Are you down here?"

We jumped apart like school kids caught holding hands.

"Yes. I am in here," I yelled back, my voice cracking a little. I looked at Amelia, and pink stained her cheeks.

"That's about as good as I can do at the moment," I said to her. "As Evers, we all have some healing ability, but it does drain us. I can try again tomorrow if you like."

"Thank you. It feels much better," she said, barely looking me in the eye.

"Okay then, Goodnight, Amelia," I said softly, the breath catching in my throat.

"Goodnight, Gloom," she replied, a blush blooming on her cheeks.

I turned and left the room before I did something I couldn't take back, and I headed out to see who wanted me. On the way back to the town, I couldn't help thinking about what had come over me. Something about Amelia drew me to her, and emotions were stirring inside me. Emotions I thought long dead. Seeing Awe near her had raised my hackles, and it took all of me to not restrain him in vines and drag him away from her. Having him in the same space and breathing the same air made me wild.

I needed to get a hold of myself. I couldn't afford to be distracted at a time like this. Especially if somehow Dread was clawing his way back here. How was I going to deal with this? I needed some help. I sighed, knowing how the conversations would go with my brothers and sisters. It would take a bit of convincing to get them to believe me. By the time I got back to Toleran, the clean-up was already underway. I could see people still looking for their loved ones. I saw an elderly lady I had always said hello to. She was crying.

"I'm so sorry for this. Is there anything I can do to help you?"

"Oh, Master Gloom. Thank you. My husband is missing. He went back in to save some of our things, and I haven't seen him since." Her sobs increased, and I looked over at the house she was looking at. There wasn't much left of it, and I didn't think if someone was in there, they would have survived.

For most of the night, we searched through the debris to try and find the missing people. In the early hours of the morning, all three bodies were found. Rage and sadness battled within me. The people of this town had been through enough these past months with the disappearances. I knew it deep in me. I was connected to this city and town on a deep level, and when they hurt, I hurt, and it was weighing on me heavily. We organised places for people to stay and put the bodies of the ones we lost in the temple.

I went back to my room and lay in bed, hoping to get an hour or so of sleep before the meeting. I ignored the light peeking through the window as sleep claimed me, and I welcomed the oblivion.

TWENTY-FIVE

Amelia

The next day, I got ready and thought about the things I had seen yesterday. The devastation of the fire, The fright of the Horned One and the resilience of the people of Toleran. A wrinkle of fear ran through me when I thought about what this meeting would be about today. I would have to tell them what I saw, and likely my power would come out. I wondered what people would think when they learnt my secret. Just the thought of telling a group of people made my skin crawl. Since it had manifested in me a few years ago, I had spent all my time trying to hide it.

By the time I made it to the war room, most of the seats were full. Bilvog, Kennock, Gloom and a few other important members of the household were seated, having low conversations. All of them looked like they were lucky to have had two hours of sleep, and most were still covered in soot and ashes, and the smell of smoke was overpowering in the room. As I walked in, I kept my head down, trying to be invisible. On the way to my seat behind Gloom, I could feel his eyes on me. Making me flushed and warming places in my body.

Blood rushed to my face, and my senses sharpened so I was aware of every look he gave me. I tried not to show the effect he was having on me and sat in my seat behind him and watched his head incline to look at me briefly.

Once I had calmed myself, I looked around the room to see who we were waiting for. Everyone was here, apart from Lilly. She must have got caught in the Comms room. I imagine she would be busy with damage control.

"Thank you for coming." Gloom stood and addressed the gathered people. "We have a situation here that needs to be addressed immediately. He looked every person in the eye and frowned. "It seems like we are missing Lilly. Has anyone seen her this morning?" He continued when no one answered, "I will fill her in later." He looked at me and nodded, and I made a note to go and find her afterwards. I wished she was here now. It would be nice to have another friendly face in the room.

"I know we have been trying to figure out who has been tormenting our city, and I think I may have some information for you." He paused for a moment as if to gather his thoughts. I knew what was coming, but I didn't want to believe it.

"I believe it is the Shadow One, Dread. My adopted brother." Gloom waited while gasps and sounds of surprise filled the room. Everyone apparently knew about Dread and what that meant. My body tingled with shock at the confirmation of what I had suspected. Dread was Gloom's brother. What had happened to their family that his own brother would be trying to attack him?

When everyone had calmed, Kennock spoke, "How could it be him? We all know the stories. He has been locked away for centuries! I thought there was no way he could return."

"I don't know how, but there has been evidence it is him. As a lot of you know, we have been finding symbols throughout the forest. They are the symbols of the Horned One, who we all know is Dread's most trusted minion. The only time I had ever seen those symbols was when Dread was active. To see them now suggests he is back or someone close to him is doing his dirty work for him. We have also had a sighting of the Horned One himself." This time, there was silence after Gloom spoke.

"But the Horned One hasn't been seen in centuries. Surely there must be some mistake," Kennock said with a frown on his face. His ears were twitching on his head, and I could tell he was trying to come to terms with what had just been said.

"No. There is no mistake," Gloom said firmly but with a sigh. "It was seen by someone I trust, who has also seen the symbols in the forest." He looked behind him and extended his arm to include me in the conversation.

It took a minute, but I realised he wanted me to stand, so I put my notepad away and walked towards him. Standing there looking at everyone, I sank into myself. I reached up and played with the necklace around my neck, and I felt my face get hot. I didn't want to tell all these people about what I had seen. I didn't think they would believe me if it did. Why should they believe me? I was just some woman Gloom brought home. I was useless, and they had no reason to trust anything I said. All the confidence I had built up since being here seemed to vanish, and I was right back there in Woodmere. Tears sprung to my eyes, and I tried to use some of the meditation techniques Gloom had been teaching me.

Gloom leaned down next to me. His mouth was so close his lips brushed my ear when he whispered, "Don't be scared. Tell them what you saw. I believe you." Before he moved away, he put his hand on the small of my back, and a calmness seemed to radiate from it. Had he used magic on me? At this point, I didn't care. I came back to myself, and the tears dried up. I ignored my beating heart and looked at the people looking at me expectantly. I looked at Tristan and Kennock and realised I had friends here, even if they were new. I spoke.

"Yesterday, I was drawn to the place where I had found the cold patch on the wall a few weeks ago." A few people nodded, and some looked confused, but I kept going. "As I got closer, I noticed there was a figure standing there. Instead of a head, it had a stag head with large antlers. It was the Horned One from the symbols. Before I could do or yell anything, it melted back into the wall. That's it. That's all I saw."

I had left out the magic because I wasn't sure if Gloom wanted everyone to know about it yet, and it wasn't really important to the story.

I hurriedly sat back as discussions on whether I had really seen him and if I was trustworthy began. Gloom stood, and when the room had calmed, he said, "I know this sounds crazy, but I believe Amelia. She has seen the symbols in the forest, so she knows what he looks like, and it is not a mistake you would easily make. I think it is time we accept this thing's out there. And Dread might well be rising. We need to increase all patrols of the area and have all patrols include a mage. I also want the mages of the city to patrol the walls inside and out to look for gems or anything foreign in the wall. This appears to be how they got in, and we need to stop it before they can again. Twice, they have made it in here. I will not tolerate a third time. We will need magic to defeat this thing."

Tristan spoke up, "If they are using the gems to get through the wall...then that means it was an inside job. Someone must have put it there."

Silence followed his conclusion as that information sank in.

"Yes. That is what we suspect. We need to be suspicious of anyone acting strange. I need everyone to keep their eyes and ears open. Nothing is innocent anymore."

"But how are we going to defeat Dread? The stories tell us a huge amount of power was used the first time. Can we do it again?" asked one of the mages. I think his name was Leiland. He was young and barely looked like he had finished school with his freckles and buck teeth.

It was a question I had been wondering about since last night as well. After being in the presence of the Horned One's power, I didn't think anyone would be able to bind it.

"It will be difficult. There are many things to work out," Gloom said, crossing his arms in front of him.

"Excuse me, but how was he bound in the first place?" Tristan asked.

Gloom sat back in his seat and rubbed his forehead. "It was a complicated and expensive process. The remaining Evers all had to give an artefact the hags used to bind him. I gave my Staff of Thorns, Awe the Sword of Light, Gentle the Crown of Glass, Enduring the Chalice of Sea, Fury the Hourglass of Time, and Crescent the Robe of Stars. These items were important to us and were needed to focus the magic. The hags used them and then hid them from us, so we couldn't use them to raise him if we wanted to. I myself only know where one is. To be honest, I don't know how we would bind him again. Without the help of the hags, it would be very difficult."

The room appeared deep in thought. I wondered what had happened to those precious items the Evers had given up. Could they be found and used again?

After a bit more discussion, plans were set, and people started leaving. All that was left at the end was Bilvog, Gloom and me. I waited back while Bilvog spoke to Gloom.

"Master, what are we going to do about this threat? Are we sure it is him? I can't believe it."

"Yes, we are sure. There is no mistaking the Horned One. He has been here, and he will be back. I think the main focus at the moment is trying to keep the city safe. Let me worry about how to deal with Dread. I need you to organise the defence of the city. Have you seen Lilly? It's strange she didn't make it here tonight. I didn't see her last night either, did you?"

"I haven't seen her this morning, but I did see her last night. She probably ended up on the other side of town helping. She will show up, I'm sure." He waved his hand in the air to dismiss Lilly. "These are certainly dark times. I am getting too old for this, Master," he said with a sad smile.

"Never. You will outlive us all!" Gloom replied, lightening the mood a little. Bilvog chuckled and headed out the door. When he left, Gloom turned to me. I walked over and stood beside him. "Come with me to see Lilly. It is strange I haven't seen her. I will write out some things to get done. You will be working closely with Martha, the housekeeper, to keep this place going while I am busy with this stuff. You two will need to keep things running smoothly. Let's go."

We decided we would try Lilly's room first. Knocking on her door, there was no answer. Gloom cracked open the door. "Lilly? Are you in there?"

Silence.

After a moment, we walked inside. Everything in the room was made from tree branches like they had just fallen from the tree. Her bed even had leaves growing out of the frame. It was decorated in autumn colours: orange, red and yellow. It was bright and cheery, just like her. I rock formed in my belly, and worry niggled at me.

After a quick look, it was obvious she wasn't in there, and everything looked like she had walked out that morning. "She must have already left for the Comms Room. Maybe she forgot about the meeting this morning," I suggested.

"It is so unlike her. But she has been busy lately. There has been a lot of stuff here to keep on top of. Let's head to the Comms Room and see what she is doing," Gloom said.

We made our way to the Comms Room. Despite the growing threat pushing on us, Gloom appeared more re-laxed. Even though he looked like he hadn't had a decent sleep in a week, his shoulders were relaxed, and he had let his guard down a fraction.

Everything changed when we opened the door to the Comms Room. We were greeted with a very different scene in Lilly's room. Everything had been disturbed. There were computers and papers all over the floor, some of the screens mounted on the wall had been smashed. Keyboards and electronics had been ripped from the wall. It was trashed. I lifted a hand to my mouth to stifle a gasp. Gloom turned into the Ever I knew. He was hyper-focused, and all the spring had gone from his step.

"Stay there and don't move. I need you to take as many photos as you can with your tablet."

I did what he said and took photos of the destruction around me. I noticed in one of the frames there was a splatter which looked a lot like orange blood on the floor. I froze in place.

"Gloom, over there. Is that blood?" I pointed it out to him and he approached slowly so he didn't disturb anything. He bent and touched it lightly with his finger. It looked sticky, and I recognized it as sap.

"Damn, this is old. Looks like whoever did this, did it last night. Go and find Kennock. He will probably be in his office. Tell him to come here immediately."

I was feeling lightheaded, and lost, that the only friend I had ever had, might be in pain or in danger. I did what he asked, hoping it wasn't Lilly's blood splattered across the room, even though I knew it was.

TWENTY-SIX

Amelia

The rest of the day was a blur. Search parties were sent out to search the castle and the city. When she wasn't found there, they were sent outside of the wall. The wall was examined, and no other stones were found, but that was a small comfort. Everyone was looking, and we all prayed we would find Lilly.

Gloom personally interviewed everyone he could, and we spread the word if anyone knew anything, they were to come to the castle and tell someone. A lot of people thought they had seen something, but it was during the chaos of the fire, so it wasn't very reliable.

Whoever had taken her had targeted her specifically, but why? We had to assume it was Dread. Why would he take Lilly? The best theory we had was she was a good target because everyone knew her, and it would send a signal that no one was safe. It would send a clear message that even Gloom's favourite could be taken. No one was safe from Dread. All day, we searched, and nothing came from it.

I could sense the pit in my stomach deepen with each passing moment she was gone. I hadn't realised till that point how much she meant to me. She had been my first real friend, and I had told her things I had never told anyone else. She had given me advice and asked for mine in return. I missed her and worried about her. It gnawed at my heart.

I could see how much she meant to everyone else as well. Everyone was doing whatever they could, and I heard story after story of how kind and friendly she was to everyone. They brought in some mages to try and magically re-create the scene. There was a large crowd gathered at the door of the comms room, but I was able to squeeze through so I could see. I was worried about what I might see happen to Lilly, but at the same time, I didn't want to miss this. Three human mages entered the room, including Leiland from the meeting, and formed a triangle focusing on the most damaged section. They took a deep breath together and lifted their arms while chanting a strange language I didn't know.

The room grew very still. There was something in here. Another presence was moving among us. All the hairs stood up on my neck and arms. I stood rigid, trying to make myself less of a target. I could tell others were aware of the energy, too as they started to fidget and rub their arms. I could see Gloom from my vantage point, and he was laser-focused on what was happening in the circle. His skin seemed pale, and he appeared to have aged since the meeting this morning.

The lights flared bright and I had to shield my eyes. Then, as quickly as they had flared, they went out. When they turned on again, sitting at her desk was Lilly. She was translucent like a ghost, and I stifled a gasp at seeing the projection while we watched her work at her desk.

Everything seemed normal. She was working when someone came through the door. They spoke before she turned and went back to work. I could see the strain on the mages faces and the pressure this was putting on them. The chanting was increasing in volume, and it drowned everything else out until it was like a drum beat in my head.

Lilly turned around again and spoke to the person at the door we couldn't see. This time, she looked upset. She said something to them and stood. I looked towards the door but couldn't see anything. Where was the intruder? Wasn't that the whole point of this? To see who had taken her?

Lilly's eyes moved as the intruder walked towards her. She looked up, and a panicked look crossed her face. It must have been the alarms ringing for the fire that had woken me. She brushed off the intruder and tried to walk past them, but they knocked her to the ground, and there was a struggle. Whoever had taken her didn't think she would be a fighter, but she was. She thrashed and fought with everything in her. She did not want to be taken. Leaves and sticks from her head were scattered around the room, fluttering in the air around her. At some point, she got a cut on her leg, which was where the blood came from. The invisible person must have covered her mouth with something because she eventually passed out.

Tears were running down my face as I watched her eyes close. I prayed to whoever was listening that she was still alive. We watched as her attacker dragged her across the room towards the door. It was slow, and they struggled, but they got there. I felt some relief when she stirred, and someone picked her up to walk alongside them. Looking at Lilly stumbling along while being held up, I noticed her attacker and the person who was carrying her couldn't be the same people. When Lilly was talking to them, she was looking down, so the attacker was shorter. Whoever was carrying her did it with ease and was the same height.

As they walked through the door, the mage's arms dropped, and the chanting stopped. Lilly blinked out of view, and it was over.

There was a moment of silence at the end as everyone absorbed what they had witnessed.

"Who took her?" Gloom asked quietly, his voice cutting through the quiet. One of the exhausted mages answered, "I don't know. They were shielded from our magic. Whoever it was is a magic user and is good at using it." He slumped to sit on the floor with the others. They were spent with sweat running down their red faces.

"Well, what was the use of that then? The whole point was to find who took her," Gloom exploded and stormed out. I had never seen him so angry. Kennock looked at me.

"You go. I need to stay here. He will need someone when he calms down."

"Okay. Good luck," I replied, wondering how I was meant to comfort him.

I followed Gloom down the hallway and into his room, where he paced back and forwards like a restless lion stuck in a cage.

"Gloom," I said. He stopped but did not face me. "We will find her. She was alive, and we will find her."

I saw his broad shoulders tighten under the black jacket. I reached up and held my grandmother's necklace, needing the strength it provided. I walked behind him and reached out a hand. I hesitated a moment, remembering what had happened last time, but I swallowed my fear and placed it on his arm. I felt him relax under my touch.

All the fight leaked out of him, and his voice cracked. "How can we save her if we don't know where she is? They took her from my home. I can't protect anyone. No one is safe."

"This is not your fault. We will find her and bring her home. We will not let them beat us."

He turned and looked at me, hiding nothing. In his eyes, I saw the real Gloom. Not the one he showed to the world but the one who thought he wasn't good enough. The one who thought he had to do everything himself and couldn't trust others. He was tired and sad and worn out.

I guided him to the table and chairs, where he slumped into one. I busied myself by getting us a drink in the familiar rooms. Once I was seated in my usual seat, we had a drink. It burned all the way down my throat, and it was a struggle not to cough it up. But I had another.

"Okay, well, let's look at what we do know. We know she was taken before the sirens. Otherwise, she wouldn't have been in there, and we saw her react to them," I said, checking them off with my fingers. "We know she knew her attacker. She wasn't surprised to see them, and we know they are on the short side. It looked like a struggle to get her out of there. I also think there were two people. The one carrying her out looked taller than the one she was talking to when they entered. Now, we have to narrow down the suspects. Also, you have been asking if anyone saw anything strange during the fire. We should see if anyone saw anything *before* the fire."

He looked at me blankly for a moment then his vision sharpened.

"Thank you, Amelia. You're right. We have more answers now than before. I need to re-question everyone and re-think who it might be."

I stood and got a piece of paper from his desk, aware of his eyes on me. "Who do you think could be the person to take her?"

Sitting there, a person popped into my head immediately. I wrote their name on the paper.

"Rak? You think he could have been involved?"

"There is something about him that doesn't sit right. A few weeks ago, I heard him talking to himself in the kitchens about how much he hated all of us and resented being here. I don't think I have ever seen him smile. Plus, he knows how much damage it would do if Lilly was taken. He would know what a blow that would be, and he is short."

"I suppose. I mean, I didn't think he would love being here. But to kidnap people from here seems a bit much. Are we assuming whoever took Lilly took the people in the village, too? I don't know, maybe you are right. He will be the first person I speak to."

"What about Bilvog? I know he has been your advisor forever, but he is short," I said, hating to bring him up. I had a feeling Gloom wouldn't want to believe it was him, but he needed to be added to the list.

"Bilvog? I don't think so," he said. "Plus, I saw him at the fire. It couldn't have been him."

I nodded and crossed his name off the list.

Gloom stood and opened his door. Outside, I could see a soldier standing there. Gloom issued an order to collect Rak and have him put in a room with guards. He requested they spread the word Lilly was taken earlier than we first suspected. Lastly, he wanted a search party ready and armed outside the castle doors in one hour. He closed the door and turned to me.

"Thank you, Amelia. You helped me see clearly." He walked around the room gathering weapons with a new purpose in his step. He strapped on some daggers and reached for a sword I hadn't noticed before. Behind his door was a longsword. It was so clean and polished I could see his reflection in it. All up the blade, it was engraved with swirling vines, leaves, and flowers. Leather was wrapped around the handle, and it, too, was engraved with vines and flowers. Gloom held it up to the light and looked at it.

"It's beautiful," I said.

"Yes, I haven't needed it for a long time, but it might come in useful tonight."

He put it back into his scabbard and hung it around his hips. He put on some leather armour that had been dyed a deep green. It, too, had swirling vines all over it, but this time, they were the spiked ones of the bougainvillaea plant. Once he had finished putting weapons and armour on, he kneeled in front of me. He took both my hands in his and rubbed his thumbs across them.

Looking into my eyes, he said, "I'm going out into the woods to find her. We're going to find her and bring her back." Tears filled my eyes for my lost friend, and I nodded. He squeezed my hand, stood and walked out the door.

TWENTY-SEVEN

Gloom

Stepping out into the forest, I looked around and motioned my troop to follow. The forest was full of things that would hurt or kill us if they got the chance, but I needed to find Lilly, and this was the quickest way to do it.

Before we left, one of the butchers in town had told us they had seen someone struggling to carry another person towards this side of the wall. They didn't get a good look because they were trying to fight the fire. They had forgotten about it till the memo went out about Lilly.

At least we knew what direction they had been going. We searched all the houses in that direction but came up empty, leaving us to search the forest. It had been a while since I had gone deep into the forest. I generally tried to stay near the wall, keeping to the agreement I had made with the Forest Folk many years ago. I would stay within Toleran, venturing out close to the wall, and they would get to keep the rest of the forest. We had followed those rules for centuries and, apart from the odd rule-bending, had lived in peace. I hoped our pact would continue.

I knew many beasts also lived in the forest, but I was ready for a fight. Anger burned through my veins that one of my own had been taken. Lilly was one of my most loved employees, and the thought of anything happening to her made me wild. She was strong, and I knew she could hold out for me to come and rescue her.

I stalked the forest, hoping to see a clue as to where they had gone. My best trackers were with me, but after an hour of walking, my anger was rising. Nothing, we had found nothing. More unsettling was that it was silent. No creatures stirred in the forest. It was unnerving. We decided to come back and look when it was light. Stumbling around in the dark wasn't helping.

Before we could return to the wall, the atmosphere changed. All of us felt it, and we stopped, trying to put a finger on what it was. I scanned the trees and brush, trying to get a glimpse of anything. I shifted my stance and grip on my sword. I heard the others do the same. I had six other members with me, and we formed a loose circle, each protecting the others' backs with grim faces.

Creatures trampled in the woods in front of us. We kept our focus and waited for it to show itself. I saw two red eyes glint in the leaves before it burst out and attacked. Redcaps.

"Shit. Watch out. Redcaps are circling," I called out to my people, and I heard a few others mutter a curse or two.

I swung my sword at the evil gnome and waited for him to get closer. The red cap he was named after was a deep red in colour. I could see the sheen of wetness on it, and I knew we weren't the first people or creatures they had hunted today.

I bounced on my toes, preparing to jump out of the way of his pointed yellow teeth. I stumbled but righted myself before I fell. The redcap advanced on me, his big metal boots leaving impressions on the damp ground. I took a chance and looked around at the others and could see about four others had emerged from the trees. My moment of distraction cost me, and I cried out as the one I had been fighting took advantage and slashed me across the chest with his sickle. I covered the wound with my hand, feeling the blood run down my front. I bared my teeth at him and slashed three times with my sword. Somehow, he managed to avoid them, and he smiled at me.

"You'll not get out of this so easily. We have victory in our veins, and we won't take a defeat today," he said, sounding confident. His voice grated against my nerves with its scratchy sound.

"Well, I am sorry to disappoint you, but you will not be dipping your caps in our blood today." I slashed and stabbed again so fast it was like a dance. My blood sang in my veins, and I remembered how much I enjoyed battle. The redcap couldn't keep up. His big, heavy boots couldn't move fast enough, and with the last slice, I cut his head clean off. Blood sprayed out in a wide arc, splashing onto the leaves and trees in the area. The look of surprise would have been comical if it wasn't so ugly.

I turned to help the others, but they had it under control. The six of us managed to defeat the four creatures with minor wounds.

When they were all dead, we piled them together off the side of the path. Something bigger would come along and get a free meal. We left, nursing our various wounds.

"Well, we were lucky they were the only thing we encountered. I swear I heard the howling of a Night Wolf a few nights ago," Tristan said.

Someone shuddered. "Many things appear to be more active in this forest. Things are changing," Bran said.

"Yes," I replied, "something old and evil. I think we will be in for a few more battles, my friends." We smiled grimly at each other.

As the wall came into view, my stomach dropped. All around the wall were the Horned One symbols. At a glance, there had to be at least fifty.

"Come on. Let's see if they go all the way around," I said quietly, not willing to admit how disturbed I was. "Don't touch them."

"What do they mean?" Tristan asked, grabbing the hilt of his sword.

"It means there is no question who took Lilly. It is the Shadow One, and he is letting me know he is back. Dread is rising," I said quietly.

We walked all the way around the wall from one side to the other. All over the ground, there were the Shadow Ones symbols. One after the other.

Walking through the wall, I dismissed the search party when we were safe, and I went to the aerie and into my room. I was exhausted and frustrated, and all I could think about was Lilly was out there for a second night, and I still hadn't found her. I opened my bedroom door to see Amelia lying in my bed. It stopped me in my tracks. She must have stayed after I left and fallen asleep. I could see on the table a list of names of who it could be, plus a list of things she could do to help. She had been busy. I stood there a moment, wondering if I should wake her. I knew at the least I should find somewhere else to sleep.

In the end, I silently removed my weapons and boots and walked to the bathroom. I took my ripped shirt off and looked at the wound on my chest. I had healed it a bit, but it was still red and inflamed. Who knows what was on that sickle he cut me with? I got into the shower and washed the dirt and blood off my skin while trying to wash away the worry and pain in my soul.

I got out, grabbed some clothes to sleep in, and walked over to the bed. Amelia was still asleep, and I decided to leave her there. I took a pillow off the bed, careful not to wake her and walked over to my lounge and laid down. Many times, over my long years, I had wished for a beautiful, intelligent woman in my bed, and here she was. Unfortunately, she didn't feel the same as I was beginning to.

I spent the next few minutes watching her sleeping as I dreamt about a life I didn't have. Something was growing between us, and though I shouldn't, I liked it. Somehow, she had become an important part of my life. I loved to watch her fire up and speak without thinking. She was beautiful and didn't know it. Seeing her in my bed felt right, and I couldn't help imagining what it would be like to wake up like this every morning. I smiled at the thought of it.

Eventually, sleep overtook me.

When I woke up, the bed was empty. I rolled onto my back and put my arm over my eyes, trying to prepare myself for the day to come. Worry chewed through me, constantly thinking of Lilly and what she might be going through. Needing to find her, I dragged myself off the lounge, tired to my bones and dressed when there was a knock on the door. I opened it, and Amelia was standing there with a tray of food.

She gave me a shy smile and set the food on the desk. Even though I knew I should be out organising what we were to do today, I couldn't stop myself from sitting with her and eating the food she had brought me.

"I'm sorry I fell asleep in your bed last night. I was waiting for you to get back, and it got so late. I thought I would lay down and close my eyes for a few minutes, and I fell asleep," she explained, looking at the table while a pink blush spread across her cheeks. I lifted her chin with my hand so I could see those blue eyes of hers. Her skin was soft and warm, and at the contact, a small fizz went through my fingers.

"Don't apologise. It was a big day. I was glad to know you were getting a good night's sleep."

We ate in comfortable silence, keenly aware of each other, when there was a knock on the door. A second later, Bilvog walked in. I saw him stop and stare at us eating breakfast together in my room. I wondered what was going through his mind. Looking at this face, I bet I could have guessed.

"Ah, good morning, Master. Amelia." He bobbed his head at both of us, still trying to work out what was going on and why Amelia was in my room eating breakfast so early.

"We have multiple search parties today going out and questioning and searching for anything they can find. The city has been put on high alert, and Lilly's parents are here to speak to you and help as well. You will meet with them later. I have added it to your diary because I couldn't find Amelia to do it." He frowned at her back.

"It's fine, Bilvog. I will look and make sure I am at all meetings today. We were about to leave." I stood to leave.

"I had an idea last night," Amelia said, and I sat again.

"Maybe Matthew, Woodmere's leader, would know some information about Lilly. We have sentries all night there. The person who took her might have gone through the real world, and they saw them. I could go and ask them. They would be more likely to talk to me than any of you."

"What a fantastic idea. Woodmere has been there a long time, too. They might have some stories about the Shadow one and can help catch him," Bilvog agreed immediately. "We should do anything to try and rescue Lilly and the others. To think of them out there, possibly with Dread, is sickening."

"I know," I said, rubbing my jaw. "But if she goes back there, they will know you weren't sacrificed. Who is to say they won't lock her up and try again? They have already tried to kill her once." I dropped my hand and folded my arms in front of me. "This sounds too dangerous. Let me get through today and think about it. Either way, if we are to even consider this, I will be going with you." I could see the fire in her eyes spark to life and smoulder.

"Look. Lilly is missing. She is the only friend I have ever had. I want to help you try and rescue her, even if that means going back to Woodmere and risking whatever they might do to me. I want to help, and they might know something. I think it is important to try every avenue. Let me do this...for her." Amelia looked a bit surprised at the end of her little outburst, but I could see the resolve in her eyes. I sighed, thinking through all the things that could go wrong.

"I'm not saying you can't do it. I'm saying let's give it another day and see what we find. Maybe we won't have to risk you. We might find her today, and there will be no reason you need to reveal yourself to that man." My mouth dried at the thought of her out there and at his mercy. "Now, I am going to see the search parties and work out our next port of call." Thinking about what the leader Matthew tried to do to Amelia made my blood boil. He should hope he never ran into me in the forest alone.

"Well, I think it was a good idea," Bilvog responded. I glared at him. "Let's think about it later, but. Let's get through today." He scampered out in front of me. I looked at Amelia and saw she was seething. "We will find her. She is my friend, too, and I won't rest until she is found. I promise." Her anger drained away, and she nodded. "I'll see you later," I said and gave her a smile that she returned. I walked out the door, hoping it was a promise I could keep.

By mid-afternoon, it was clear we weren't going to find any more clues about what happened to Lilly. It was time to go out and bring her home. I called an emergency meeting with the essential people, and we gathered to discuss our next move.

I stood at the end of the table and waited for the chatter to die down. Everyone's faces were creased with worry, and everyone looked tired. At the table were Amelia, Kennock, Tristan, Bilvog, Elred, the head mage and a few other soldiers and mages that were important. Once it had quietened down, I spoke.

"Now I know we are all worried about the people that have been taken, and I think it is now time to act. Tomorrow morning, I want a group of twenty people ready to travel through the forest, and we won't leave until we have found our people and brought them back." Everyone around the table nodded, and I could see a new determination spark in their eyes. "We have a general direction from Vivian the hag, so we will begin there. I want a mix of mages and fighters with the group. Do not underestimate them. Don't forget they have managed to get in here twice and take our people, so we need to approach this with care." I paused for a moment, getting my thoughts in order. "I have also contacted some of the other Evers, and Ashes and Gentle will be joining us. They will be here in the morning. Bilvog, I need you to ask Martha to pack enough food for a couple of days. Right, I think that is it. Are there any questions?"

Everyone appeared to be thinking, but no one spoke. Just before I was about to dismiss them, Amelia raised her hand.

"I want to come too," she said, standing out of her seat. "If you are going to find Lilly, I want to be there. Also, I can be useful in a fight." Some of the people around the table frowned, wondering how she could be useful, but I kept my eyes on her.

"Amelia, I don't think it will be necessary. I think it would be best if you stayed here and kept things running."

"I would like to come. I can be useful, and I won't get in the way."

Impatience sizzled through me, and I spoke without thinking, "This is not the time to discuss it. I have said no, and that is my final decision." I heard the sharpness of my voice and winced inside. Amelia put her head down and sat, her face turning red. Immediately I wanted to apologise but now wasn't the time. I had too much to organise and get ready for what was to come. I pushed it to the back of my mind as I dismissed everyone. I watched as Amelia walked out, and I made a note to speak to her later.

For now, I had to prepare to possibly come face to face with my brother.

TWENTY-EIGHT

Amelia

While sitting on the balcony after the meeting about rescuing Lilly, I went over it in my mind. My emotions were raw after Gloom had shot me down so harshly. I thought we had moved past that, and it was a shock to be spoken to like that. I was disappointed, and there was a constant churning in my stomach. Anxiety over not being able to go with them. Something inside me felt like I should be there to help.

I was looking out at the lights winking on in the city and the people wandering around when I heard a knock at my door. Answering it, I was surprised to see Gloom there. He looked at me and gave a small smile. I didn't return it. My emotions peaked, and I felt the coldness of my power start to run down my arms. I used a breathing exercise Gloom had taught me to keep it at bay, and it complied.

I stood at the door, not opening it wide enough to let him in. "I wanted to check on you after today. I didn't like the way I spoke to you this afternoon. I wanted to come and, well, apologise."

He looked so uncomfortable it was obvious he didn't say sorry very often, and I wondered who the last person he apologised to was. He was fiddling with the bottom of his jacket and kept pushing the hair out of his eyes. Seeing him so uncomfortable, my anger softened, and I let him in. We sat in the armchairs near the fire.

Finally, I broke the silence. "That's okay. I'm sorry I pushed you in front of everyone, but I'm coming. You know I could be useful in a fight. I can help you. This is the whole reason you made me come here. To use my powers to help you."

"Amelia, you have basic control of your magic. I can't put you in such a dangerous position if you can't defend yourself." I opened my mouth to argue, but he cut me off, "Look, I've been thinking. I will allow you to come, but we will need to train on the way. If I don't think you are ready, you will not be entering the fight. Is that clear?" I nodded, and he continued, "I will not put you in danger just because you think you are ready. I will decide that." I nodded again and tried to keep the smile off my face. He saw and gave me a small smile back before we settled into our chairs.

We sat in comfortable silence for a bit, watching the fake flames dance in the fireplace. The room was dark and cosy, with small amounts of light emanating from the mushroom clusters. It was private and restful. I remembered something that had been niggling me since going to see Vivian.

"So, Destin. Where did Gloom come from?" I smiled at him, hoping to loosen him up a bit. He smiled back.

"Destin is my real name, I suppose. When we became the Evers and guardians of our realms, we took on other names we thought suited us and our realms. I'm not sure who started it, but my brothers had always called me gloomy. I was the youngest and was always being picked on by one of them. I was a quiet child who didn't trust much."

"Not much has changed then," I chimed in with another smile.

"No, I suppose you are right," he said with a chuckle. "Anyway, when I took on the forests and Toleran, I thought Gloom was fitting."

"So, did you get to choose your place? And what exactly is an Ever's job?"

"The others did. It went in age order, so Awe was first and chose the sun, Enduring chose the sea and so on. In the end, the forests were all that was left, but I didn't mind. I have always liked trees. They provide protection and solitude, you know?"

He sighed and snuggled deeper into the chair. I nodded because I did know. For a lot of years, the forest was where I had come to escape. To be away and to just be me. I loved the trees and the privacy.

"These days, being an Ever isn't so important. People have moved on, and a lot of people think of us as 'old Gods.' I am in charge of this forest, and I make sure it isn't destroyed. Back when we were at our peak, we would listen to the prayers of the people and support them if we could. These days, there are only a few villages like Woodmere that worship us." I wondered what would happen when no one worshipped them anymore.

We sat a while longer, feeling like we were the last two people in the aerie. The room was so warm and cosy. I thought about what he had told me. Yes, he could be gloomy, but he was also loyal, and kind, and always doing what he could for his realm. He helped put out the fires and often went out walking through Toleran, listening to what the people had to say. He was much more than gloomy.

Before I could tell him that, he stood and stretched. "Right, well, time to go and finish getting ready for the morning. Will you need any help to pack?"

I thought about it and realised I didn't need very much. "No, I think I should be alright. Is there anything in particular I need?"

"No, just some clothes to train in. Try and keep it light. We will likely be carrying the bags for a few days. I'll see you in the morning at the front door after dawn." He looked at me, and in the soft firelight, it looked like he wanted to say something else, but he just smiled and walked out.

After he left, I noticed my heart was beating like a drum, and I was smiling like an idiot. I shook my head and started to pack. I grabbed comfortable clothes I could walk all day in and sleep in to save room. I packed warm clothes and decided to wear my boots. I included my leather outfit to fight in, too, as it added a bit of protection. Basic toiletries were the last things in there. I thought I did well, but I still had to kneel on my bag to get it closed. I picked it up and dreaded having to carry it on my back. I wondered if there was magic to help with that.

After a few minutes, I was interrupted by another knock on the door. Butterflies jumped in my stomach, and I wondered if it was Gloom returning to say what he hadn't earlier. I opened the door and was surprised to see Bilvog standing there.

"Amelia, can I speak to you for a second?"

"Yes, of course. What can I do for you?" I asked, trying not to show my disappointment.

"I was thinking about what you said before about going to Woodmere. Do you think they could help us?"

"Well, I don't know. If they knew anything, it would be in their best interest to tell us. They aren't going to want to get on the bad side of an Ever, and this affects them as well. If everything about Dread is true, he will be more of a danger to them because he hates humans so much."

"Yes, you are right. I think it is a path we must take. Do you think they will listen to you? Like Gloom said, there is a risk they will try to hurt you again."

"It's a risk I will take. I want to help."

"I think we should be taking any route we see. Ah, but I saw Gloom a moment ago, and he informed me you will be coming with us. If we are leaving tomorrow morning, it might be difficult. Perhaps we should wait until we get back, hoping, of course, they don't have any information useful to us." He ran his fingers through his beard and tapped his staff on the ground. "Mm, that is a tricky one. I will let you decide, Amelia. Seeing how you are the one taking the risk." He smiled at me and left before I could say a word.

I closed the door and thought about what he said. Surely, if Woodmere knew some information, it would be better to know before we leave tomorrow. I looked at my watch. Could I get there and back without being seen? I knew Gloom would be pissed when he found out I had left by myself without a guard but what about Lilly and the others. We needed to know if Woodmere could give us any advantage.

The symbols had been found in my world, so they might have come across the Horned One or know about Dread. I needed to go.

TWENTY-NINE

Amelia

I looked around the room for anything I could take with me to Woodmere. Not knowing what to prepare for, I strapped my dagger to my thigh just in case. By now, they would be finishing dinner and getting ready to go to the temple for night prayers. I was curious to know what everyone had been told of my disappearance.

I picked at a few bits of lint nervously on my coat, putting off the time I would have to leave. I tried to ignore the complex emotions that were racking my body. It felt like my whole body was tingling and numb at the same time. I would be facing some tough memories walking into that place after I had done pretty well forgetting them and moving on. I tried not to think about what Gloom would say. I was sure it wouldn't be good. My worry was he would forbid me to go with him tomorrow. I hesitated with my hand on the door. Was this worth the risk? Yes, I decided. This is what I could do to help.

I buttoned the long black coat that looked a lot like Gloom's and stepped out of my room, putting a black beanie in my pocket. I nodded and smiled at people I passed, making sure I acted normal and did not draw attention to myself. Luckily, people were used to me wandering around at all times doing errands for Gloom, so it wasn't strange I was out and about.

I made my way out of the aerie and headed towards the wall.

I stood near one of the large trees outside of the light, pulled on my beanie to hide my blonde hair and waited for the guards to turn. As I was about to dart out and say the password, one of the guards stopped, and I had to skid back into my hiding place. I stood, heart racing to see if he had seen me. When no one shouted out or came to find me, I peeked around and took the risk. I walked towards the living wall and muttered the password, *voyant,* hoping it hadn't changed or everything would be wrecked at this first hurdle. I was relieved when the vines and branches parted, letting me leave Toleran. I leaned against the wall, ignoring the spikes and looked to make sure there were no sentries watching as I darted into the cover of the trees.

It was cooler in the forest, and it was getting dark. I travelled through the forest as fast as I could, keeping to the trees but staying close enough to the path so I didn't get lost. I didn't want to deal with the Forest Folk today if I didn't have to.

My heart thundered in my chest, waiting for the Horned One to step out and catch me at any moment. Every shadow and movement sent a spike of panic through me. Not for the first time, I wondered if what I was doing was a stupid idea, but I knew in my heart if I could save Lilly and help the people of the town, I would do anything. I might have been taken there when I didn't want to go, but in the last few months, Toleran had become more of a home than Woodmere had ever been.

I could see ahead the portal to the Jagged Thorn Forest. Looking around one last time, I said the word. The portal glowed green, and I stepped through, back to the real world and the people who had left me to die at the whims of a God.

I stepped out into the once familiar forest, dizzy and unsteady on my feet as the effect of the portal took hold. I had grown up near this place, but it was foreign after being in Toleran, the land of the Evers. There was no path on this side, and I ducked and weaved through the thorns that tried to catch me. I had forgotten about these thorns, and I grew a new hatred for them. They tore at my clothes, and I was covered in cuts within minutes.

As I made my way closer to Woodmere, something was different in the air. It took me a few minutes, but I finally put my finger on it. It was smoke. I was confused at first, and then it dawned on me. I hurried to the clearing where my whole journey had begun. The pole was still there in the ground, but the ropes had been cut away and were gone. I took a moment to look at the place where my town had abandoned me, hoping a God would come and take me. I held the tears back as the feelings from that day came rushing back.

The helplessness and fear threatened to drag me under, but I held it back. I felt my power at my fingertips and almost released it like I had that day tied up, but I held it back and, in that moment, became stronger. I now look back on that event as something that had likely changed my life for the better. Since that day, I had found friends and a community that liked and supported me. Even though I had been taken to a whole other realm with strangers, I was less afraid for my safety there than I had been in the town I had lived in most of my life.

I held my necklace and sent a prayer to my grandmother. "I did it. I'm happy now."

With a new resolve, to save Toleran, I finally lifted my eyes and saw black smoke rise from the trees. A fire. Coming from Woodmere. I took a breath and ran towards my former home. As I broke through the tree line, I froze in place. Woodmere was burning. Everywhere I looked, there were flames and people running. It was like the fire at Toleran, but it was bigger. Every house was ablaze.

My eyes sought out the people running around. Fear and panic on all their faces. My heart went out to them. Even though some of them had hated and shunned me, I had still grown up with them, and I didn't want anyone to go through this. I looked over to my old house and noticed it was burning. My heart sank, and before I knew it, I was running towards it. So many memories of my grandmother in that house were likely being turned to ash. I wondered if they had cleaned out the house after they abandoned me or if someone else was living there now.

The closer I got, the more I noticed it was *really* on fire. Most of the roof and back of the building was in flames. I wrenched the door open, ignoring the heat of the handle, and looked inside. Everything was gone. It was empty. Tears sprung to my eyes, and I didn't realise how much I had wanted the things in there till I couldn't have them. I wiped my eyes and closed the door, wincing at the burn on my hand. I looked around and couldn't help but see how unorganised everything was. Where were the water buckets?

At that moment, I needed to help the others put the fire out before everything was consumed. My stomach dropped, and I looked around frantically. The children. Where were the children? I could get them out into the forest, far enough away from the flames. I turned and ran right into a hard body.

Looking up, I saw it was Matthew. The leader of Woodmere and the one who had decided my fate. My body turned cold. Not from my power but from fear. This was the man who had driven my parents away from the only place they had known. He had tormented every person in the village and was the cause of so much pain. My body shook, and I couldn't speak.

As he recognised me, I saw hatred and fear flash in his eyes. "You! What are you doing here? You should be dead."

My senses came rushing back to me. This man had no power over me now. I was no longer going to be frightened of him. I was not useless.

"How could you have done that to me?" Anger roiled inside of me, and a different coldness spread throughout my body. I barely kept it in check.

"You are the reason this is happening. You were meant to go to the Ever Awe. He is unhappy with our sacrifice. I knew you would be unworthy of him, but I thought he might take you anyway. You are the reason all of this is destroyed!"

I took a step back, seeing the madness in his eyes. I was pinned between the burning wreckage of my old house and him. I readied my power in case I needed it as a last resort. "This isn't my fault!" It was a losing battle trying to reason with him, so I tried a different argument. "Where are the children, and are they safe? I can help you." I said, hoping the thought of the children would help him come to his senses.

"Help us? You are the reason this place is burning. You and your foul magic." He spat the word. "We should have gotten rid of you and Hazel years ago before you poisoned my followers."

My world narrowed to a pinprick. "What do you mean get rid of Hazel? My grandmother died from a heart attack."

He laughed. "A heart attack? Not even that could kill that disobedient old bitch! I had to get rid of her before she filled everyone's heads with stories of what it is like on the outside. She was turning them against the Evers and leading them into sin. No, no, no. She had to go."

I felt the blood drain from my face and my body tingled. "You...you killed her?" Rage and grief welled up in me. He had done this. He had taken the last family member I had from me. My stomach churned, and I held back the vomit, threatening to rise. I was trying to get my breathing under control when I felt his hands on me. I snapped out of my sorrow and struggled.

"Maybe if I get rid of you now, Awe will forgive us and stop this fire," he said in his madness. My brain was trying to work out what he was talking about when he started pushing me back. Back into the burning house.

By now, I could feel the flames heating my back, and the crackle of the inferno filled my ears. I looked behind me and could see the whole house was consumed by the fire. I struggled and kicked and screamed, but nothing I did would stop Matthew from pushing me backwards. Smoke filled my lungs and eyes, and I coughed, trying to get some fresh air into my body. By now, I could feel the heat lapping at my ankles and knew I was inches from the flames.

"No, please, stop," I wheezed out, but he ignored me. Fear had taken over my body, and all I could feel was the pounding of my heart and the heat of the flames. Finally, he left me no choice, and I did the only thing I could do in my fear. I raised my hands and pressed them to his chest. I released my power.

His mouth opened to scream or yell at me, but was cut off. My power poured into him, unhindered and easy, and I watched as the colour leaked out of him. His face went from alive and red from the fire to ashy and grey. His skin and clothes turned grey, and his body started shrinking, wasting away bit by bit. I watched, horrified, as the man who had tormented me and many others in my town shrivelled away till he was a skeleton and then quickly dust.

Horror washed over me that the man who had made Woodmere and my life miserable was now gone. I had never used my power on another person before, and I looked at my hands, terrified of doing it again. I felt sick that I had killed someone. I had never wanted to hurt anyone with my power, and now I had done the unforgivable. I dashed away from the burning house, stepping over his ashes on the ground as they blew away on the wind.

I looked around and saw no one had seen what happened. Hopefully, they would think he had run away like a coward. It wouldn't be too hard to believe. I moved away from the pile of dust rapidly blowing away and pushed the emotions about what I had done deep inside of me. There would be time to open *that* box later.

I walked out into the open and scanned the village. People were still running around with water, trying to put out their homes or find loved ones. No one took much notice of me, or if they did, they gave a shocked look and kept on going. I didn't know who needed my help the most. While looking around my eye caught on a creature in the distance. Blending into the trees and watching me was the Horned One. As we looked at each other, I remembered the hag telling me he was hunting me. Was I the reason he had done this? To draw me out? Here I was, all alone with no one to help me. I pulled out my dagger, knowing it would be no use against him. My power seemed to be all out, and I cursed myself. I had not controlled it better.

He ran.

I jumped and whirled around, unsure of the best place to go. I needed to get out of there. He was running for me, and I knew if he caught me, it would be all over. I pumped my legs and willed myself to go faster. I made it to the edge of the forest and dared a look behind me. Woodmere was still burning, but I could see people trying to put out the fire with water, and I felt a small amount of relief that they had started to fight back. But coming up fast behind me was the Horned One. His antlers glowed orange in the firelight, and his long arms and legs were moving at such a speed I knew I could never outrun him. But I needed to try.

I ran faster and faster, not caring about the spikes and thorns tearing at my clothes and skin. Somewhere along the way, I lost my beanie, but I kept running. I could hear the beast crashing behind me. I risked another look and noticed it was slowing. Its large antlers were getting caught in the branches of the trees. This was my chance. I could hear it huffing, and a frustrated scream let loose behind me. My belly liquified as the sound tore through me. I scrambled faster and faster, not looking at the ground beneath me. I was making distance between us, and there was a little spark of hope I could outrun it even though it was still after me. A smile stretched across my face as I realised I was close to the portal. A little further to go.

I pushed myself as fast as I could, chest heaving and lungs exploding. I was going to make it until my foot caught on a spiked vine lying across my path. I tripped and felt the pain of the thorns wrapping around my foot. The air rushed out of my lungs, and they felt bruised from the impact. I lay on the ground, trying to breathe, but nothing was working.

Finally, I heaved in deep breaths sucking in dirt and leaves along with it. I pushed myself up with pain radiating from my leg where the long spikes pierced it. They dug deep into my flesh, and I knew there was no way I could pull it out. They were too deep. I could hear the beast getting closer. I whimpered and tried to cut the vine with my dagger, but it was thick and woody. The Horned One appeared through the trees and started huffing like it was laughing at me.

I scrambled back and tried to ignore the pain in my legs, but it was no use. I was completely at his mercy, and I was terrified.

THIRTY

Gloom

S itting in my office, I was going over the last few details about our mission tomorrow. My vision was blurring, and I put the paper down onto one of the stacks that were littering my desk. All the things that could go wrong were spinning around in my head. I was relieved that Gentle and Ashes had agreed to come with me tomorrow and ferret out Dread. I was even more relieved that they had done so without me needing to tell them what a failure I had been so far.

My blood hummed with the need for revenge and to get back at the people who had hurt my community. There would be no forgiveness shown to the people who had come in and took people from their homes in the middle of the night. No mercy shown to the ones who had set houses on fire, not thinking about who might be inside. We would eliminate them.

I stood, feeling my body get hotter the more I thought about them and went to look out the window at my city that was slowly recovering from the ordeals thrust upon them. Watching people walking along the bridges spanning the trees and going about their lives the best they could made my body cool and the more rational part take over.

Once I was calm, my mind turned to something else that had been occupying it.

Amelia had been in my thoughts a lot lately. We had spent a lot of time together, and I was surprised at how much I relied on her counsel and advice. I didn't know if it was because she was a good listener or what, but I had been opening up to her and telling her things I hadn't discussed in years. I felt safe around her and was trusting her in a way that was scary but also...nice.

As it had often, my mind stumbled on something whenever I thought about her. Amelia wanted to be free. Living here and being with me would make her anything but. I had already decided once we had defeated Dread, I was letting her go. Even though it would break my heart to see her walk away, it was what was best for her. A selfish part of me did worry when that happened, I would again become my namesake. Gloom.

Since she arrived, feelings had been growing in me that I hadn't had for a long time. I had always been untrusting and unwilling to rely on other people. I always looked for the worst and never made any close relationships. I had felt lighter and had smiled more in the last few months than the last few centuries. I didn't want to lose that. I didn't want to lose *her.*

Busting through the door and interrupting my thoughts, Tristan appeared.

"I'm sorry to interrupt, Master...but Amelia...she has left."

I stood up straight to listen to him as my stomach clenched.

"Explain," I barked at him. I bit my tongue, trying to control the fear and anger surging through me. How could she leave? She knew the risk with the Horned One out there. Why would she leave Toleran? Leave me?

"I was coming back from visiting with Mary and my son, and I saw her sneaking through the wall and into the forest. By the time I caught up, she was going through the portal. I ran right back here to tell you. Do you want me to send out some soldiers to find her and bring her back?"

I was already moving towards the door. "What portal?"

"The one on the North side," he shouted back to me.

"I'll go. I'll bring her back." I raced through the castle, avoiding everyone to get to the portal as fast as I could. I ran through the forest, not seeing the trees around me, everything a blur in the darkening woods.

I made it to the portal and shouted the password so I didn't have to slow my running. As soon as I made it through, I could smell smoke and worry crawled through me. Where was she? Had she gone back to Woodmere? It wasn't lost on me that I had been thinking about letting her go, but as soon as she left, I couldn't let it happen. I realised I needed her, and I wasn't letting her go without a fight. If I could bring her back, I would tell her how I felt and see where this would lead after we trapped Dread.

The damned forest tore at me and stung. Luckily, I healed fast, so it wasn't a worry. I was a blur running through the trees. Then, I heard a sound that made my heart skip a beat. A roar of rage exploded through the quiet. I knew at once it was the Horned One. I had fought him before, and I would never forget that sound. I pushed myself harder, and as I rounded the corner, I saw him.

He was stalking towards Amelia, who was sprawled out on the ground. I saw red and moved to stand in front of her. I heard her trying to get up, but I blocked her out and focused on the Horned One.

When the Horned One looked at me, he widened his stance and snorted at me. We both knew this wasn't going to end without bloodshed. I sized him up for a moment, and without warning, I shot vines out from the ground to wrap around his arms, legs, and antlers. They pulled his body from side to side. I knew they wouldn't hold him for long, but I needed to give Amelia time to get away.

The Horned One bucked and threw himself around and, with his great strength, broke free. I stepped closer to put more distance between me and Amelia and prayed she would get up and run.

The Horned One rushed me, and, too late, I dodged. One of his antlers caught my arm and ripped through my clothes and skin. Memories flashed back about those horns and another fight. I remembered when they had pierced my face the last time we had battled. I could still feel the warm blood dripping into my mouth while I wondered if he had taken my eye. I shut out the painful memory and focused on the here and now. Blood poured down my arm, but I ignored the pain. I used his momentum to slam him into the nearest tree. There was a loud crack as the bone hit the wood, and the tip of one of his antlers chipped off.

He let out a roar of rage, and while he was distracted, I went to check on Amelia.

"My leg. There are vines around it," she said in a shaky voice.

I looked to where she pointed, and I could see one of the nasty thorny vines had dug itself into her ankle. The Horned One was recovering from its injury and I didn't have much time. I looked at her eyes and, without warning, gripped the vine and pulled it off her. Amelia let out a scream as the thorns ripped through her skin. The scent of blood filled the air, and I threw the vine away in disgust.

I looked at her, wanting to say more, but I didn't have the time. I said one word, "Run."

I watched her stumble to standing and limp towards the portal. The rage in me calmed a notch, knowing she was going to be safe, and I turned back towards the creature. Cold calm and focus settled over me, and I smiled. He ran at me again with his head bent low. Again, I wasn't quick enough, and he managed to catch me under my arm. He flung me through the air, and I slammed into a tree trunk nearby. The thorns growing around it dug in deep, and I let out a scream of pain. The thorns punched through my skin, but I didn't think they had hit anything vital. My back was on fire, and stars flashed in front of my eyes, and I gritted my teeth. Every breath was agony, and for a moment, I worried a thorn had punctured my lung. I braced myself as I pulled myself off and stood slumped over, trying to recover. The thorns were dripping with my blood, and I cringed.

In my head, I heard the clear, deep voice of the Horned One. My body jerked in shock at hearing his voice after one hundred and fifty years. "Give up, Gloom. He will win. He has learnt from the last time you all trapped him, and he won't make the same mistake again. He will be victorious. He will not hesitate to kill you all to reach his goal."

"I will never give up while I have people to protect. Dread will not win."

I pooled my power and sent it out to all the bougainvillaea's spiky vines the forest was famous for. My body shook with the effort, but I never took my eyes off him, knowing one moment of weakness could be the end of me. My vines shot out and headed right for the monster. He bellowed in rage in and out of my mind as thousands of sharp thorns penetrated his skin. He tried brushing them off, but they kept coming, peppering him over and over again like thousands of small arrows. He snorted at me. "This isn't over," he gasped out and ran off.

I watched him running away and made sure he didn't double back. It almost seemed too easy.

As the forest returned to its normal rhythms, I turned towards the portal, determined to find out what Amelia had been doing out here. I took a couple of steps, and she appeared from behind a tree. I stalked towards her, forgetting my exhaustion, and crowded her. "What the hell did you think you were doing out here?"

THIRTY-ONE

Amelia

Gloom was standing so close I could smell the metallic scent of his blood, and his heavy breathing drowned out all sound. He was beaten and bloody, and I could see the fight still in his eyes. I stood still, waiting to see what he would do next while I tried to calm the frantic beating of my heart.

"I...I went to see if anyone from the village had any information for us before we leave tomorrow. That's all."

He stood closer. I had to crane my neck to look into those green eyes that had turned stormy. "So, you snuck out in the middle of the night to a town that hates you, through a forest where you knew there was a monster trying to capture you and didn't tell me?" By the end, he was yelling at me, and I flinched away.

When he said it like that, embarrassment flooded me, and I knew how foolish I had been. I took a moment to steady myself, hoping my voice didn't waver. "Um, yes?"

He stepped away and ran a shaky hand through his hair. "God, Amelia. How could you be so stupid? What if something had happened to you? Who would have helped you?"

Anger replaced my embarrassment, and it boiled inside me. "I don't need anyone to help me. I can take care of myself, thank you very much! I'm not some little kid who needs your protection."

He raised his eyebrows and pointed to where he had found me on the forest floor. "Clearly," he said with so much sarcasm I couldn't help but roll my eyes.

"Well, I would have gotten out of that. I was about to blast him for your information. What is it to you anyway? I was doing it to help you! They might have had some information."

"What is it to me? What is it to *me*?" he said, thumping his chest. "Don't you know I am falling in love with you?" His eyes widened, and his mouth fell open.

I looked at him with a fluttering in my stomach, knowing my face was turning red. Not from embarrassment but from the attraction. His eyes drifted from my eyes to my lips, and my mouth suddenly dried. I ran my tongue over my lips, licking them. Gloom groaned, and the next thing I knew, his lips were slamming down on mine. I greeted them eagerly.

Passion overtook us, and we were out of control. I gasped into his mouth as he lifted one of my hands and pinned it above me, pinning me into the tree harder so he could press himself against me until nothing could come between us. My other hand bunched in his shirt, and I tried to pull him closer, though it was impossible. He growled into my mouth, and shivers broke out all over my body, and it had nothing to do with the cold night air.

He broke the kiss long enough to mutter my name, "Amelia," as his hands landed on my hips, gripping them tightly. A haze had filled my head, and nothing in the world could distract me from him at this moment. For the rest of my life, all I wanted was to see, smell and touch Gloom, and I would be happy. I had been with boys in the village before, but this was different. It was like he was branding my soul, and we would forever be joined now. I was breathing hard now as I let the sensations wash over my body. He had pulled up my shirt, and his hands were on my bare back, and it felt like fire where he touched me. I moaned, surrendering myself.

He looked at me with lust and love in his eyes as we connected again passionately. I moaned again as he bit my bottom lip, and all thought left my body.

As fast as it started, he ripped himself away from me. I stood there looking at him with lust clouding my vision and flowing through my veins.

"What...What are you doing?" I walked over to him, intending to continue, but he backed away again.

"I can't. I can't take you for the first time under this tree even though I want to. I want to be in a nice, warm bed and be able to take my time exploring every inch of your body. The things I can do to you can't be done under a tree where anyone can see."

My toes curled, and images flashed through my mind of all the things I wanted to do with him.

He smiled back at me like he could read my mind. "I want it to be memorable. Not a quickie out in the forest." We took a moment to gather ourselves.

His smile turned into a frown as he lifted his hand to my necklace. "What is this?"

I looked down at the necklace I normally kept inside my shirt. "Oh, my grandmother gave it to me. She said it had been in the family for generations. It's my good luck charm." I smiled thinking about my grandmother and all the things she had done for me.

Gloom looked at it closer, and a smile spread across his face. "Yes, Wendy. That was her name." He had a faraway look on his face.

I was surprised he knew her name. "That was my ancestor who owned it originally. Wait, did you know her?"

"I gave her this. We were friends. She was about seventeen years old, and like you, she was trapped in that town and sought out the forest for solitude. One day, I was walking on this side of the portal and met her. We chatted, and I found her very interesting. For a young woman, she had a great understanding of the world around her. We would meet in the forest and chat and play games. We did that for a few years until she told me she was to be married. She was miserable and cried for hours. She knew even then, when she became a bride, she would be trapped there and never be free. I gave her this to remember me by. And," he opened his jacket and showed me the pin on the inside, "I kept this. I often think about her, and I wish I had done something to help her. I regret that I did nothing."

"Wow. How strange I am a descendant and have the necklace," I said, turning it over in my hands with a new appreciation.

"Not strange. It was fate. It waited until it belonged to the right person before it came home. I have waited for you for so long."

Warmth spread through me, and tears pricked my eyes. I closed my eyes and leaned against his chest while he held me. This. This is what I had always dreamed about. Someone to call my own. Could this be true? After a minute, he pulled back and smiled at me. Tucking the necklace back in the front of my shirt, he said, "So I suppose we should head back. We have a very busy day tomorrow."

"You're right. After what I have seen in Woodmere, there is no way they are going to get away with it. They were innocent people, and they have lost everything. It was awful."

Gloom raised my hand and kissed it. "Do you want to help them? Anything you want to do, say it, and I'll do it."

I thought for a moment, grateful he would give me the choice. "I would like to help them. Not everyone was bad, you know. With Matthew gone, I'm sure they will be different."

Gloom's eyebrows rose. "Matthew's gone? What happened out there?"

We walked towards the portal hand in hand. Neither of us was in a rush despite needing a good night's sleep.

"There was a fire. Everything is gone. I would be surprised if anything is still standing. I went to look in my old house to see if there was any of my and my grandmother's stuff in there I could save. It was empty. As I turned to see who I could help, Matthew was there. He blamed me for the fire and confessed to killing my grandmother." Tears were running down my cheeks, and my breathing quickened as the impact of everything came crashing down. Gloom stopped, and I could see the concern in his eyes. "He tried to push me back into the burning house. He wanted to kill me so Awe would forgive him. I lost it. I hit him with my power, and he collapsed. I watched as he turned to dust and floated away." My voice dropped to a whisper, and I confessed something that had been hiding inside of me, "I was glad. He was an evil man and needed to go, but I killed someone." I sniffed and tried to control myself. Gloom reached up, wiped the tears from my eyes, and kissed my eyelids.

"He *was* evil, and now he can't hurt anyone else. It is always hard to hurt someone, but he was going to kill you. It was self-defence."

I looked at him and said a silent prayer of thanks. "Thank you," I whispered. He kissed me again, and we walked through the portal to Toleran.

"So, what are we going to do now?" I asked, looking at our linked hands.

Gloom smiled gently. "As much as I would love to shout it from the treetops, I think we need to be discreet. We have an important mission tomorrow, and we need to be focused." He looked at me intently. "Please don't think I don't want to be with you. That is all I have dreamt about for the last few weeks, but we need to focus."

I blushed at his words, and while I, too, wanted to tell everyone, I understood where he was coming from.

"Okay. I understand," I said, disappointed all the same.

"Don't worry, we won't tell anyone either," said a voice behind us.

Gloom whirled around so fast I barely registered it. I could see his hands were faintly glowing green.

"Stand down, Gloom. It's just us," said the Lord of the forest, his queen standing next to him. "We came to tell you we know about your plans tomorrow. We will do our best to keep all the beasties away, but we can't guarantee you will travel without incident."

"Hello, Lord and Lady. Thank you for your help. It is most appreciated," Gloom said in a reverential voice.

The Lady stepped out of the trees and approached me. Her power overwhelmed me, and I struggled to not take a step away from her. It pushed against all my senses and caressed my nerves. I stood my ground and looked at her respectfully. I bowed my head.

"Amelia. This trip is going to be important for you. Be strong and hold onto what you know. Don't believe everything you see and hear, and it will serve you well." She reached up and cupped my face. "You are more important than you know, and he will need you in the coming days," she said softly and close to my ear.

She smiled at me and walked back to her husband. Gloom stepped next to me and put his hand on my back as if to reassure himself I was there.

The Lord looked at the Lady with a question in his eyes but said nothing.

"Good luck. You will need it," he said. They vanished.

As soon as it was clear they were gone, Gloom looked at me, worry in his eyes. "Are you alright? Did she hurt you?" He put his hand where the Lady's had been.

"I'm fine."

His brows furrowed.

"It's fine, Gloom," I said, smiling and placing my hand on top of his. "I sensed nothing bad from her. Please, let's go before someone else sneaks up on us."

He sighed. "You are right. One last thing, though." He picked me up, and I wrapped my legs around him. We kissed while we smiled and soaked it all in. I ran my fingers through his hair and wondered when I would be able to do it next and if this was all a dream.

He set me on my feet, and we walked into Toleran, looking the same but forever changed.

THIRTY-TWO

Amelia

Travelling through the forest was slow going. We were a group of over twenty people, plus Ashes and Gentle, who had arrived this morning. We were loaded with a week's worth of rations each and equipment to cook and camp with. We had a rough direction of where to go, but we were still mostly in the dark. Gloom had warned us about the dangers in this forest, and we kept a wary eye out for anything that might come our way.

This was the deepest I had been in the forest, and it was unnerving. There was a stillness that felt heavy and oppressive. Every minute of the day, it was like we were being watched. The trees were silent around us, watching and waiting. I wondered if the Forest Folk followed our progress and if we would remain undisturbed.

Gloom and I did our best to appear to be normal. It was hard. Any chance we got, we would sneak away for a quiet moment or just be together, holding hands. It didn't happen often, but when it did, it was magical. We were both still floating on cloud nine, even though we didn't know what we would be walking into. I felt guilt over being happy at a time like this. I kept Lilly in my thoughts and hoped we would find her so I could tell her about Gloom and me. I thought she would approve.

On the second day, it started to drizzle, making the ground slippery and people's moods short. The whole day, all I could hear was Bilvog mumbling and cursing the weather. I was tempted to agree with him. It was uncomfortable, and I was glad I packed my big coat because it didn't take long for everyone to be soaked and muddy. The rain running through my short hair gave me the chills. Along the walk, I watched as Bilvog picked twigs and leaves out of his long beard while the others were quiet and serious.

After we made camp that evening, Gloom collected Ashes, Gentle, and I and we walked into the forest. After leading us out of sight of the camp, he used his power to weave the vines and plants around us until we were in an arena completely closed off.

"Ashes, Gentle. I want to show you something." He looked at me, and I could see uncertainty in his face. It took everything I had not to reach over and take his hand.

"The reason Amelia is with us is she has some powers. I want to show you now, so you won't be surprised when we are fighting."

The other Evers looked confused but agreed to stand against the plant wall as I prepared myself to demonstrate.

I was standing still and waiting when vines shot up underneath me to wrap around my legs. They climbed up my body, locking me in place. Even though I knew it was Gloom, panic began to rise in my body. I pushed it down and focused my power. Thinking about the vines entangling me, I focused my energy on pushing against all my skin, not only my hands. The vines around my legs loosened, and when I looked, they were black and starting to flake away. I smiled. That was new.

I heard a gasp and looked at Ashes and Gentle. Both looked on in shock, but before they could say anything, Gloom interrupted.

"We don't know where the powers came from, but they will be able to help us in the fight to come." Something about the way he was talking was strange, and I couldn't pick up on what he was really trying to say. His eyes were intent, and I could see Ashes and Gentle were also a bit put off by it.

Eventually, Gentle moved closer. She was like an angel. She had long blonde hair, which looked like it had never had a tangle. On top of her head sat a silver circlet with leaves and feathers all around it. Her eyes were bright blue, and her full pink lips were smiling gently. Above her top lip, she had a beauty mark, and she was dressed in a long sky-blue dress, reminding me of what Greek goddesses wore. Across it, clouds drifted lazily, reflecting the sky. It was nearly see-through and fluttered about her like it had a life of its own. There was no doubt she was the Ever of the air. The rest of us were covered in mud, but she was clean.

"Amelia. When did this power start?" she asked in her sweet voice.

I hesitated a moment, intimidated by these beings in front of me, but I now knew I could do hard things, and talk to the other Evers. "I have always had it, but in the last few years, it has been stronger," I answered, slightly intimidated by her presence.

"Gloom. Why didn't you tell us before? This is something we all should have known about. We could have helped you," she said.

"Of course, he didn't want to tell us. He didn't want to out his little pet here." Ashes moved to stand next to Gloom, and I could see the tension radiating off them. Ashes was tall with black shoulder-length wavy hair and a large widow's peak. His skin was bronzed from the sun, and he had dark, almost black eyes. His large, straight nose stuck out over a black moustache and beard that tapered and ended in a point. He was wearing billowing plants and a linen shirt, both orange in colour, with a wide belt of leather around his middle, and I could see gems and jewels on all parts of his body. He was beautiful and exotic and terrifying, and there was something dangerous about him. Like he was slightly mad.

"You only brought her, so Awe didn't go and take her while you weren't home. Because if that is all she can do, it won't be a lot of help." He sniggered as he turned to look at me with his cold eyes. "Can't be going up against big bad Dread if you are useless," said Ashes, throwing his hunting knife from hand to hand. He took a few steps out into the open and spread his arms wide to invite me to join him. He was so cocky. I wanted to, but I looked at Gloom to see what he was thinking. He nodded to me, but I could see some worry in his face.

I stepped out, ready to face down an Ever. I looked at Ashes standing there like he didn't have a care in the world. I wanted to make him care. He had been baiting Gloom since he got here, and I was sick of it. I took my jacket off and dropped it on the wet ground. The cold bit into my skin, but I didn't want to be hindered by it.

I took a moment, and when he just looked at me waiting, I held out my hands and shot a long string of magic at him. The grey streak, barely visible, wound around and targeted his back.

He laughed mockingly as he dodged it easily. "That's it? You are going to need more than that to kill the Shadow One. Something like this would be useful." He clicked his fingers, and out of nowhere, I was surrounded by a swirling dust storm. I was standing in the middle of a tornado, and I couldn't see anything in front of me. I held my hands up to protect my eyes and tried to breathe through the grit and dust the desert Ever was kicking up.

A howling noise filled my ears, and I struggled to hear over the top of it. I wondered how he was doing it. Was Gentle helping with the wind, or did they all share some similar magic? I could hear him laughing on the other side, and I turned towards the noise. Kneeling on the ground, I closed my eyes and sent out my decaying power through the ground. I watched as the grass around me started to die as it travelled out towards the laughing voice of Ashes. The wind was circling all around me, and I hoped I had targeted the right person.

Suddenly, the sand stopped and fell to the ground like a curtain. Looking at Ashes, I could see a trail of destruction leading right to him. He did not look so confident now.

"Well, that was a good trick, but I won't fall for it again," he said, his lip curling.

I smirked at him, glad I had managed to get one up on him and moved around the circle.

"Let's see how you like this one," he shouted as he threw balls of sand at me. I dodged and dived, managing to avoid them. I was very happy that Gloom had made me run all those mornings. Without his training, I never would have been fast enough. The adrenaline and power coursing through my body was amazing. I had never felt so alive. I risked a look at Gloom, and I could see worry still on his face. Next to him, Gentle was also watching Gloom but with a small smile.

That glance cost me. In the seconds I was distracted, Ashes sent another ball of sand at me. It hit my shoulder, ripping through the thin sleeve of my T-shirt and blasting my bare skin. I screamed as the sand rubbed all the skin off my body, leaving a red raw patch. It stung like a thousand needles, and I was too scared to touch it, knowing it would make it worse. I heaved in a few deep breaths and waited for the pain to pass. I could see Gloom running over and yelling at Ashes. Looking at Ashes, he looked super satisfied with himself, and anger boiled inside of me. I wanted to get him back. I was embarrassed I had dropped my attention. I was no better than him. I was feeling cocky about tricking him and had let my guard down. I held out my arm to stop Gloom and stood as straight as I could. I blinked back the tears from my eyes and fixed Ashes with a stare.

Gloom stopped but didn't step back. I could sense his presence a few feet behind me, and it grounded me. Ashes gave me a smirk. "So, you want more, do you? I have plenty more to give. You should come back with me. I could teach you all kinds of tricks."

I snorted. "I don't think so." Before I got the words out, I sent a blast of power to a tree overhanging the clearing. A large branch snapped off the now brittle trunk and was falling on top of Ashes. He looked at the last second and managed to dodge it, but while his attention was on the branch, I sent out a ball of power straight for his chest. His eyes widened when he realised what I had done, and he was thrown back a few feet and landed on his back.

He didn't move. I got a sick feeling in my stomach, and fear clenched my throat closed. Memories of Matthew drying up and blowing away filled my mind. Had I just done that to Ashes?

Gentle must have been worried, too, as she ran over, calling his name, and knelt beside him. By the time she had lifted his head, Gloom and I were there too. My heart was racing, and panic was surging through my body. Had I killed him? Could you kill an Ever?

His skin was drained of colour. Where the magic had hit him and spread out, it was all grey, including his clothes. As we watched, it spread up his neck, turning his bronzed skin a sickly white.

"Ashes! Wake up!" Gentle was yelling. She slapped his face, and in front of our eyes, the colour started to come back to him. The grey was fading, but his shirt remained bleached of colour. His eyes snapped open.

"Oh, thank you. I was worried we had lost you there for a minute." We all relaxed until we looked into his eyes.

They were focused on me, and rage had filled them. I stood, and my heart kicked up a beat. I had pissed him off. I took a step back while he scrambled to stand up. I kept putting distance between us. I didn't want to be anywhere near him when he had that look on his face.

"You! How dare you! Who do you think you are?!"

Gloom and Gentle tried holding him back, but in his rage, they couldn't stop him. Gloom came to stand between us, but it did nothing to draw his attention away from me.

"I'm sorry, I'm sorry. I didn't mean to," I blubbered, clutching my necklace with my uninjured arm.

"Well, now you are going to pay." He raised a hand, and a ball of sand formed. I knew if he hit me with that, it would do some serious damage I might not recover from. I cowed behind Gloom, waiting for it to hit me.

When nothing happened, I peeked around Gloom and saw he had shot out vines to wrap around his arms and legs, pinning him in place. The wind picked up, and I watched as Gentle created a forcefield around us, stopping anything from passing through it. Leaves and sticks were flying everywhere. My hair was blowing around my head, and Gloom's coat was flapping wildly in front of me. I pressed myself into his back to keep from being blown away. I could hardly hear anything over the howl of the wind wall in front of us.

"Now Ashes," she said, "there will be none of that. You wanted to see what she is made of, and it looks like she is made of strong stuff. I won't have you killing her here in this field before dinner." I could see the strain on Gloom's face from holding him still, and I hoped Gentle could get through to him. After a few tense moments, he dispersed the sand ball and relaxed. Gentle released the air shield, and I was able to hear and see better. Eventually, Gloom relaxed the vines, and I moved out from behind him. Ashes was still staring at me, but the bloodlust had gone from his eyes.

"I'm so sorry. I didn't mean to do that."

He smirked again, but it wasn't as confident as it was earlier. "I think you have a weapon there, Gloom. Let's hope she can do it better and actually kill Dread when the time comes. She is going to need a lot more training before she will have a chance to do that. Shame we don't have time for that. Let's hope she doesn't end up killing *us* by accident." He straightened his clothes and stalked off into the forest towards the camp, not looking back.

"Huh. Quite impressive, Amelia. I haven't seen him go down in a fight for a long time. It won't hurt him. His ego is bruised that a small, mostly human girl defeated him. Well done. He will cool off. He is quick to anger but quick to forgive. Don't worry about him." She walked over to stand next to us, and a beautiful spring breeze brushed over my sweat-slicked skin.

"Well, I am off to have some dinner. Oh, wait. Let me look at that." She held her hand above my injured arm. It warmed, and the stinging stopped. When she took it away, it was an angry red colour, but most of the pain was gone.

"Thank you. Do you really think he will forgive me?" I said, not wanting to be on Ashes' bad side.

She waved a hand. "Of course. He really is a big teddy bear." She laughed and walked out the opening and towards the camp.

Gloom bent over and helped me put my jacket on, and I burrowed down in the warmth of it. By now, it was almost full dark, and I was looking forward to a meal and a warm sleeping bag.

"Are you really okay? You took quite a hit," Gloom said, moving to stand close.

"Yes, I am fine. It hurt, but it feels better now."

"Good. I thought you did a good job. That was some good control. Maybe we will be in with a chance when we find Dread," he said with a smile, trying to lighten the mood, but I could see he was worried. I took his hand, not caring who saw.

"We will win. We will find Lilly, and we will destroy Dread."

He smiled weakly at me and squeezed my hand. "Come on. I am starving."

THIRTY-THREE

Amelia

Every delay and rest we took grated against my nerves. It seemed like Lilly had been gone forever, and we were never going to find her. We trudged through the forest, hoping the scouts would come back with something while we tried to ignore the rain and the cold.

On the third morning, people noticed there were tracks circling our camp. Someone or something had been surrounding us at night. And it was big. Looking at the footprints, it was obvious to the Evers and I that it was the Horned One. I saw worry cloud Gloom's eyes as he tried to work out the best way to deal with it. All we could do was post more sentries, especially at night. A pit of anxiety and worry filled my stomach. I chewed my lip so much it was bleeding, and any little sound made me jump. I stayed as close to Gloom as I could.

That night, as we were lying in our sleeping bags, every movement was suspect. I was jolted awake multiple times by the sounds I heard in the forest. Each time, I thought the Horned One was looking down at me. Fortunately, I was wrong, and I didn't see him, but I was startled to wake and see the Lord and Lady of the forest wandering through our camp. Everyone else looked asleep, and the sentries were further off. The fire had burned out, and I could hear

Tristan snoring a few beds away. I lay as still as I could and watched their progress out of the corner of my eyes.

"Making their way, I see. It won't be long now, and we can be rid of that creature," said the Lord, his long blue velvet cloak trailing in the dirt.

"Mm," said the Lady, who seemed to be the only light in the dark forest.

"What? You don't think they can do it?"

"I think they can defeat the Horned One, especially with the girl. I'm not so sure about the other one…Dread. I think they will need our help before this will be all over."

"I think you are right there, my dear. We will have to begin thinking of the price we will ask," he said with a sly smile. They had made it halfway around the camp, and I did my best to look asleep.

The lady smiled indulgently. "Yes. It will be a large one. I know we should stay out of it. It's of no consequence to us, but I can't help but feel for them. I didn't enjoy watching the humans being destroyed the last time. I don't think I want to watch it again."

"You and your soft heart. I worry once the humans are gone, what is to stop him from turning his evil gaze on us? Perhaps you are right. If they ask, we should help…Within reason."

The Lady turned toward the Lord and kissed his nose. "Such a generous man."

The Lord melted. There was no other way to describe it. His whole body softened, and he only had eyes for her.

They continued their walk around the camp. I watched through slitted eyes as they passed my bed. The Lady looked at me and winked. I hadn't fooled her.

"Come, my love. Let's go and have a drink," she said, and they disappeared back into the forest. I sat up and looked around the camp to see if anyone else had seen them. All were sleeping except one. Gloom was sitting up, looking at me. Looking at me the same way the Lord had looked at his Lady.

The next breakfast, the scouts returned to camp. "Master, we have found tracks. We followed them, and there is a mansion a few hours west. It looks abandoned, but the tracks lead right to it. I think it's what we've been looking for."

Gloom nodded and stood. "Right, everyone. Break camp and load up. Looks like we have a lead. Make sure your weapons are at the ready and be alert."

We broke camp, and a strange buzz was running through the people. Finally, this was it. We travelled in tense silence. Even Bilvog had stopped complaining. I hoped when the moment arrived, I didn't run out of courage. Everyone changed into their fighting clothes, and I put on my leathers. Gloom wore his leather armour, and even Bilvog was wearing leather pants and breastplate, and it looked strange on his small form. Could he even fight? I guess I would find out.

Before dark, we arrived. The rain had let up, but there was still a light mist covering the land in a strange white sheen. Staying in the cover of the trees, we got our first look at the house.

It once would have been a beautiful house to live in. Although house might not have been the right word. It was more like a mansion with at least two stories. It was built with large white stones that glowed in the fading light. They were marred by vines that looked like they were trying to strangle it. I could see the remnants of a rose garden behind a small stone wall, and out the front of the mansion was a large fountain made of the same white stone, sitting in the centre of a driveway. I wondered what vehicles would be travelling out here in the middle of the forest. The fountain was a mermaid being stabbed by a triton, and it was haunting and tragic. There were chips missing from it, and the water had long since evaporated, leaving the white stone covered in black and green smudges. The whole building was crumbling and overgrown, and there was an off feeling about the place.

We could see light through some of the windows and movement occasionally passing in front of them. It gave off an eerie vibe, especially with the mist clinging to everything. Where did this come from? Was it from my world? There was something about it that repelled visitors. Thinking about going into the house made my stomach cramp, and my instincts were screaming not to go in. My thoughts were interrupted by Gloom.

"I think the best course of action will be to spread out and wait till it is fully dark before we enter," he said to us all gathered. "Let's keep an eye on the place and see if we can get a count of how many are inside. I want you in small groups, and no one goes anywhere alone. They know these woods better than we do, and we must be aware in case they're planning an ambush. This was too easy," he muttered with a frown.

We split up and spread out so we could cover most sides of the house. Each of us with at least one other person. Bilvog and I stayed with Gloom. We watched the other groups sneak off and disappear into the forest. There was an air of anticipation, and once we were alone, it hit me: I would be going in there, and I had no idea what we would find. I focused on my mind and let the familiar sounds of the forest calm me. Crickets and birds sang like they didn't have a care in the world, and I envied them. Meanwhile, in my mind, I was thinking about how I was about to go in there and quite possibly kill someone. It reopened the dark part of me that had appeared when I killed Matthew. There was a darkness in my soul now that had "murderer" branded on it. By the end of the night, there would be more. Would the darkness eventually fill my soul? I didn't want to find out.

I could hardly stay still with the adrenaline coursing through my body. With Bilvog there, I couldn't say any of the things I wished I could to Gloom, but I knew he knew how I was feeling. I prayed we would have the time we wanted to love and laugh together. It would be a cruel twist of fate to find each other only to have it taken away. I locked away my heart and focused on the task ahead of us. After a few quiet hours of waiting, we regrouped to discuss what we had seen and come up with a plan.

"This seems wrong," Kennock said. He had a frown on his face, and he kept pulling on his left ear. "There aren't enough sentries. All up, we have counted five people. Does it seem enough to anyone? If they do have our people in there, you would think they would be more heavily guarded."

"Well, this should be a nice, easy victory, and we can all be home before breakfast. Let's go," said Ashes, cocky as ever.

"Maybe they think being this far out, they don't have to worry?" I asked. I agreed with Kennock. Something was off. Everyone ignored Ashes. "It does seem foolish, but with the Horned One, they might think they have enough defence," said Bran.

"Hm, you might be right," Gloom said, "but I think we need to proceed with caution. Expect anything and everything. Even though this is a rescue mission, it's also a kill first and ask questions later situation. Once the captives are found," he swallowed, "in whatever condition they're in, we get out of there. We can fight them all another day. Our people are the first priority. Are we clear?" Everyone nodded and agreed, but my stomach was feeling queasy. Would it be that simple?

We decided we would all go in groups and enter through all the doors we had seen when we were watching the house. We would spread the Evers out so there would be one on each floor in case the other groups needed them. Once our people were found and it was time to leave, someone from the group would light the flares we had passed around. That would be the signal to leave. We would evacuate and meet back at our camping spot from last night.

We spread out, and everyone moved in.

THIRTY-FOUR

Amelia

We found the door we were to enter. It led out into a small courtyard which once housed a beautiful garden. Now, it was overgrown and dead. A birdbath painted blue lay smashed and broken in the centre, along with a beautiful curly iron table and chair set that was toppled over and bent.

We crouched at the edge of the small wall surrounding it, keeping our heads and voices down. I took the time to centre myself and ground into my power. I felt it awaken and flow into my hands at the ready.

"Are you ready? This is not going to be easy. If you can't do it, tell me now, and there will be no hard feelings," Gloom asked. There was no judgement in his gaze, only focus and determination.

"I'm ready," I said and nodded my head, hoping I wasn't lying to myself.

"Alright. Stay low to the ground and take cover when you can."

We all nodded and readied ourselves to go inside. As one, we stood and leapt over the small wall and crouched in the darkness before we took off again, each finding cover behind bushes and trees. My legs were burning by the time we stopped. I silently wished at that moment to be a gnome like Bilvog, so I didn't have to crouch as much. As if he had heard me, he looked at me and gave me a small smile. For the first time since we had left, he looked happy. Maybe it was all the excitement and the fact we were finally taking action, but I felt the same and gave him a feral grin, my body full of adrenaline.

We waited to make sure there was no one on the other side of the door, and we snuck to either side of it. I took the moment to ready my power again, and then Gloom opened the door, and we were in.

As my eyes adjusted to the light, I was shocked at what I was seeing. The room was completely trashed. There were piles of garbage and food in the corners with who knows what mixed in with it. On the walls, the wallpaper was peeling, and patches were missing. In the corners were cobwebs, and there was a rotting smell everywhere. It looked like this room was once a sitting room, but now the furniture didn't resemble furniture anymore. Most of the legs were missing from the lounges, large gouges were slashed in the cushions, and they were stained with things I didn't want to think about.

The mansion was silent. The only thing I could hear was the muffled sounds of the other groups infiltrating the building all around us. We had planned for each group to take certain rooms and see what they could find. Our job was to try and find the basement as it was the most likely place Lilly and the others were being held.

We made our way through the sitting room, wincing every time one of us trod on a creaky floorboard. My heart was thudding so loud that I was surprised we weren't discovered immediately. I wiped my sweaty hands on the front of my shirt and shook them out, trying to release some of the tension that had built in my body.

Leaving the sitting room, we entered what should have been the dining room. There was a large table pushed against one of the walls, and a huge chandelier hung from the centre of the room. It was beautiful, and I could easily picture it back in the day when this room was used to host amazing dinner parties. Now, however, there were crystals missing from the chandelier lying broken on the ground. All around were broken chairs, and I wondered what sort of people would destroy them for no reason.

Walking through, our feet crunched with each step as we trod on debris. In the quiet mansion, it sounded like an army walking over gravel, and I cringed with every step. I was keeping my power within reach, but it was taking a toll. My arms were getting heavy, and sweat was forming on my lip. I wiped it away and grit my teeth to keep going.

As we reached the door on the other side of the room, we heard sounds on the floor above us. We froze as we heard shouts and things being thrown around the room. It sounded like everything in there had been picked up and tossed about. I realised that was Gentle's floor and was likely exactly what had happened. With her wind power, she was likely throwing them all over the place. After a minute or so, the sounds died out, and it was quiet. Gloom looked at us and nodded his head. I could see the worry in his eyes, but we had all agreed to keep to our mission, even if we heard fighting. All the groups were very capable, and we had to find the captives. There were people in here, and we had to be careful. They could be anywhere.

We continued and opened the door. It led into the kitchen. The kitchen was decorated in black and white with lovely pale green wallpaper. This was the first room we had seen not completely destroyed. There was evidence people had been cooking here as dishes were strewn about on the counter, and some of them actually looked clean. In the sink was dirty water, and large pots were on the stove. I took the risk of lifting one of the lids to see what was in it, and it looked like some kind of stew. It was cold, and a layer of fat had congealed on the top. I quickly put the lid back and grimaced.

Walking through the kitchen, there was a table and chairs set up at the end and a couple more doorways leading off into other rooms.

"One of these doors must lead to the basement," Gloom said, his voice seeming too loud in the quiet room as he headed for the closest one. "Most houses like this would have had extra food stores down there."

I nodded and went toward the door closest to me while Bilvog was behind the counter, opening cabinets and looking around. As I reached for the door handle, my brain was a bit slow in processing what I was seeing. The door was ajar, and I could see a glint of metal inside. I opened it, and a man in a brown cloak reached out and grabbed me. I screamed as he spun me around and pressed me to the front of his body. I clawed at his arm, which was wrapped around my throat, pinning me there. I tried to kick him in the legs but couldn't get them.

Panic was filling my mind, and I was running on instinct. He quickly put a knife to my throat, silencing me. I looked on in horror as five more of them came out of nowhere and took hold of Gloom and Bilvog in the same way. All of them were wearing scratchy brown robes, and all were bald with a strange symbol on their heads. We were outnumbered.

"And what do you think you are doing here then? I'm pretty sure I haven't seen you here before." The one holding me sneered, his hot breath on my ear.

"We are here for our people. Where are they?" Gloom yelled, anger painted all over his face. The man holding him tightened the knife at his throat till a dribble of bright red blood dripped from his neck. While we were being held, the other cult members were tying our hands, leaving us unable to use our powers. The rope wrapped around my wrists brought back memories of being tied to the pole. I twisted my hands, trying to get free, but they were tight.

"That is enough out of you," he said, narrowing his eyes. "It's time to go and see the grandmaster, and he will decide what to do with you." They led the three of us through the door Gloom had been about to open. He was right. There were stairs leading down.

We walked with one of the cult members leading the way. Then Gloom, me and Bilvog. I turned to see behind us, and the last thing I saw was one of the cult members sneering and waving as he closed the door, leaving us in the dark. I stumbled on the stairs, but the man pulled me in close so we didn't fall, and we kept going. My skin crawled where he touched me, and I worked hard at keeping calm. Towards the bottom, a wall sconce was casting a yellowish light that did nothing to illuminate the space around us.

I could see ahead of us the stone tunnel went on and on. The floor was smooth from the constant foot traffic, and it dawned on me how long these people had been using this house as a hideout. We walked down, and I wondered who would be waiting for us on the other side. Who was this grandmaster, and what was his role in this? The tunnel was small and tight, and the men holding us could only just make it through, the walls brushing their shoulders on both sides. Because of the smallness of the tunnel, it was impossible to try and escape. I took each step, knowing I might not make it out of here. I didn't want to die in a stone tunnel. I wanted to see the forest again and feel the fresh air on my face.

I let my powers simmer so they would be ready when I needed them and focused on watching Gloom's head in front of me. Despite being held, he was walking with his back straight and head high. I could hear my heart beating in my chest, but I told myself this was how we got to Lilly. Surely, this grandmaster would know where she was. We would get free. Gloom might be captured now, but he is an Ever, and they are powerful. Not to mention the others were in the house. We would get free. Frantic thoughts swirled around in my head, and I tried to still myself and think clearly.

The tunnel went on forever, and every now and then, other tunnels branched off. There was a whole network down here. As we passed them, I could see other cult members darting in and out of other passageways, and I lost count of how many there were. There were definitely more than we thought, and I tried to keep track of our path so we could get out again.

Finally, we came to a large wooden door. The cult member at the front used the ram-head-shaped knocker and waited for a reply. Someone knocked on the other side, and he nodded. He looked over our heads to all the other members with him and opened the door.

The first thing that hit me was the smell of blood. The second thing was the dark stains covering the floor and walls of the stone room. The third thing, was a being attached to a long metal chain as thick as my wrist. The thing moved, and I cringed as it rolled over to look at us. My eyes widened, and my breath caught in my throat.

Lilly.

THIRTY-FIVE

Gloom

A roaring sound filled my ears as I looked at the beaten body of Lilly. How could they have done this to her? I moved towards her, but my captor tightened the knife at my throat. I ground my teeth together, hating being powerless but knowing I had to bide my time.

Next to me, Amelia had tears streaking down her face at the sight of her friend. For that alone, I would make them hurt. For what they did to Lilly, they would die. My power begged to be loosed, but I clenched my fist to keep it in check. I forced myself to wait for the coward to show his face. Then, I would destroy him.

I watched as Lilly looked at us, hope shining through her black, swollen eyes. I did my best to give her a reassuring smile, but my stomach churned looking at her injuries. I could see the desperation, pain, and relief at seeing us in her eyes, and I hoped I could live up to it. I followed the chain and found it tied to a large throne made of thick, twisted vines and branches. It was empty.

"Gloom." I looked at Amelia and saw confusion and fear written all over her face. "Where did they take Bilvog?" I tried to look around but couldn't see the whole room.

"Stand still," the man holding me growled in my ear.

From what I could see, she was right, and Bilvog was gone. My stomach dropped. Had I failed him, too?

"Where is he?" I asked through clenched teeth.

"Oh, we took him to have a bit of fun. Don't you worry," the man holding me said with an evil smile.

"What are you doing to him?" I roared. He didn't answer, but I could hear him laughing in my ear. I struggled, but his grip held tight. I thought of the stalwart gnome who had been there for my family for years and years. I vowed I wouldn't leave till I found him, too.

I heard movement behind me, and more members of the cult filled the room. The room soon filled with men and women wearing brown robes and bald heads. The symbols tattooed on their head were meaningless to me, but I memorised them so when I got out of here, I could work out what they meant. My heart sank as the last group to arrive came with all my party with them. They must have put up a fight because they were all bruised, and there was blood on all of them. I was pleased to see a lot of members of the cult were also wounded, and I smiled. We were all pushed to the front of the room to stand in front of the throne and Lilly. She made moves to get closer to us, and I could tell every movement brought her pain. A puddle of her blood surrounded her, most of it dry.

My heart broke to see her struggle, and I heard a sob leave Amelia's throat next to me. I could hear my people muttering with pity as they, too, recognised it was Lilly there in front of them. I cringed inside for Lilly. She would hate to know people were pitying her. Darkness snaked through and filled my body, and all I could think was how I was going to kill everyone. I let it flood my body and calm my mind. One of the cult members spoke.

"The grandmaster arrives," someone said with reverence. They all bowed, and our captors forced us to bow as well. It grated my pride to bow to anyone, especially someone who had done such terrible things to one of my friends, but I did it. It went against everything in my body to kneel to the person who was trying to destroy everything we had done. I could hear someone struggling next to me. Ashes. He wouldn't go down without a fight. The air whooshed out of his lungs, and he grunted before he, too, knelt on the ground.

The room was silent apart from Lilly's ragged breathing. It echoed through the chamber, and every inhale sounded wet and painful. When I didn't think I could take any more of her rattling breathing...footsteps.

I could hear two sets of footsteps. The grandmaster had entered from a door in the back of the room, and he had someone with him. I strained my eyes, trying to see him while the man held me down with firm hands. I wanted to see the man who had done these terrible things to my city. Who had come in and stolen my people, tortured my friend and was trying to resurrect the most evil and heinous creature?

The footsteps grew louder until I could see who it was. The Horned One walked in front. Its long black limbs getting closer. His stench hit me, and I swallowed, trying not to gag. In this small place, it was overpowering. As he passed us, he snorted, leaning close enough that hot air glided across the back of my neck. My lip curled, and I longed to stand and fight him. But I stopped in my tracks.

The second set of footprints walked in front of me, and I saw the grandmaster's shoes. My blood ran cold. I knew those shoes. They were small black leather shoes. I closed my eyes, and a heaviness settled in my stomach. I looked up, and my suspicions were confirmed.

The grandmaster of Dread's cult was none other than Bilvog.

THIRTY-SIX

Gloom

He smirked at me through his beard, then turned and walked to his throne. As he walked past Lilly, my gut clenched when he jerked the chain she was attached to and dragged her closer to the throne. She whimpered and cringed away from him, and I hated him more for what he had done to her. I stared in disbelief as he sat on the throne and surveyed us like a king.

"Welcome, welcome! I hope you haven't been too injured while touring my home. I can see Ashes took a few hits, although I'm not surprised. You never take the easy way. Please stand. You can release them. They won't be going anywhere." He spoke like he didn't have a care in the world. I couldn't believe he could act like that when he held his friends captive and tortured and possibly killed others.

"What the hell is going on here?" roared Ashes, standing up.

"That's no way to speak to the grandmaster. Show some respect," his guard growled as he punched Ashes in the stomach. I made sure to memorise his face.

"What is going on here," Bilvog answered, "is I am SICK AND TIRED of being your lackey! For years, I have served you all. I have been in all your kingdoms and advised and steered you right. You never once appreciated me for all I could do. So many of my ideas and plans you denied and ignored. I moved to the next person, hoping they would hear me and see me for what I really am, and you never did. I am not some little man you can push aside."

"What are you talking about, Bilvog? We never ignored you. We took your council every day," Gentle said with pain in her voice at the betrayal. Gentle had always had a soft spot for Bilvog, and I could see her shaking and trying to hold herself together.

"I don't think so." Bilvog sneered. He pointed his staff at her, and I winced inside. "I could have made your realm the most powerful Gentle, but you constantly ignored my advice, instead choosing to listen to your brothers and sisters. Letting all those humans in to tarnish this realm. They are not content to destroy their own realm. Now they have to take ours? Well, you will be sorry when you see what's coming for you. Your little mountain top will crumble, and you won't be able to do anything about it." He laughed with a glint of madness in his eyes. Gentle paled at his words. Had he already done something? Worry for her realm wormed into my body.

At last, I found my voice. "So, it was you who stole those people from Toleran. Why? What did you do with them?" I demanded, thankful my voice didn't waver. My body seemed to be tingling in shock, and my brain couldn't comprehend that the person who had betrayed me was Bilvog. I could never have imagined that it could be him that fooled me.

"Careful now, Gloom," he said in a soft voice. "I am not your subject here. I have the power." He wiggled in his throne and sat up straighter as if to prove the point. "But yes, it was me. I needed them to...accomplish certain tasks. Don't worry. They did what they were supposed to and were killed without suffering. That's really all you can hope for in the end, isn't it?" he asked with a shrug. I bristled at the casual way he spoke about those brave people who died.

"How could you do that to people you knew? Innocents!" I asked, the pain in my heart lacing my voice.

"I will do what needs to be done!" Bilvog snapped. "Not all were innocent. Many of them had wronged me. Talking to me like I didn't matter. Like they didn't have to obey me. I am the senior counsel, and they *ignored* me. All of them were human lovers and supported their coming here to Toleran. That could not be allowed to happen." He leaned back on his throne and took a moment to compose himself while he stroked his beard. The familiar sounds of the bells in it making me sick.

"However, it was unfortunate, I will admit, but if we are to change the world, some people have to die," he continued.

I couldn't believe these words were coming from his mouth. How could he possibly think killing innocents was okay for any reason. I had spent my entire time as the Forest Ever trying to protect my people, and now, to have been betrayed by one of my closest advisors was unthinkable. My mind was still reeling that the person we had been looking for all along was Bilvog.

"So, what is the end game here, gnome? What's your grand plan?" Ashes asked.

"Since you asked Ashes, my followers and I will be raising Dread. He was the only one out of the rest of you losers who had any respect and appreciation for me. With him in charge, I know we will change the world and not do the same old things. We are going to do amazing things together. If a few people have to die, then so be it. I know with my guidance to help him through this modern world, we will change everything," he finished with a smile on his face, and it made me want to vomit. This was actually a dream for him.

"Pfft. You're crazy if you think he isn't going to kill you as soon as your usefulness has run out. I hope I will be there to see it. You have chosen the wrong team here, Voggy," Ashes said. Bilvog's eye twitched at Ashes' nickname for him, and a thrill ran through me at inflicting some damage.

"You have no idea what you are talking about," Bilvog snapped again. "We are going to make the world as it should be. All these humans are good for nothing. All they do is breed and destroy everything they touch. Why can't we make them useful? We could rule them to do whatever we want! They will be powerless against Dread and his followers."

"So, you want to enslave humans? That is ridiculous. We have lived in peace for hundreds of years. Why change it now?" Gentle asked.

"Why not? Dread wanted to go ahead and kill them all again, but *I* convinced him to keep them around to do the dirty work. Most of them could be useful, and the ones that aren't, well, we will dispose of," he said, looking and gesturing to the Horned One standing near his throne. "Now, if you don't mind, this is getting tiresome. It is time to finish this little information session and get on with the job."

It took everything in me not to run and rip the little man apart, but I had to think about Lilly. The Horned One was right there, and I couldn't risk him killing her while I dealt with Bilvog. Even though our captors had released us, our hands were still bound, so I was pretty much useless. How were we going to get free? Bilvog hopped off the throne and walked toward Lilly.

"Now, my dear. It seems like your saviours are here. But they won't be saving much, I am afraid." He knelt and pushed some twigs that had fallen in front of her face away, breaking some in the process. She shrunk away, and a part of me broke to see this strong dryad be so beat down. Her birch bark skin was paler than normal, with the black sections looking more grey than black. She had cuts all over her, and tufts of leaves were missing and littering the ground all around us, smashed into the blood coating the floor. Her eyes were swollen, and more than one finger was broken. Her clothes were tattered and barely covering her. She whimpered as he knelt.

"Now, now, Lilly. We both know I have never been your favourite. In fact, I know for a fact you are quite good at talking about me to people whenever you get the chance. Yes, chat, chat, chat. One of the many things I hate about you," he said, his face twisting into an image I had never seen from him. When had he turned into this evil, spiteful man? He was so twisted and distorted that I didn't understand how I could have missed it. Lilly whimpered again, and I took a step closer, ready to rip her away, no matter where the Horned One was standing.

But I never got the chance.
"Get away from her!"

THIRTY-SEVEN

Amelia

I was shaking all over, trying to control my rage. How could he stand there and be so cruel to her? I walked towards them, but before I could get far, Gloom spoke, "Amelia, stop." I looked at him in disbelief when I noticed his eyes flick the Horned One standing near the throne. He also had taken a step forward. I knew if it came to him or me getting to Lilly first, he would win, and it wouldn't be to rescue her. I reined in my outrage.

"Let her go, Bilvog." I had kept quiet while he spoke earlier, but I wasn't going to stand there and watch him kill my friend. I had to try and do *something*. "Please, let her go." Having to beg this monster left a foul taste in my mouth, but I would do anything to get Lilly out of there safely.

The tension in the air tightened. People were shifting positions all around the room. Out of the corner of my eyes, I could see cult members moving to cover the exits, and I knew there was no way we were leaving without a fight. I focused back on Bilvog and Lilly.

"You," Bilvog bit out. He spat on the ground at my feet and wiped his mouth. "You are very lucky to be alive, little girl. Don't worry, I know all about your powers. I probably know more than you do. No doubt Gloom here didn't tell you much. Wanting to keep you in the dark so you don't learn the truth. I bet he never told you where they came from. Such a power like yours is extremely unique. One look and he would have known, but he has kept it from you. Haven't you Gloom?" he said with a satisfied smile and a gleam in his eye.

I turned to look at Gloom, and he was looking at me with sadness in his eyes. My breathing became difficult, and dizziness washed over me as my stomach dropped. Gloom knew. He knew where these powers came from and had kept it from me. He knew I had been searching for answers in the books in the library. I had asked him, and he had *lied* about it. He had had plenty of opportunities to tell me and never had. Now, I had to find out from Bilvog. I blinked the tears of betrayal out of my eyes and looked back at Bilvog. I straightened my spine and prepared myself for what I was sure he was going to say.

"Oh yes. I know exactly who it is. And so do they," he said, gesturing out to the other Evers.

"Who is it?" I demanded of him, my voice hard as a rock. I saw Gloom look at the ground out of the corner of my eye. A strange silence filled the room, like everyone was waiting to hear what they already knew. It was like they couldn't believe it until he confirmed it.

"Poor little human. Trying so hard to be important. Well, if no one else wants to tell her, I will." He looked around gleefully, waiting for someone to speak.

"That's enough, Bilvog. If you want to hurt someone, here I am. You don't need to hurt Amelia. This has nothing to do with her," Gloom finally spoke.

"Nothing to do with her? She is here, isn't she? She demanded to be included in this, so she has made herself involved. Really? I don't know why you are all so worried. It should be a point of pride in her insignificant life."

My body tingled. I knew I was about to find out something I couldn't unknow. This power had been inside of me my whole life, and for much of it, it had to be hidden. It had caused me more trouble than good until a few months ago. Since then, I had learnt some measure of control, and it was no longer as much of a burden as it once was. Did it matter who it came from? In the end, I didn't think it did as much as before.

I looked at Bilvog. He was so smug, and I could tell he was dying to tell me. Just so it would hurt me. I froze my face and vowed I would show no emotion when he told me. I would not give him the satisfaction.

"Get on with it, Bilvog. I don't care anyway," I said, trying to sound convincing.

"Fine, fine. Well, I'm sure the rest of you have guessed by now, so it has lost some...impact, shall we say." He sighed heavily and dramatically. "Amelia," He fixed me with a fake sympathetic look, "the person you get your powers off is none other than the Ever you are here to defeat. Dread."

I knew it. I knew it had to be him. I felt sick that somewhere along the line, one of my ancestors had been with him and gotten pregnant. What a hypocrite. I couldn't imagine it was consensual. I kept my features neutral so he wouldn't know the disgust I felt, but he turned to Gloom instead. "And yes, I know all about her powers. Did you think you two were practising in private? I know all about your little training sessions. I also know you were training more than your powers, too." My face heated with embarrassment and anger as he turned the special thing we had into something to be ashamed of.

"You can't do any better than this lowly human? Even if I didn't have many other reasons to destroy you, that would be all it would take."

He looked to see Lilly had been creeping away from him inch by painful inch. She was looking at the ground in front of her, creeping closer and closer to us. She didn't notice Bilvog had seen her and was too slow to move her broken body out of the way. Bilvog reached down, grabbed the chain, and pulled her back to him. She grabbed the clasp around her throat and gasped as it jerked her back by her neck. She started to cry, and tears ran down my face, sadness and hopelessness crashing over me. To watch a once vibrant, happy, and kind dryad be broken and bound was torture, and I knew I would never get the image out of my mind, no matter how much I tried. It was imprinted on my soul alongside the dark patch from Matthew.

"Now, I think that's enough talking. The Shadow One needs more energy, and I am going to give it to him." He clicked his fingers, and the collar fell off her neck. Lilly tried to suck in deep breaths even though we could see how much it hurt her to do so. Bilvog reached a hand into his robe and pulled out a black steel dagger. The hilt of it was made of bone with one large black stone in the bottom of it. The blade was large and curved, and it had some sort of a shadow or smoke curling around it, shifting and swirling. He held it high for a moment like he wanted everyone to see it. I heard Gentle gasp softly, and when I turned, there was devastation on her face. Gloom and

Ashes looked shocked and startled as well. Clearly, they knew this knife and what it could do. I watched and waited, my stomach churning and turning sour, knowing what I was about to witness.

I knew what he was going to do but was powerless to stop it. I saw Gloom jump forward, but the cult members behind us grabbed and grappled us so we couldn't move. A roaring sound filled my ears, and I realised it was coming from Gloom. He was trying with everything he had to get free and make it to Lilly. The man holding him was struggling, and another came to help, but it seemed like he would still break out.

But he was too late. Bilvog raised the knife and whispered something close to Lilly's ear. I screamed out her name as he brought the knife down on her neck.

THIRTY-EIGHT

Amelia

Blood splashed across her face and the stone floor. I watched as the eyes of the only friend I'd ever had flickered out. As she took her last breath, I thought of all the ways she had been kind, funny and caring towards me. I hated that the last thing she felt was pain and fear. My heart broke as I sobbed, unable to do anything to save her. Next to me, Gloom had stopped struggling and was staring at the body of his friend. He looked like the ground had fallen away from him, and he was suddenly adrift.

Bilvog looked at the dagger and smiled. He dropped Lilly on the floor like a bag of rubbish, and I cringed as she hit the ground hard, her body painted orange from her blood. He held the knife, and the smoke encircling it poured off it. It sank to the floor and started to rise, taking the form of a man. The smoke swirled and danced until we could see the image of a man clearly. He was tall and naked.

Even with smoke as a body, I could clearly see he was well-muscled and handsome. He had curly hair that tumbled around his shoulders and a wide mouth. His square jaw was chiselled, and he looked like a statue. The only thing marring his beauty were his eyes. Even though they weren't clear, they were cold and empty. He looked at Bilvog and smiled slightly. Gloom and the other Evers were staring with open mouths, shocked at who they were looking at. Dread. Their brother.

Dread looked over at them, and the smile vanished. He raised a hand like a wave, but before he could do anything else, I saw Gentle raise her bound hands and the smoke was blown away. Gentle lowered her shaking hand and straightened. So that was Dread.

There was silence as everyone processed what they had seen. They had just seen the image of a monster they had only heard about in bedtime stories, used to scare them. Where had he come from, and did this mean he was back for good?

Bilvog turned and faced us. "Now, wasn't that a good visit. As you can see, there is nothing you can do to stop him. He is gaining power as we speak. Give up. Death will be quick and painless."

Ashes growled at him. "If you believe that, you are more deluded than I thought. There is no way we are letting him get away with destroying the humans again."

Bilvog didn't answer but simply bent and wiped Lilly's blood off the knife and onto her dress. My face heated to see him treat her so poorly. The atmosphere in the room changed. Seeing him do that had broken the stupor over the room from seeing Dread. Now, our people were angry and filled with vengeance.

Lilly was much loved by the people of Toleran, and I knew, like me, they were having trouble understanding how one of our own people could do that to her and the others.

Looking at Bilvog, he, too, was aware of it. He stood slowly, keeping a wary eye on us. I could see Gloom's chest rising and falling as his fury built. The cult members were shifting on their feet, waiting to see what would happen. Perhaps they realised they were stuck in a basement with at least four magic users filled with rage. Bilvog put the knife back in his robe and looked towards the Horned One.

"Kill them all."

The Horned One nodded, and he stalked toward us as Bilvog backed away towards the door he had entered.

I watched him go as a cold calm settled over me. The man behind me, holding me, relaxed his grip for a second, and I sprung. I reached my hand back and touched his leg. I let my power go and focused all my hate and energy on sucking the life out of him, never taking my eyes off Bilvog. There was no way I would let him get away.

My magic syphoned the life out of the man I was touching and destroyed the rope binding my hands. I turned around and watched him as his skin turned grey and eventually flaked off his bones. At the end, all that was left was a pile of dust. I swallowed, turning my emotions off and shoving them down deep. I needed to be cold and focused on getting out of here.

All around me, my friends were doing their best to get free. Gloom was struggling with the two that held him back earlier. I pulled out my dagger and rushed up to them. I stabbed the dagger into one of the men's necks, and the warm blood splashed across my arm. I gasped as the hot liquid covered me, and I clenched my teeth against the disgust and shock I felt. I was not going to let these monsters get away after what they had done.

As soon as the one I had attacked went down, I cut Gloom free, and he extended his arms to the side. He yelled out a deafening yell, and sections of the wall crumbled as vines weaselled their way through the mortar between the bricks. Vines and branches came pouring in, devouring everything they touched. The vines smothered the closest person and jammed themselves into the throats, eyes and nose holes, suffocating the man swiftly. Once dead, the vines backed out, covered in blood and flesh, and I knew I would be seeing that image in my nightmares. I didn't give myself too much time to think about it before I was taking off after Bilvog. He was who I wanted.

As I was running after him, I saw dirt and sand whip up and swirl around the room, blocking all the exits. We were in the middle of a cyclone, and there would be no escape. The sound of wind fought with the shouts of people fighting, creating a deafening clash in the underground chamber. Around me, there were balls of power flying around as the mages we bought used their power to destroy, and I did my best to ignore the blood and gore that was splattering the room.

I caught Ashes' eye, and he grinned at me before he hacked off a cult member's arm with a scimitar in one smooth movement. Blood soon coated the floor and the people in the room.

Once Bilvog realised his means of escape had been cut off, he turned towards the fight, his body shaking. His eyes searched out the Horned One, but he was occupied with Kennock and Tristan. Seeing he was alone in this battle, he seemed to find some resolve in his cowardly body. He rushed back to the throne and pulled out his staff from behind it. I knew from some experience it held magic, but I had never seen it used as an attack weapon. It looked different. Before, it was carved from smooth wood, but now it seemed to be made from the bougainvillaea vine. The vines looked twined and knotted, and the whole thing was covered in thorns. It was unfamiliar, and yet it nagged at me.

I heard behind me Gloom mutter, "No, my staff?" It clicked that Bilvog was holding Gloom's Staff of Thorns. One of the artefacts used to bind Dread.

Bilvog saw me coming and raised the thorned staff towards me. Green light shot out of it, and fortunately, my training kicked in before my brain, and I managed to dodge out of the way on instinct. The heat blasted past me, and a fissure of fear danced down my spine. I wasn't trained enough to be in this fight. This was life and death, and I wasn't sure I could survive.

Standing, I slipped on some of the blood on the floor, and while I was distracted by my thoughts and the blood, I didn't see the second bolt coming. I screamed as acid landed on my thigh and immediately ate through my leather pants and skin. Pain erupted as my skin bubbled and peeled away. It was stinging so bad I couldn't focus on anything around me, and it was getting fuzzy at the edge of my vision. My skin was turning black, and I could hear it sizzling. I screamed again, and Gloom appeared before me. I clutched onto him, needing to hold onto something as pain overtook everything.

"Amelia. Oh, Amelia." He put his hands over the burn an inch from the skin. I tried not to move, but it was unbearable.

I shook uncontrollably, but eventually, I felt a coolness instantly lower my pain, even if it was by a fraction. I tried to power through the pain, breathing heavily through my teeth as Gloom worked his magic. Everything else was blocked out apart from the pain in my leg and Gloom trying to make it better. He lifted his hands from my burn, and it was no longer bubbling and melting, but it looked horrific. The top layer of skin was melted away, and all that was left was the deep red of muscle. I choked back a sob and scrunched my eyes closed, wanting to be anywhere but here.

"It's okay, Amelia. It will get better. Shh, shh, we need to keep fighting. We aren't safe here." He picked me up, and my world swam as he carried me, then leaned me gently against the wall of the room. I took the weight off my leg, but it didn't seem to make any difference to the pain.

Hearing his words helped me swim out of my stupor, and I looked around me. Everyone was still fighting, but things were not good. It looked like half of our people were injured. Watching the cult members, they fought with a wildness and ferocity I had never seen. They were like caged animals trying to get free. Our people were struggling even with the Evers and their powers.

The Horned One strode through the people, ramming them and throwing them around like they weighed nothing. His horns glinted red in the lantern light, and it dripped down his skull.

"Okay, Okay." I gritted my teeth and leaned on Gloom's arm as I tried to support my weight. My muscles strained in my leg, and I cried out. I steeled myself as I tried to straighten up. I knew I wouldn't be able to walk, so I worked on standing. Gloom stabilised me until I gave him the nod to let me go. I couldn't put my leg flat on the ground, and I knew what a liability I had become.

Gentle was using her power to fling people away from us, but I could see she would be needing help soon as they were becoming too much for her. I looked into Gloom's eyes, and I saw he, too, knew we were losing. He looked at me like he was trying to memorise every inch of my face. He leaned down and kissed me gently. "I love you. I won't let you die here." Before I could say anything, he joined Gentle in protecting me.

Tears streamed down my face, and my throat felt tight, and I felt hopeless. My body was like a lead weight, and I was finding it hard to stand. I stared at the carnage with vacant eyes. What was the point? Maybe it was time we gave up.

I saw Bilvog. He was firing his acid spray at anyone close enough, and it was doing terrible damage. I watched as grief warred inside of me. All these people had been killed. Such a waste. Imagine if Dread got free. How many more people would die for nothing? I was no longer the scared girl cowering in the corner. I had friends and a city, and I needed to fight for them like they were fighting for me. My attention turned back to Bilvog, and I thought of all the evil he had done. All the pain he had caused. He had lured us here and kidnapped innocent people. It was time he paid.

I built my power, and while his attention was turned away, I shot at him. I focused all my pain and strength into it, and I watched as the dark power slammed into the side of his body. He yelled out and fell to his knees, dropping the staff. I could see the rot spread out from his right shoulder all the way to his foot. He looked at me, full of hate, while I stood tall and stared him down.

He reached into his robe and held the dagger. He slashed a cut on his palm, and the black smoke encircled his hand and absorbed the blood into it. Colour returned to his face, and he managed to stand. Somehow, the dagger had healed him or gave him the power to heal himself. My rot stopped spreading, but I could see his hand and wrist remained grey and lifeless. He clutched it to his chest and yelled out, "Kill that human now! I want her dead! Kill her!" with a level of madness and hate I had never seen before.

He turned away towards the door, clutching his useless arm, and stood there waiting for a break in the sand cyclone to make his exit.

I heard Gloom shout out, and I whipped around to where he was helping Gentle fight off the cult members. Time slowed as I watched the Horned One charged at Gentle. Gentle was too slow and didn't see him until it was too late. He charged with his head down and horns leading, but Gloom saw him coming, and without hesitation, he leapt in front of Gentle to protect her from the attack.

The Horned One slammed into both of them, and I saw Gloom's side get gored by the horn. I cried out as they fell and landed in a heap. The Horned One disentangled himself and looked for his next victim. He let out a deafening roar, and I had to cover my ears. He turned on his heel and ran back into the dwindling fight in the middle of a blood rage, leaving Gloom and Gentle to bleed together on the floor.

They were not moving. Blood gathered around them, mingling and pooling together. I could hear the raspy, shallow breaths I was taking, and my head grew light. I stood there waiting for them to wake up, but nothing. Not a twitch. He couldn't be gone. Not after I had just found him. I wouldn't give him up now. Our story had just begun, and we had a lifetime to live. There was no way that could be over now.

I got on my hands and knees and crawled over to them, gritting my teeth against the pain. Every movement was so painful tears sprung to my eyes, and I worried my teeth might crack with the pressure of gritting them against the pain. I made it to them but had to crawl through their blood to reach them. I swallowed and waded through. It was warm, and the sight of the sticky blood on my hands was disgusting.

So much blood.

It coated my leathers, and I slipped, swallowing back the vomit building in my throat. I put my hand on Gloom's side, where there was a large hole from the horn, and I could feel the steady flow dribbling out of it. Immediately, my hand was soaked in his blood, and it wouldn't stop. I knew the Evers had a small amount of healing power, but Gloom had already used his to help me. Could he still heal himself? He was pale and unmoving.

"Gloom! You have to wake up! Come on. Wake up. Don't leave me now."

I bent my cheek to his mouth but could feel no air, and his chest wasn't moving. I shook him, tears running down my face, knowing but still unable to believe he was gone. My world shrunk small, and I focused on each breath. This couldn't be happening. Slowly, a sound seeped into my brain. It came from very far away. Laughing. Someone was laughing amidst all the carnage. My focus widened until I was back in the throne room again. The smell of smoke, blood, and death all around me. My senses were overwhelmed, and I had trouble focusing.

I looked over and could see one of our mages on the ground with a sword wound slashed across his belly. His eyes wide and lifeless with shock while his guts were spilt out on the floor. I knew he had a family at home, and my stomach sank for them. People were littered on the floor. So much life, just gone. All to stop a mad God rising and killing half the people on the earth. So many lives were destroyed.

I followed the laughter until I saw the Horned One. He was laughing at us a few feet away.

"This is it, little girl. You are losing, and now two of your precious Evers are out. There is no way you can win. Give up, and let us kill you all quickly, and be done with it," he said. His gravelly voice was hard to understand in my head, and I felt a spear of pain from the power of it.

I scowled at him and leaned in to kiss Gloom on his cheek. "I love you," I said to him, hoping wherever he was, he knew that. I looked at Gentle and was sad to see her also unmoving. I wished I had had more time to get to know her. I steeled myself and stood as tall as I could with my leg. I clutched my grandmother's necklace, hoping it would give me the strength to do what I was about to try. I wobbled but managed to root myself to the earth. I could see Ashes fighting while looking at his fallen brother and sister. The pain on his face was hard to look at, and I shut it out, focusing on the Horned One in front of me.

"We will never give up, you monster. We will do everything we can to stop you from raising that bastard. I will not give up knowing he intends to kill my people. None of us will."

"There is no point. Look around you. You are outnumbered. He will rise, and it will be glorious."

"Glorious? He is going to kill thousands of people. How can you think that's a good thing?" I raised my voice so the others around me could hear. "Don't these *human* followers realise what a hypocrite he is. He is only using them until they are no longer useful. Then he will kill them all."

I gathered my power and pooled it. There wasn't much left, but I scraped every last bit in my body, willing to kill myself if it came to it. My back muscles were straining, both from standing on one leg and from the effort I was putting in readying everything in my body. I glanced around again, getting an idea where everyone was, and prayed I didn't hurt any of my own people. I risked a look for Bilvog but noticed the sand cyclone had stopped at some point, and the door out was open with no sign of him. He had escaped.

I let the disappointment and anger that washed over me gather in my hands. I looked at the Horned One and the cult members around. I pooled all I had, and with a scream filled with grief, disappointment, anger, and sadness, I raised my hands and fired everything I had in me at my enemies. I saw the Horned One recoil in pain as it hit him. I watched as the huge deer horn that was his head crumbled into a fine powder and fell to the floor. He screamed in agony, and I smiled.

Then all was dark.

THIRTY-NINE

Amelia

Someone was shaking me awake. My head flopped, and I scrunched my eyes, wanting to tell them to go away, until I recognised the voice.

"Amelia. Wake up. Come on. It's time to wake up now." The urgency in his voice made me crack them open, and a shape took form in front of me. I made out the dark hair with horns and the moss-green eyes looking at me with worry and wonder.

"Gloom," I said, relief coursing through me. "You're alive. I thought you were dead," I croaked out weakly. I buried my head in his shoulder and sobbed as all the emotion of the last few hours avalanched into me. I had seen more people die today than I ever wanted to again, but I knew there would be more to come in the future. For right now, I held onto Gloom and soaked in his scent.

"Amelia. What did you do to him? They are all gone."

"I...I don't know. I knew I had to kill them right now, or they were going to kill all of us. I had to protect you all, so I let it all out. Even if it killed me." I looked into his eyes, and they softened. Before he could speak, I heard a voice over his shoulder.

"I have never seen anything like that. It was quite a thing to see," said Ashes, no hint of his usual sarcasm. "She vaporised them all. One minute, they were here. The next, gone." He shook his head. I could see he had taken quite a beating. His tanned skin was pale, and he had patches of blood soaking through his shirt and pants. I didn't know if it was his or someone else's.

"Gentle? Where is Gentle?" I said, finally lifting my head from Gloom's shoulder and taking a good look around the room.

"I'm here. I am okay. I was stunned. I was able to heal Gloom and bring him back. He is far from good, but it will do until we have a rest. I am glad you are alright," she said with a smile on her face.

"I was so worried about you," I said, offering a smile. "Who else is hurt?"

The circle of people got quiet. I saw Kennock come forward and was relieved to see him still alive.

"I'm afraid not all of us made it. Half of our team died. Bran and Tristan among them," he said with a catch in his voice. Looking around, I could see a few people moving and cleaning the fallen around the room. I saw Tristan, and a sob built in my throat. He had been so kind to me, helping me with my jobs and just being a niceh person who had turned into a friend. I sat there stunned. All those people I had come to know and trust, gone. Just like that. I couldn't stop the tears from falling as I thought about the future they should have had, and now they wouldn't get.

I stood with Gloom's help and limped over to where Lilly was lying. I could see someone had laid her out and cleaned most of the blood from her body, but it couldn't hide the damage that had been done to her. I knelt beside her and took her black and white streaked hand. "I'm really going to miss you, Lilly. You were my first friend, and I will never forget all the ways you helped me. I will get him. I promise. He will not get away with this." I kissed her hand and cried again, knowing I would likely never find another friend like her.

The trip home was long and hard. We had found a few things in the mansion to help us on our way. Warmer clothes, food, medical supplies, and things we could use as stretchers for our fallen. Still, it was hard. Everyone who had survived was injured, and trying to take our supplies and the fallen was proving to be more difficult than we thought. We did talk about leaving a few behind and coming back for them, but no one wanted to leave them in this evil place. Plus, it would not be right to return without them where their families were waiting.

We also searched the place for any information on where Bilvog might have gone and what his next move would be but found nothing. Whatever had been here was taken or destroyed. We also found the bodies of the people that had been taken from Toleran. We cleaned and dressed them for the trip home, and our hearts were heavy.

When we woke on the first morning through the forest, we saw, on the edge of our now small circle, some hand carts. Inside were fresh linens and medical supplies. I looked into the forest and saw the Lord and Lady standing on the edge. I bowed my head to them, and they nodded in return and faded into the trees. I had a feeling we would be getting a visit from them soon, but I chose not to think about it, grateful for their help. The handcarts made it much easier to move our friends, and we made faster work on the rest of the trip.

Gloom and I healed gradually, but every morning, Gentle or Ashes would tend to our wounds, healing us with the power they had. We no longer tried to hide our love. After what we had been through, we didn't care if people knew. No one said anything, but we got a few sweet smiles. I wondered how well we had kept it a secret on the way and realised probably not well. Every night, we would lie together, and it was like a dream. To have his arms around me and be enveloped by his scent while we were sleeping was heaven and torture. I couldn't wait to get back to the castle and into a private room. I had told myself not to be guilty over this freedom, but it was hard. So many lives ruined. But I wasn't going to hide any longer. This was special, and I was going to treat it like that.

The last morning, Gentle and Ashes announced they would not be joining us at Toleran.

"We shall go back to our own realms now. With Bilvog on the loose, we need to be vigilant," said Gentle. I thought of the threat Bilvog had made to her and nodded. "Yes, it is probably a good idea to go and make sure your people are safe. Thank you for all your help. There is no way we would be here without you. With Bilvog free, please be careful out there," I said, giving them a smile.

"Don't worry about us. We are much more capable than you lot are. I'll pass on the message to Enduring and Crescent. Tell them to keep an eye on everything."

"Thanks, Ashes. It looks like Dread might have more help than we thought. We may be in for a long fight," Gloom said with a sigh. Everyone agreed, and we waved them off with the promise of meeting soon.

We arrived in Toleran in the early afternoon. One of the soldiers with us had gone ahead and gathered everyone we needed to see. We arrived, and all of Toleran was waiting for us, heads bowed and respectful. A hush had fallen over the town, and everywhere I looked was bowed heads and tears. While making our way haltingly through the town, petals and flowers were falling around us, creating what looked like a beautiful, coloured snow tumbling around us.

I looked up to see people lined up on all the bridges and platforms, dropping them in respect for the fallen. We carried in the carts with our people who didn't make it. People came forward and laid flowers and ribbons on the carts as they passed. It was a sad and solemn welcome back home.

We made it to the palace, where the family members of the fallen were waiting. My heart broke, looking at them all, watching our sad procession. So many lives ruined. The effect of this battle would be felt for years, and tears filled my eyes at the waste. On the way in, Gloom stopped and talked to all the people there waiting. I watched as he spoke to them all by name and offered to help in any way. The families were heartbroken, and I couldn't stop the tears from falling. The grief was overwhelming and oppressive, and my heart went out to them.

Gloom handled it well. He had time for every person there. He listened while they yelled, held them when they cried and spoke when they needed words of comfort. That is why the city loved him. He loved them, and he hurt when they hurt. My love for him grew more than I thought possible. The rest of the afternoon was spent comforting and offering support to the families. The sadness weighed on everyone heavily, and we knew what we had lost and how little we had gained. All we had done was stop the Horned One. It didn't seem to balance, and I wondered if it would ever feel enough.

FORTY

Amelia

After everyone had gone back to their houses, we dragged our tired and aching bodies back into the aerie. I went to my room, had a nice long bath, and washed off all the dirt and grime that had gathered on my body over the last few days. I washed my hair twice and soaked until the water went cold. I opened my wardrobe and put on some comfy yoga pants and an oversized T-shirt. I was warm and comfortable, but something was off.

Even though I was bone tired, I was restless. I sat on the lounge in front of the fire and absorbed everything that had happened in the last few months. My life had changed in so many ways. I had found a home, people to call my friends and found love. But I had also encountered heartbreak, loss, and grief. The emotions warred within me, and I wasn't sure which one was going to win.

I looked around my room and wondered where I stood here now. Gloom said he loved me, but does that mean we are a couple? Am I still his assistant? Is this still my room? I had no answers. In the forest, before we left, there was so much passion between us, and my body warmed in place thinking about it. But had we fizzled?

We had hardly had a moment to ourselves since then. I sat up straight. If I didn't know, then I should find out. I was sick of being meek and mild. I no longer want to be like that. I want to ask questions and demand answers. I stood. It was time to go and see Gloom and sort this out. This was the new Amelia, and I wasn't in Woodmere anymore. I walked to the door, confidence and determination fuelling my steps. I opened the door and ran right into Gloom.

"Oh, crap. Sorry," I said.

He smiled at me, and I melted inside. I knew how lucky I was to see his smile, knowing not many people got to see it. "I came to find you. I finished with my meeting, and you weren't in our rooms."

"Our rooms?"

"Well, yes." He took my hands. "I want you to move into my rooms...well, if you want to," he said with uncertainty in his eyes. I squeezed his hands. Thinking about the confident man I had first met, I never thought I would see uncertainty in his eyes.

"Yes, of course I want to move into your rooms. I was coming to see you to find out where we stand. I wasn't sure. We haven't had much time to talk since this all began."

He looked at me surprise filling his face. "Where do we stand? I love you, Amelia. I want to spend every minute with you and never be apart." He cupped my cheek, and I leaned into it. "Amelia, you have changed me. You have brought light to my darkness, and I can see again. I can see a future for me and us. That's where we stand if you agree."

I felt complete as he looked into my eyes, and I could see the future all laid out, and it was more than I ever dreamed I would get. Something in me clicked into place in the spot Matthew and Woodmere had broken. This was my home, and I was loved and going to be happy for the rest of my life.

I reached up, put my hands on both sides of his face, and pulled him lower so I could kiss him.

The kiss promptly deepened and turned into something different. Gloom buried his hand in my hair and held me closer. I pulled myself closer to him, getting as close as I could. Gloom broke the kiss long enough to bend over, pick me up, and carry me to the bed. He laid me down gently and looked at me from head to toe. My whole body came to life seeing the hunger in his eyes. Keeping his eyes on me, he slowly took his jacket off, throwing it on the floor behind me. I sat up on my elbows to watch, my body practically vibrating off the bed.

We both took our time undressing and savouring each other as we came together and showed our love. Looking into each other's eyes, love shone back at us, and we expressed that with our bodies. We took out time until passion overtook us, and by the end, we were spent, but I knew beyond any doubt that this was where I was meant to be. Here in his arms in Toleran.

"Well, that was nice," I said sleepily with giggle.

He opened one eye. "Nice? Is that it?"

"Okay, it was a little bit better than nice."

He grabbed me and pulled me in tight so my head was lying on his shoulder. I wrapped my arm across his hard stomach and sighed in happiness.

"Well, it looks like I will have to work harder to get better than nice next time," he said.

"Perhaps you will," I said, smiling as I fell asleep.

FORTY-ONE

Amelia

The next few weeks, we spent most of our time re-organising the kingdom. We had lost a lot of important members, and with the threat of Dread on the rise, we had to prepare in any way we could. I stayed on as Gloom's assistant. I wanted to stay busy and be useful and not be lying around all day, and I enjoyed seeing other people. It didn't take long for people to realise Gloom and I were a couple, and I was worried people would treat me differently. For the most part, they didn't, and I was glad. I knew it would have to change eventually, but for now, while we were recovering, I was happy to not make anything too official.

I poured a lot of time into my training, which no longer had to be in secret. I never wanted to feel like a burden again, and I wanted to be able to fight alongside the people I loved and be useful. Something had unlocked in me after defeating the Horned One, and my magic flowed and obeyed me in ways it never had before. Physically, I was getting better as well, and I was learning how to fight with a sword and loving it. I loved the power and confidence that came from knowing to defend myself and others that I had never had before.

Toleran was slowly recovering from its losses. We held funerals for the people who had been lost, and quietly, the people of Toleran were healing. I missed Lilly every day. It was an ache in my chest. I would see something or think to go and find her to get her help, and I would realise she was gone.

The day after our return, Kennock spoke to Gloom and me over breakfast.

"Master, it seems Rak managed to escape while we were away. The others tried to chase him down, but he seemed to have vanished."

Gloom's eyebrows lowered. "Well, that is a problem. Inform Ashes right away. If Rak is returning home, Ashes might have some trouble on his hands."

Kennock nodded and left us.

"Why would that be a problem?" I asked as Gloom continued to stare at his food, looking worried.

"Rak was here to ensure his father did not cause any trouble. Shomari and Ashes have had a long feud, and he is a powerful mage who would like to overthrow Ashes. He came very close last time. Ashes needs to know if Rak has returned and lost that leverage." We finished breakfast in silence, and I wondered how powerful the mage was if he had almost overthrown Ashes.

We prepared as much as we could, thinking about the war to come. The other Evers all came and helped where they could and spent many hours together, locked up, trying to find solutions. I met Enduring the Sea Ever and Crescent the Moon Ever. Both were friendly, but I could see they wondered who I was to have caught their brother's eye. They seemed happy for us anyway.

The only Ever not to arrive was Gentle. She was hesitant to leave the mountain she called home while Bilvog's threat hung in the air. They had begun searching the mountain for anything strange but so far had found nothing. I had heard from the others that Gentle had been the closest to Bilvog and was taking his betrayal hard.

I was worried about what would happen when Awe found out about us. After all his threats, I thought he might be mad or even dangerous. Gloom assured me he wouldn't care. It didn't take him long to arrive.

"Ah, Gloomy! How are you all coping?" Awe asked as he strode in uninvited, interrupting dinner.

"Awe. How nice to see you. Please sit," Gloom said while dismissing everyone else at the table. The only ones remaining were the other Evers and myself.

"I see everyone arrived, and no one told me. I am offended," he said while sitting and helping himself to a plateful of food, his golden hair shining in the lamplight.

"We knew you would be here sooner rather than later, so we didn't want to waste our time," said Crescent in a bored tone as she flicked her short silver hair over her shoulder.

"Well, thank you very much." He looked around the table while chewing. "And who do we have here? What are you still doing here, my little sacrifice? Haven't you gotten sick of being here in the forest yet?"

Before we could say anything, Ashes spoke, "Can you believe this is Gloom's new *girlfriend*?"

My cheeks heated, and Gloom put a hand on my knee under the table and smiled at me.

Awe froze with the fork midway to his mouth. "Is this true? I can't believe it. I mean, I can see what you see in her, but are you sure, Emily? Do you really love Gloom?"

I saw out of the corner of my eye, Enduring giggling, her bubble gum pink hair covering her face.

"My name is Amelia, for a start. And yes, I love him," I said, looking him in the eyes. "I'm not going anywhere."

"Good luck to you. You will need it with this mopey idiot. We call him Gloom for a reason, you know," he said good-naturedly. The rest of the meal passed with laughter, arguments, and a few tears. This is what a family was meant to be. People who cared, and though they didn't always get along, you knew they loved you. Not like at Woodmere when any small infraction would see you beaten. This is what I had had with my grandmother. I had wanted this for so long, and now I had it. I held my necklace and thought of her and how she would be so proud of me and who I had become. I wished she could be here to see it.

Gloom and I had decided to try and help the people of Woodmere, too. Many of them had chosen to stay, but they were no longer so insular. Matthew's most hardcore followers had fled after the fire. Some of the children went to the local school, and I was happy to see them branching out. We sent people and supplies to help them rebuild, and slowly, I was repairing some relationships. It was healing and hard but worth it.

While at a meeting with the other Evers, Gloom told everyone he had seen Bilvog with the Staff of Thorns, one of the artefacts they used to bind Dread. They had no idea how he had got it, but the fact he had it meant he was one step ahead of us. Discussing the situation ahead of us, we decided we should all go after the artefacts. Perhaps they could be used again. We decided it was worth doing if it meant Bilvog wouldn't get them.

We discussed going and seeing the hags to see if they would help again, but the price they had to pay last time, they were reluctant to pay again. I had tried to find out what the price was, but they were keeping it close to their chests. They spoke about approaching the fey they shared these realms with. It was decided they would do that under extreme caution and only if nothing else came up. All the Evers were going to return to their kingdoms and look for any information about Dread and what he and Bilvog might be up to.

Gloom and I had decided to not put our lives on hold. We were going to live and love until the threat made itself known again. And then we would fight.

FORTY-TWO

Bilvog

Invisible and clutching my black and shrivelled arm, I stumbled out into the darkness of the forest. I could hear the fighting had died down, but I wasn't a fool, and I knew they would be out looking for me.

What a failure! Dread would be displeased. I shuddered a little, thinking about what he might decide to do with me when he was at full power. It was a delicate line I was walking, and I never forgot who I was serving.

As I was running, my invisibility wore off, and I was now exposed. Pain seared through my brain, and I stumbled to my knees. I wondered if I had been shot with an arrow, but it was worse.

"You have failed!" a voice thundered through my brain, and I clutched my head with my good hand as tears started running down my face.

"You used the soul knife for yourself? How dare you!" the voice boomed again. Every word seemed to rip through my brain, and I was shaking uncontrollably.

"I'm sorry, Master. I'm sorry!" I whimpered like a pathetic child.

"You are forgiven—this time. Make sure to have a vessel ready. I will not take a second failure," the voice said as it faded from my mind.

I whimpered in the dark and sighed as my brain was mine again. Fear flooded through me as I realised what Dread could do now. Was he still in my thoughts, riding along with me?

I made my old body stand and kept walking through the forest, clutching the soul dagger. I needed to rest before I could continue to the shrine. There, things would change. I would bring Dread back, and everything would change.

Everything.

Thank you so much for finishing Gloom and Amelia's story!
If you enjoyed this book, I would sincerely appreciate it if you could take the time to leave a review. It would mean so much to me!
If you would like to keep up to date on the rest of the Evers Saga, join her newsletter at www.blparkerbooks.com

Connect with Brooke online

Website and Newsletter – blparkerbooks.com
Facebook – facebook.com/blparkerbooks
Instagram – instagram.com/blparkerbooks

Acknowledgements

So many people helped me finish and bring this book to you, the reader. First of all, thank you to Emma, my alpha reader and the one I bounce ideas off. You have been so helpful with every draft you read and I wouldn't have got here without our Writers Extraordinaire Messenger Group.

Thank you to my beta readers who picked out the mistakes and helped to make this book better than it was before you got it: Clara, Mia and Kelsie. Your feedback was SO helpful and really helped me unlock new ideas.

Thank you to my ARC and Street Team for helping me, an unknown author with no following, reach my fingers out a bit further.

Lastly, thank you reader for taking a chance on me and Gloom and Amelia. They will only get better from here and I hope you stic around and see what happens!

About the Author

B L Parker is a young adult fantasy writer who loves a slow burn romance and dark evils rising. Her favourite author is Juliet Marillier and hopes to one day meet the Good Folk. She loves karaoke and her go to song is Hit me with your best shot.

She enjoys playing Dungeons and Dragons with her friends and spending time with her partner and two boys, and when she isn't doing these things, you can usually find her watching true crime, The Office or Parks and Recreation. She loves trying new crafts and always has a new hobby on the go.